Sunrise Side of the Mountain

By

Linnhe McCarron

This is a work of fiction. Names, characters, places, and incidents are either the product of the author's imagination or are used fictitiously, and any resemblance to actual persons living or dead, business establishments, events, or locales, is entirely coincidental.

Sunrise Side of the Mountain

Also By Linnhe McCarron

The Riverwood Series
Fool Me Once (2018)
A Bitter Wind Blows (2019)
Signs of Life (2019)
Ride A Pale Horse (2020)
Far And Away (2020)
The Hand of Fate (2021)

DEDICATION

For SallyAnn

Chapter One

Avery Markham sat at her kitchen table. She'd been alone for less than a year, struggling to get through the days, one day at a time. Her laptop was open, and she stared at a map of the United States. She was fifty-one years old, a young widow, with decades of living still ahead of her. She could go anywhere; where would she go? She'd never particularly liked Iowa, would never have chosen it, and now had no compelling reason to stay.

She took a sip of coffee, inhaling deeply, appreciating the rich, bitter aroma that was such a familiar part of her morning routine. Restless, she walked to the window, pulling the edge of one curtain slightly back, gazing out at the lightening sky as if it might hold the answer.

Where have so many years gone?

She remembered the first time she saw Andrew Markham. He did not make a favorable first impression.

Avery Beall grew up in New Canaan,

Connecticut, the only child of wealthy, well-educated parents. Carmeline and Palmer Beall placed a premium on quality education, enrolling their daughter in pre-K at the New Canaan Country Day School, just a few miles from their secluded estate.

Unexpectedly, Palmer Beall's Manhattan law firm transferred him to their London office, a significant promotion, when Avery was thirteen. The move came the summer after she completed the eighth grade, and Avery accompanied her parents abroad, returning to Connecticut for her enrollment at The Hotchkiss School.

Avery and her cousin, Hailey, had applied to several private prep schools in New England and had been accepted at most of their choices, but both girls chose to remain in Connecticut. The Bealls were confident that Avery's aunt and uncle would provide a stable home for their daughter during school breaks. Both sets of parents eagerly accepted plans for the two girls to spend summer vacations from school in England during their high-school years.

Although the cousins were only four months apart in age and had been extremely close all their lives, they went their separate ways when Hailey was accepted at Stanford, an application she considered a long shot.

Avery loved crime novels and hoped for an eventual career with the FBI. She researched the best schools offering an undergraduate degree in criminal justice and decided on Northeastern. She had remained in Boston and was in her first year at Harvard Law when she encountered Andrew Markham.

The weather was as bleak as her mood when she spotted a parking space right in front of the bakery near the law school campus. The corners of her mouth turned up with glee as she pulled her car forward, shifted into reverse, and turned the wheel, preparatory to backing in. Her momentary pleasure turned to shock and then to fury as a sleek silver Porsche Targa slipped in nose-first.

Avery opened her driver's door, stepping partway out, slush seeping through the thin soles of her leather ankle boots within seconds.

"Hey!" she called. "That's my space! I was just about to back in."

"Sorry, sorry," the Porsche's driver called back as he thumbed his key fob. The car emitted a chirp, its headlights flashing briefly.

"Asshole!" Avery yelled. He raised his arm over his head and waved, acknowledging he'd heard but clearly having no intention of doing anything but continuing on his way.

Entering the room where her civil procedure class was held, Avery slammed her books down on the desk. Yanking off her scarf and gloves, she slung her jacket over the back of the chair and fell into her seat.

"Whoa! Someone's in a bad mood," Joseph Christensen, her seatmate, observed. "Didn't you sleep well?"

3

"I slept just fine," she retorted. "What I didn't do is get a cup of coffee because some asshole took my parking place, right in front of the bakery."

Wordlessly, Joe slid his cardboard takeout cup over to her. "It's black. And hot; be careful."

Gratefully, she took a tentative sip and then another. "Thank you."

"Supposed to snow tonight," Joe said, making conversation in the minutes before the professor arrived and class began.

"Looks like it's going to start any minute," Avery said. "I don't care. I'll be holed up all weekend, studying."

"Me, too." Joe nodded. "I've got a torts test on Monday."

The next time Avery encountered Andrew Markham, he was ahead of her in line at a coffee shop in Harvard Square a few weeks later. This time, she was looking forward to treating herself to a cup of hot chocolate and a pastry after getting her grades for the winter term. She had done gratifyingly well in all her courses and deserved a reward, she thought.

"I'll have two large hot chocolates with extra marshmallows," she heard the man ahead of her tell the barista. A moment later, when he turned to hand one to the petite blonde at his side, Avery recognized him as the driver of the silver Porsche. She scowled, but nothing could dampen her mood after seeing her GPA.

"I'll have a medium hot chocolate, no marshmallows, and a cheese Danish," she said.

When the server held a cup under the spigot and depressed the pump, the carafe gurgled and spat, but no liquid emerged.

"I'm so sorry," she told Avery apologetically. "We're out. I can make some, but I'll have to heat the milk, and it will take a few minutes. If you want to have a seat, I'll bring it to you as soon as it's done."

"Are you fucking kidding me?" Avery muttered under her breath, realizing that the Porsche's driver had just snagged the last of the hot chocolate. Aloud, she said," No, sorry. I don't have time to wait."

"Take mine." The Porsche's driver had witnessed the exchange and held out his cup. "I owe you." Tilting his head at his companion, he added, "We can share hers."

If he had not winked, Avery might have taken his offer, still feeling aggrieved by his arrogant appropriation of the parking place he had surely understood she intended to back into. But the wink was the last straw. Ignoring his outstretched hand, she set the Danish she held back on the counter. Pulling her wallet from her shoulder bag, she laid a twenty-dollar bill on the counter and sighed deeply.

"It's not your fault, and I'm trying not to take it out on you," she told the barista. "This is for the Danish; keep the change.

Six months later, Avery Beall was living with

Andrew Markham.

Four months after that, she and Andrew Markham were married.

The following month, having completed her first year at Harvard Law, Avery Markham dropped out.

Now, decades later, Avery stared down at the simple gold band on her left ring finger, lost in memories.

She'd spotted Andrew on campus several times and had gone out of her way to avoid him. One day, she walked out of Langdell, exhausted by a long day of grueling classes in the enormous tiered classrooms on the upper floors.

"Let's run over to The Pub and grab a sandwich before study group," Lauren Thatcher suggested, shifting the weight of her bulging backpack. "I could use a break."

Avery half turned as an icy blast flung stinging ice pellets against her cheeks. She tugged her scarf up to shield her lower face and pulled her knit cap down.

"God, I'm sick of winter! I hope this is the end of it. Hard to believe this is spring semester. But to answer your question, I think I'm going to pass on the study group and get home before the streets turn to a sheet of ice."

"Did you drive in today?"

"No, I was running late and didn't think I'd be able to find a parking place, so I jumped on the shuttle. It's just a couple of blocks. The temperature doesn't really drop until after dark, so it should be okay for another hour or so. But I think I'm just going to call a cab."

"Well, I guess I'll microwave something in the kitchen at the dorm and do some reading for an hour before study group," Lauren said, swiftly amending her plans. She turned to go back into the building and through the underground tunnels that connected the buildings in the law school complex. Avery had already pulled her phone out as she started down the steps. Looking up, she suddenly reversed course, catching up with Lauren and tugging at her arm.

"What?" Lauren gasped.

"I changed my mind," Avery said as they both hurried through the building. "Let's go to The Pub. I'll call a cab later."

"What was that all about?" Lauren asked.

Avery yanked open the glass door and picked up her pace as she speed-walked down the corridor, ignoring the question and hoping Lauren would drop the subject.

The two women settled into a booth in The Pub's cozy red and wood-paneled interior, and Avery shrugged off her outerwear.

"Hey," a voice called cheerfully just as their waitress walked away, tucking the two menus under her arm. Alina Lennox plopped onto the bench next to Lauren, nudging her over with her hip and setting her Coke on the table. "You guys going to study group?"

After about forty-five minutes, Lauren requested the check. The waitress returned and said, "Your bill has been settled, compliments of the gentleman in the far corner." She motioned to a four-top on the other side of the room. There were three men seated at the table, and one was looking at them expectantly. Alina gave him a big smile and a small wave.

"Sweet!" she exclaimed. "Who is that? You know him?" She looked at Lauren. Noting the blank expression on her face, she swiveled her gaze to Avery, who was stony-faced.

"Is that someone you know? Lauren doesn't seem to recognize them, and I've never seen any of them before. Why would that guy pay for our meal?"

Avery stood abruptly, mortified when her chair tilted on two legs. She caught it moments before it toppled, righting it with one hand and snatching her coat with the other. She slung her purse strap over her shoulder and hefted her backpack, marching toward the exit with Lauren and Alina in her wake.

She caught Andrew Markham's knowing wink out of the corner of her eye and steeled herself not to react.

The study group started right on time, but Avery was so irritated she had trouble concentrating. She didn't know Andrew Markham's name, had no idea whether he was enrolled at Harvard, or why he seemed to be popping up everywhere she went.

Lauren pulled Avery's notebook toward her, and

surreptitiously scribbled a note. *"You okay?"* she wrote and slid it back in front of Avery who nodded.

"What's going on with you?" Lauren asked in a low voice when the session broke up.

"You know, I'm not bitchy by nature," Avery told her wearily. "That guy who paid for our lunch just rubs me wrong. He snagged my parking place a couple weeks ago which shouldn't be that big a deal but I was already running late. I'm so tired all the time and I feel so pressured. If one tiny thing goes wrong, I just lose it."

Lauren smirked. "Welcome to law school. You and everyone else."

"Then he scored the last cup of hot chocolate at the Coop the day I got my grades and wanted a treat to celebrate," Avery explained. "He tried to make amends by offering me his but I blew him off. I felt bad later but I'm always on a hair trigger and I don't even recognize myself sometimes."

Avery's law school life was too overwhelming to spend any time thinking about anything or anyone tangential to her grueling schedule and crushing workload, and she quickly forgot about the mystery man. Soon after the school year started, she'd applied for the FBI's Honors Internship Program, a paid ten-week summer program. Thousands of applicants vied for those coveted positions. Avery was thrilled to be called into the Boston field office for an initial interview, having made it through the preliminary selection process. Her application met all the criteria, but Avery was well aware that a conditional offer would largely depend on the current skills the FBI needed. She studied the headquarters and field offices available and analyzed the job openings, hoping to maximize her chances by requesting the six locations most likely to produce her desired outcome.

She took and passed the polygraph and the mandatory drug testing. Her background check was in process, and Avery had no qualms about it turning up any information that would disqualify her from receiving a Top Secret security clearance.

Throughout Avery's four undergraduate years as a criminal justice major, she belonged to the school's mock trial association, where she put her skills to good use and gained valuable insight into the process of bringing criminals to justice. Now, in law school, her punishing schedule didn't allow time for extracurricular pursuits. Still, occasionally volunteering to serve as a witness or a juror for Harvard's mock trial association continued to hone her comprehension of the legal nuance she'd need as she began preparing for the mandatory moot court competitions that would start at the end of January, soon after first-term finals were over.

Avery put in sixteen-hour days, holding herself to a rigid schedule as she studied for exams.

"Avery!" her aunt had said in dismay when she declined to spend Christmas in Connecticut. "You *need* a break from school, a change of scenery. You need to relax and catch your breath," she counseled. But Avery knew Hailey would be home for the holidays and would want to party. As much as she hated to disappoint her aunt and would miss seeing her cousin, she knew she wouldn't get any studying done if she went.

"The dorms are closed when school's not in session, so I'm checking into a hotel," she told Hailey in an infrequent phone call. "I won't have any interruptions or distractions, and I can just order room service meals when I get hungry."

"It sounds grim," Hailey said flatly. "I don't know how you do it. Once I graduated, I never wanted to see the inside of a classroom again."

"It gets better after the first year," Avery said. "It won't always be like this."

"Of course not," Hailey teased. "After you grind your way through three years of pure torture, you can put in those sixteen-hour days for another six or seven or eight years trying to make partner in some soulless corporate firm with hundreds of lawyers."

Avery sighed. "I can't think of anything worse. That won't happen," she said resolutely.

"Your dad's hoping you'll get an offer you can't refuse, and you'll see the light, you know."

"It won't happen," Avery reiterated. "I think I've got a good shot at the internship I applied for. I know exactly what I want."

"What you *think* you want," Hailey said. "But, do you think Palmer Beall, Esquire, footed the bill for your expensive education so you could wind up as a government grunt? Your dad will have plenty to say when the time comes. People would *kill* for the kinds of strings he could pull on your behalf."

"I know." Avery sighed again. "But I'm not his "mini-me" however much he'd like me to be."

When exams were over, and grades were handed out, Avery's knees went weak when she dared to look at the sheet of paper she'd been handed. Clearly, her hard work and endless hours of study had paid off as her efforts were rewarded. With stellar grades, she had a good shot at becoming a prospect for an invitation to participate in Law Review. She had debated the enormous commitment of time in addition to her regular coursework but, in her hearts of hearts, she knew she coveted the honor as much as everyone else in her class. But, now, the pressure was off, however briefly, until the end of January when she began to prepare for the moot court all first-year law students were required to participate in.

"They need jurors for the mock trial on Friday night," Lauren Thatcher told her one afternoon soon after the 1L's received their grades. "Alina and I were thinking we'd like to do it, just to get more familiar with Ames. Any interest?"

"That's not a bad idea," Avery said. "It sure wouldn't hurt to feel more at home in the courtroom when we have moot. Ames is pretty intimidating. Yeah, I'm in."

On Friday evening, the three women grabbed a

bite to eat before making their way through the underground tunnel connecting Wasserstein Hall with Austin Hall, where the Ames Courtroom took up an imposing space on the second floor. The tunnel connecting the law school buildings was almost deserted at that time of day, but Avery saw a figure she thought she recognized far ahead.

"Is that the guy who paid for our lunch a few weeks ago?" she asked her companions.

"What guy? What are you talking about?" Lauren frowned.

"Him," Avery insisted, pointing, but the tunnel ahead of them was empty.

"Oh," she said. "Never mind." *I must have imagined it.*

But she hadn't imagined it. When the three women entered the jury room, they were the last to arrive. There were two other first-year law students from different sections that Avery knew in passing. When the jurors introduced themselves, Avery learned that six were undergraduates, four law-school hopefuls, and two who didn't have dates or anything better to do on a Friday night. Avery clenched her jaw with annoyance when she realized the twelfth member of the jury was indeed the driver of the silver Porsche, the man who had so highhandedly paid for her lunch.

"It *is* him!" she hissed to Lauren. "I saw him in the tunnel ahead of us."

"You're right; it is," Lauren said just as Alina

13

broke away and made her way over to him.

"Thank you for treating us to supper at The Pub," she told him. "We were on our way out and were running late, so I didn't have a chance to thank you at the time."

"You are so welcome," he replied. "My pleasure." He was looking over Alina's shoulder as she spoke and caught Avery glaring in their direction. A slight, satisfied smirk quirked his lips up at the corners as he made eye contact with Avery. She quickly made her face expressionless and turned away, but her shoulders were rigid, and she was clearly displeased.

"What the Hell is he doing here?" Avery asked rhetorically. "Who the Hell is he anyway?"

Lauren provided the answer a few days after the mock trial. She held out her cell phone, showing Avery the image on her screen.

"I took this picture in the Coop yesterday. He's a writer. This is his latest book. He's written a bunch of mystery/crime novels, and his author photo is on the back cover. Hardbacks," Lauren added, clearly impressed.

"So, what's he doing hanging around the law school? How'd he even get in?" Avery demanded.

"I asked someone who was at the checkout, buying his book. He's a visiting professor in the English department, doing a couple of creative writing seminars. He's been giving lectures in the psych department and even at the med school, describing how he uses forensics in formulating his plots."

"Andrew Markham? Is that his real name or his pen name?" Avery scoffed. "Not that I give a rat's ass."

Chapter Two

Avery determined to put the obnoxious and irritating 'Andrew Markham' out of her mind and turned her focus to academics, studying, and preparing for her moot court appearance. Since students worked in pairs, Avery was under pressure not to let her partner down, not to give in to her nervousness during oral arguments.

When the day came, she was as prepared as she could be. She and her partner had examined every aspect of the case, discussed their strategy, and Avery had practiced and polished her opening statement. She laid out her clothes ahead of time and had set out her briefcase and her shoulder bag with her keys, money, fully-charged laptop, and everything else she'd need to get her through the evening.

Avery and her partner both made a concerted effort to arrive well ahead of schedule and met just outside the door of the Ames Courtroom. Both were dressed tastefully and professionally, Avery in an understated olive skirt suit and Sherry Van Cortland in charcoal gray.

Although the moot court endeavor was not officially graded, feedback was given. The most driven students used it as a stepping-stone for the qualifying round of the Ames Moot Court Competition they'd be eligible for in the fall of their second year.

"Hey." Sherry peered at Avery, concern etched on her face. "Are you okay? You're not crying, are you?" She rummaged in her briefcase and pulled out a travel-sized pack of tissues, extracting one and handing it to her.

Sherry laid her hand on Avery's forearm and squeezed reassuringly, "Don't be nervous. We're as prepared as we could possibly be. We have to have a positive attitude. You know, expect that it'll go well, and it probably will, the old self-fulfilling prophecy."

"No, it's not that," Avery said hastily. She held the tissue under her left eye, blotting the tears about to run down her cheek. She blinked rapidly and explained, "I think one of my contacts worked its way up under my eyelid. I can feel it." She blinked again several times in succession, hoping to dislodge it.

"Don't rub it, "Sherry cautioned. "We're early. You have plenty of time to run to the ladies' room. Take it out and put it back in. Or take them both out and just wear your reading glasses." Avery nodded and left the room.

An hour and a half later, Avery was limp with relief when the ordeal was over. She and her partner had prevailed over the opposing team, with the verdict rendered in their favor. Delirious with this tangible measure of her success, Avery was amenable to Sherry's suggestion that they go out for a celebratory drink.

"We could go over to Milstein for the reception," Sherry said. "They'll have drinks and food. Everybody says it's a great opportunity to network, but I've had all I can take for one day. I just want a change of scenery and a chance to relax and celebrate. So, let's get out of here and go to Juris Doctor."

"I saw a flier for live music every night this week at Justice Junkies," Avery countered. "I would love a glass of wine. Let's just sit and listen to some music for an hour."

"Alright!" Sherry agreed enthusiastically. "It's only a few blocks, and it's not very cold tonight, but I'd never make it in these shoes. Let's call a cab and get on with it. I am so ready for something normal, just for a few hours."

The bar was named for its proximity to the law school, but few law students had the time to patronize it. The two women had no trouble finding two seats at the bar, and the bartender came right over.

"I'll have a glass of chardonnay," Avery told him, but Sherry flapped her hand, motioning him to disregard Avery's order.

"Tequila," she insisted. "Two shots. *Casamigos Reposado.*" Avery's eyes widened in alarm, but

Sherry grinned. "Trust me. Some tequilas burn like Hell, but this one is extremely smooth." The bartender set a small dish of lime wedges between the two women.

"You probably won't even need salt and lime," Sherry told Avery. Lifting her glass, she threw the shot back and slammed her glass down on the bar. Avery followed suit.

Sherry nodded at the bartender, and he set two more shots on the bar. Avery lifted her glass and said, "To Ames." Sherry laughed and said, "To us," clinking the rim of her glass against Avery's. The two women downed the shots in unison.

The bartender raised his eyebrows in a question. Sherry gave him a rueful look. "This is eighty proof and goes down dangerously easily. I think we'll switch to margaritas."

The band began their first set and the room filled with students from Harvard and nearby colleges, a few businessmen on their way home, and several groups of women. After about forty-five minutes, the bartender slid two fresh margaritas in front of them.

"From an admirer," he told Sherry and pointed to a dark-haired man seated alone at a small table. She turned and made eye contact, smiled, and mouthed, "Thank you." He took that as an invitation to move to the empty stool on Sherry's right. Soon she was engaged in a lively conversation with him. Avery took a small sip of her drink and rotated her head, stretching her neck.

"Rough day?" a female voice inquired, and Avery turned to the left. A very attractive blonde woman had settled herself two stools over, draping her coat and the strap of her shoulder bag over the seatback. Since the row of stools was unoccupied when she'd arrived, Avery had set her own coat, her shoulder bag, and her briefcase on the empty stool next to her. Realizing that the bar was now nearly full and she should free up the seat, she retrieved her shoulder bag and coat, relocating them to her own seatback. She placed the briefcase on the floor at her feet.

The blonde misread Avery's intent and scooted over to sit on the stool next to her. *Is she hitting on me? Please, Jesus, no!*

"You look like you've had a rough day," the blonde said again. "I work in the law library. I've seen you in there a few times."

"1L," Avery replied and hoped her curt response would discourage further conversation.

"Ohhh," the blonde said, nodding knowingly. "Ames. I recognize that look. How'd you do?"

"Will you excuse me?" Avery turned to tell Sherry she was going to the ladies' room, but her friend was on the dance floor, swaying to a slow song with her arms wrapped around the dark-haired man's neck, her head on his shoulder. Avery had a feeling she knew how Sherry's evening would end.

When Avery returned fifteen minutes later, the blonde told her, "Your friend left. She said to tell you she'd call you tomorrow." Avery's lips tightened in displeasure, and she decided it was time to head home. She pulled her wallet from the side pocket of her shoulder bag, but before she could scrabble through the coin purse for a dime and use the pay phone to call one of the local taxi services, the blonde laid her hand on Avery's arm.

"You're not leaving so early, are you? I just ordered you a drink. You didn't tell me how your tournament went, but I figured you either needed to be consoled, or you needed to celebrate." Avery glanced at the bar and saw another margarita. The blonde reached over and slid it in front of Avery.

"This is my favorite song," a deep voice said in her ear. "May I have the pleasure of a dance?" Avery half-turned, and the man grasped her elbow, tugging her up and off the barstool. When she faced him, she saw to her dismay that it was none other than the driver of the silver Porsche.

"No," she said. "No, I really have to go."

Still holding her elbow, he steered her onto the dance floor and turned her to face him. "You looked like you needed rescuing."

"No, I—"

He placed a fingertip on her lips. "Shhh."

Glancing back over her shoulder, Avery saw that the blonde had decided not to waste a drink and moved the untouched margarita next to her own half-finished glass. In an instant, Avery decided the lesser of two evils was to remain on the dance floor, expecting the woman would consume both drinks and leave.

An hour and a half later, Avery and the Porsche driver—Andrew— were still on the dance floor, her arms around his neck and her head on his shoulder.

Avery woke with a start the next morning, and sat bolt upright, terrified that she might have slept through her alarm and would be late for her first class. Bleary-eyed, it took her a moment to focus, and she realized with growing horror that she was not in her own bed in her own room. *Where—? What the—?*

She sucked in a deep breath, held it for a moment, and exhaled slowly through pursed lips. Her head was pounding, and her eyes felt gritty. Her stomach roiled, and there was a bitter, unpleasant taste in her mouth. Her eyes traveled slowly around the room as she tried to get her bearings, and her gaze fell on the still-sleeping figure next to her. *Was that—?*

Her mind instantly rejected the possibility she'd gone home with her companion from the night before. Frantically, she looked over his shoulder, searching for a clock. *No clock.*

She squinted at her watch, which read nine-thirty. *What day is it? Shit!* She groaned and lay back on the pillow, her arm over her eyes, shielding them from the bright stabbing sunlight.

"Heyyy." The figure rolled over, facing her, and Avery saw that she was in bed with Andrew Markham, renowned author, visiting professor, driver of the silver Porsche. *This can't be happening!*

Please, please let this be a dream.

"Give me a minute to pee," he told her, "and the bathroom's all yours. I'll leave the toothpaste and a new toothbrush on the vanity for you. There's shampoo in the shower. I'll have coffee ready when you come downstairs." With that, he threw the covers back, stood, and strode naked across the room. Avery closed her eyes as he gathered some clothes and waited until the silence told her she was alone. Cautiously, she opened her eyes and slowly sat up. The sheet pooled around her waist and her worst fears were confirmed. She, too, was naked. As the events of the previous night came back to her, her face flamed. *I don't even know him, and I certainly don't like him. How could I let this happen?*

Avery closed her eyes again, fervently wishing she could magically will herself back in her dorm room and avoid the inevitable morning-after scene before she could make her escape. The room spun when she stood, and she steadied herself with a hand on the nightstand. Gathering the articles of her clothing from the floor, she made her way slowly into the bathroom. In addition to the toothpaste and toothbrush, there was a bottle of aspirin and a plastic glass left out for her. *That was thoughtful,* she admitted to herself, *but I still don't like him.*

Avery felt marginally better after she'd splashed her face with warm water and brushed her teeth. She swallowed three aspirin and dragged her hairbrush through her tangled hair. She dressed swiftly and, steeling herself, made her way down the stairs and into the kitchen. Andrew stood by the counter, eating a bagel that he'd slathered with cream cheese.

"I have a class in a half-hour," he told her. "I didn't realize it was so late. I've called a cab to drop you—um—wherever you live." He handed her a travel mug. "I don't know how you take your coffee, so I added milk and sugar."

Avery preferred her coffee black, but that was the least of her concerns. Wordlessly taking the cup, she nodded her thanks and left. The car pulled smoothly to the curb just as Avery reached the sidewalk. She sank into the back seat, grateful that the driver did not have the radio on. As he accelerated into traffic, she lifted the travel mug to her lips. She inhaled, taking a tentative sip and finding that she welcomed the unaccustomed sweetness of the beverage at this moment.

"Harvard Square?" the driver inquired in a heavy Boston accent.

"No. Um, I'm going to Harvard, but it's North Hall, on Mass Ave. Two blocks north of the law school."

"Gotcha'."

About half of the first-year law students opted to live on campus, and most were in the dorms connected to the classroom buildings through the underground tunnels. North Hall was a former hotel purchased by the university and repurposed as student housing, the only one featuring ensuite baths. Avery had considered the pros and cons of each of the possibilities and found that she couldn't bear the thought of communal bathrooms as well as the noise and lack of privacy she'd endured as an undergraduate. Although it was only a short distance from the law school, Avery had a car. Her father had insisted on trading in the one she'd had since she got her driver's license at sixteen and leasing a new all-wheel-drive vehicle for her.

"Let us help you, darling," her mother had urged. "You're our only child, and we're so proud of you."

Avery's room had a studio fridge, a small microwave, and an automatic coffeemaker. She accepted her aunt's gift of laundry service, and her law-school life ran smoothly.

Or, it had until today. The building was customarily deserted in mid-morning on a weekday, but, to Avery's chagrin, she encountered several people as she made her way to the elevator. She kept her head down, and her eyes averted, letting them think she was preoccupied with something she'd forgotten, rushing back to the dorm unexpectedly.

Avery felt considerably better after a long, hot shower. She downed three more aspirin and thought about eating before her long afternoon class. Her stomach was still unsettled after a night of unusually heavy drinking and little sleep. She settled on a carton of blueberry yogurt.

"Where *were* you this morning?" Lauren eyed Avery up and down. "Are you okay? You don't look so hot."

"I'm okay," Avery equivocated. "I was up half the night with terrible cramps. I made the mistake of shutting off my snooze alarm, and I fell back to sleep. I would have had to walk in halfway through class."

"You read the cases, didn't you?" Lauren asked.

"No, it's not that. I took some Motrin, and I'm in slo-mo. I'm just not a hundred percent. The thought of getting called on just did me in."

Lauren's gaze was sharp. "But you're okay now?"

"Better."

Avery hated dissembling, deliberately misleading her best friend, but there was no way she'd confess she'd gone home with someone who'd picked her up in a bar. On a school night.

"I'll live."

But three weeks later, Avery wasn't so sure she wanted to live. Two parallel blue lines. It felt like her life was over. *I am so screwed, literally and metaphorically.*

Flu had run rampant through the law school, so Avery attributed her queasiness to its onset. She expected chills and achiness, but there was only the faint unremitting nausea. But then, one morning, the smell of coffee turned her stomach, and she bolted for the bathroom, reaching the commode with seconds to spare. Standing shakily after throwing up only bile, holding the edge of the vanity for support, she stared at her wan complexion and terrified eyes, and she knew. *Thank God, it's Saturday, and I don't have classes! But, what am I going to do on Monday? And Tuesday? And every weekday for the next—twelve weeks?*

Avery ran a cool stream from the faucet and rinsed her mouth, trying to marshal her thoughts. Flipping the lid down, she sank onto the toilet seat and held her face in her hands. *The first trimester, that's what it's called.*

Resolutely, she turned the shower valve full-on and let the force of the water beat down on her neck and shoulders. In slow motion, she stepped into clean underwear and dragged on her oldest, softest pair of sweats. Her mind was racing, but she counseled herself to wait until she'd purchased a pregnancy test and confirmed her suspicion. *Or not. Please, please, let it be not.*

"Avery, hey." A 1L who lived on the floor below greeted her. She was in a different section, and Avery knew her only by sight.

"Hey." Avery turned away and kept her eyes focused on the floor. "Sorry," she mumbled. "Just got over the flu."

"Oh, poor you. I know that feeling. It hit me hard a month ago. I missed almost a week of classes, and I felt like crap for two weeks after that. I didn't think I'd ever get caught up."

"Yeah, it's been going around. I missed a few classes."

The elevator reached the ground floor, and the

doors parted.

"Well, I hope you feel better." The student smiled sympathetically.

"Thanks. I'm sure I will," Avery responded, forcing cheer into her voice. *I doubt it, but I'll know soon enough.*

In the privacy of her bathroom, with her worst fears confirmed, Avery consulted the calendar feature on her phone.

"Beginning of April to the middle of May," she mumbled. "I'll only be six weeks when the school year ends. I won't show, and no one will know. So, April, May, June, July…November, December, January. I'll be six months pregnant when school starts in the fall, and I'll be due at the end of—." She gulped and began to hyperventilate. *I'll probably go into labor during first-semester exams!*

Avery took several deep breaths, calming herself. *I can't be pregnant, and I won't have an abortion!* Tears leaked from the corners of her eyes. *How am I going to get through this?*

She thought back to the night at Justice Junkies, and her cheeks burned. *How could I have been so stupid? I did this to myself.*

Chapter Three

"You didn't do this to yourself!" Palmer Beall's voice boomed in Avery's ear. "Have you told the young man involved?" he demanded.

Her mother interrupted. "You've never mentioned a boyfriend. Is he someone in your classes? A law student?"

Avery closed her eyes, vacillating between mortification and exasperation. She wished she could have told her parents in person, could see their expressions, and read their body language. She expected that her mother would be supportive and her father outraged.

There was silence on the line as the Bealls waited for their daughter to provide further details.

"I—," Avery faltered, her voice quavering. "No, not a boyfriend. Not a law student." Her sentences were choppy as she struggled to explain. "Someone I met. Someone older."

"How long have you known him?" her mother asked.

"How much older?" Her father didn't miss the

tiniest detail, his legal skills honed over a lifelong career.

"Um—. He's a visiting professor," Avery managed.

"In the law school? Dear God, not one of your professors, I hope."

"Please don't grill me, Dad. This is hard enough," she pleaded. "He's an author, a guest lecturer in the English Department."

"It's about to get a lot harder," Palmer Beall said flatly. "You have some big decisions to make. Your choices are abortion, give the child up for adoption, or raise it as a single mother."

"You could get married," Carmeline Beall offered.

Avery snorted. "Getting married is the very last thing I intend to do, baby or no baby," she spat.

"Don't take that tone with your mother," Palmer warned his daughter. "You're the one who made this mess, and she's only trying to help."

"You're right. I'm sorry, "Avery apologized and gulped back a sob.

"Oh, honey," Carmeline said. "Are you feeling all right?"

"What about the father? It's only fair that you tell him." Palmer was adamant. "If you decide to bear this child, he'll have to pay child support."

Avery closed her eyes, the blood draining from her face. She'd been pacing as they talked, but now her knees felt weak, and she sank onto the edge of her bed. She was gripping her phone so hard her knuckles were white.

"What do you think the father will say?" Carmeline asked in a low voice.

"How well do you know this man?" Palmer asked.

Avery felt her throat close. Her mouth was suddenly so dry she could hardly speak.

"I—." She swallowed hard. "I—. I barely know him," she admitted wretchedly. "We were at a bar—." She heard her father's snort of derision and struggled to explain.

"It was right after moot, right after we won. Sherry—my partner—wanted to celebrate with a drink, so we went to Justice Junkies. I was just going to have a glass of wine and listen to some music for an hour. I just wanted to relax. But Sherry ordered tequila shots, and I guess the alcohol went straight to my head. Then she left with some guy who started buying her drinks, and this woman started hitting on me—." Avery heard her mother gasp and closed her eyes again, knowing how this sordid tale must sound to her parents.

"So the visiting professor asked me to dance and said it looked like I needed rescuing. The band was really good, and we just kept dancing."

"Drinking and dancing and, and then you went home with him," Palmer summarized. "With predictable results."

"Surely you're on the pill!" Carmeline wailed. "Or

the patch. Or some sort of birth control." Her tone hardened. "Didn't this fellow ask or take precautions himself?"

"Oh, Mom. Do you think I haven't been over that a hundred times in my head? I knew how hard Harvard Law would be. I expected to work hard and have no time for a social life, so I didn't get a new implant when mine was removed. The one I had was almost five years old. It's only good for five years. Do you think I haven't kicked myself and wished for a do-over a hundred times?"

"So you were completely unprotected," Palmer stated flatly. "And this fellow didn't think to use a condom. Well, I suggest you get yourself tested for STDs before you go any farther."

"Dad," Avery implored. "I feel lightheaded. Can I call you back? I just can't talk about this anymore right now."

The second conversation was no less difficult than the first, but at least her parents had some time to process the information. Avery's father wasted no time in getting to the point.

"It's obvious you won't be returning to Harvard or any other law school for your second year. Assuming you've ruled out abortion—*or have you?*" Palmer took Avery's silence for assent. "Assuming you've ruled out an abortion," he continued, "your mother and I suggest you take a leave of absence and come to London when the school year ends. You have only—

what? Six weeks until exams? You'll stay with us until the baby is born. If you surrender it at birth, you'll recover and return to Cambridge to continue your studies."

Avery made a strangled sound.

"Or not," Carmeline quickly amended.

"Not," Avery said. "I won't give my baby away. I can't; I just can't. I would wonder and worry every day for the rest of my life whether it was cared for, loved, and happy. I have a good education without a law degree, so I should be able to have a career and raise a child. A lot of women do."

"Nevertheless, the father will provide child support," Palmer Beall warned his daughter. "To choose otherwise is foolish and foolhardy. I'm guessing he'll demand a paternity test, this man, whoever he is—."

Avery made another strangled sound.

"Yes, it's humiliating; I understand that." Palmer continued, his voice devoid of emotion. "It may be a necessary evil. I suggest you apprise your partner of this development and set the process in motion as soon as possible."

"I will, Daddy," Avery said in a small voice. Palmer Beall was an imposing figure with a no-nonsense manner, and it had been years since she'd used this childish form of address.

"Take care of yourself, " he said gruffly. "Let us know your plans."

"We love you, darling," Carmeline added quickly.

Avery glanced at the clock and realized she'd have to hurry to make her study group on time.

"You okay?" Lauren asked when Avery slid into the seat she'd saved. Lauren studied Avery, a slight frown line forming between her eyebrows.

"I'm fine," Avery assured her friend.

"No, you're not. You look like you haven't slept in days. Have you *seen* the circles under your eyes? You're not stressing about exams, are you?"

Avery shook her head.

"I won't make Law Review but you're on track, with your grades," Lauren said. "So, if it's not that, what is it?"

Two men strode into the room and flung themselves into the two remaining chairs. Avery pulled her laptop from her backpack and set it on the table in front of her, opening it. The room fell into silence as chatter ceased, and students prepared for another intense session. As hard as it was for her to concentrate on the material, Avery was relieved to be out from under Lauren's scrutiny, for the moment at least. The two had bonded almost instantly, and Avery knew she wouldn't be able to keep such a momentous occurrence from her for long.

"You have time to grab a pizza?" she asked Lauren when the session ended.

"Sure. I could use a little break. I'll call it in, and we can eat in my room. Want me to see if Alina's had lunch yet?"

Avery shook her head. "Not today. I talked to my parents this morning, and there's something I want to run by you."

"Wow. With a five-hour time difference, it must have been *dawn* in London."

"Just about. My father is an early riser, and he likes to be the first one in the office. I wanted to catch them before he left for work."

"Are they okay? Your parents? No one's sick, I hope."

"That's not it. I've got something going on in my life that I needed to tell them about."

The two friends speed-walked through the tunnel and made their way up the stairs to Lauren's third-floor room. Lauren slid her key card into the reader with a deft flick of her wrist and swiftly pulled it out. Both women dropped their backpacks on the floor next to the single bed.

"Yeah, I know, it's a postage stamp," Lauren complained. "Stairs, no A/C, communal bathrooms. It wouldn't be my choice, but it's gotta be the cheapest room in Gropius."

"This will be The Bad Ole' Days when you graduate from Harvard Law and start making big bucks," Avery reminded her.

"Hold on a sec'." Lauren cut her off. "I just got a text. It's probably the pizza guy. My phone's on vibrate." She pulled her cell from the pocket of her khakis and glanced at the screen. "Yup, it's him. I'll be right back."

"Take this," Avery extricated some bills from the pocket of her own khakis and held out a twenty. "I'm buying; pizza was my idea."

Lauren returned with the box, holding it gingerly by the edges. "Damn, it's hot!" She flipped open the lid, and the room filled with the redolent odors of tomato, cheese, and pepperoni. Avery had been hungry for the past hour, but at the sight of the food, her stomach heaved. She took shallow breaths through her nose, hoping to quell the sudden surge of nausea.

Lauren opened a desk drawer and removed two paper plates and a few napkins. She was still holding them out when Avery leaped to her feet and bolted over to the desk, grabbing the wastebasket and vomiting into it. Lauren handed her one of the napkins, and she wiped her mouth with it as Lauren retrieved a bottle of water from her mini-fridge and offered it. Avery pressed the cold bottle to her forehead for a few seconds before unscrewing the cap and taking a cautious sip.

Lauren's eyes were wide with concern.

"You're white as a sheet. Are you sick?" she asked. "Do you have breast cancer or something? Is that what you needed to tell your parents?"

Avery shook her head, her expression wretched. "That might be preferable," she stated flatly.

"Don't say that! What could be worse? Well, ovarian cancer, I guess. Or pancreatic. Or a brain tumor."

It's not cancer. You remember the guy who paid for our lunch at The Pub? Before exams last semester?"

Lauren frowned. "Barely. What about him?"

Avery looked up and met Lauren's eyes. She nodded slowly.

"No! You're not—? You didn't—? That guy? You slept with him? Seriously? I thought you didn't like him."

"I didn't. I don't."

"Avery Beall, are you telling me you're pregnant? By some guy you don't even know and don't like? What the Hell?"

"After moot," Avery explained. "Sherry suggested we get a drink. We won our case, so she wanted to celebrate. We went to Justice Junkies because they had live music." She stopped speaking and swallowed hard.

"And?"

"Age-old story. I had too much to drink. Well, I didn't really, but I don't drink much, and it went straight to my head."

"So you went home with him? Oh, my God. Sweet baby Jesus!" Lauren stared at Avery, trying to process the information. "And now you're knocked up. Aren't you on birth control? Didn't he use a condom?"

Avery didn't speak, her face crumpling as she struggled not to cry. Lauren pulled her in for a hug, rubbing Avery's back with long soothing strokes, offering comfort.

When Avery sank back onto the edge of the twin bed, Lauren pulled her desk chair over and sat facing Avery, their knees nearly touching.

"Does he know?" Lauren whispered.

"No. My parents know, and now you know."

"What are you going to do?"

Avery drew in a deep breath and looked Lauren square in the face.

"I know what I'm not going to do," she said resolutely. "I'm not going to have an abortion."

"When are you due? What about law school? How will you manage?"

"Right around Christmas. I can get through this semester. Take a leave of absence, maybe. Go to London and stay with my parents until the baby's born, I guess."

"Then what?" A thought occurred to Lauren, and she reared back, her shoulders stiff. "Does he know? You haven't told him, have you? Whatzisname?"

"I'll get a job." Unconsciously, Avery's hand rested protectively on her still-flat belly.

"Lots of women are single mothers," she said defensively. "I don't want anything from him. I got myself into this mess, and I'll get myself out."

"He'll have to pay child support. It's the law."

"Yeah, the law," Avery snorted. "Not if he doesn't know."

"That's not fair," Lauren protested. "I don't give two shits about him. I meant not fair to the kid. Every kid deserves to know who his or her parents are. Plus, you'd want to know the health history on his side of the family."

Now tears slid slowly down Avery's face as her heart wrenched. "I hate this."

Lauren nodded. "The sooner you get it over with, the less time you'll have to dread it or stew about it," she counseled. "You can't afford the distraction, not with exams coming up. And you can't go to class hungry." Lauren produced a lemon yogurt which Avery ate slowly with a plastic spoon while Lauren inhaled three slices of pizza.

Avery didn't have a phone number, an email address, or a physical address for Andrew Markham. She thought she remembered his street name and was pretty sure she'd recognize his apartment building. Her thoughts would dwell on her situation until she had a plan if the afternoon was any indication. Avery's mind kept going around and around during her classes, and she found it impossible to concentrate. She decided to skip her second study group.

"Stop here," she told the taxi driver, pulling some bills from her wallet. Andrew's silver Porsche was in its designated parking space, just as she remembered.

She stood in the building's vestibule for several minutes, summoning the courage to confront him with what she was sure would be unwelcome news.

"Andrew, it's Avery Beall," she said firmly into

the intercom.

"Avery, hey. This is a surprise."

You don't know the half of it, buddy!

Ten minutes later, she sat in a deep comfortable armchair across from him, a diet Coke in a tall glass on a small table at her elbow. She took a tiny sip, meeting his eyes over the rim of the glass.

"I have something to tell you," she said, sliding her hands beneath her thighs to keep them from trembling. "Something you're not going to like." His eyes bored into her as he waited for her to continue.

"I'm pregnant," she said flatly, forcing the words through stiff -lips.

He nodded slowly, his eyes searching her face. She kept her head bent, focusing on her knees, avoiding his penetrating stare. She swallowed hard, audibly.

"Avery." He leaned forward and pulled her hands out, holding them in his own, surprising her.

Her head snapped up, and she yanked her hands free. "I don't want anything from you! Not. One. Fucking. Thing!"

The ferocity in her tone startled him, and Andrew reared back.

"Well, that may be, but I'd say we're in this together. Why don't you tell me what you want to do? How long have you known? You must have given this some thought already."

"It's not a matter of what I want to do. It's a matter of what I'm going to do. Which is to finish my first year of law school. Then I'm going to fly to London to stay with my parents until the baby comes. At which time, I'll get a job and raise my child."

"As a single mother? That won't be easy, and I'm not sure it's fair to the child. Paid caregivers will essentially raise him or her. That's not something I'd want for my child."

"Who says it's your child?" Avery snapped.

Andrew laughed aloud. "Well, if it isn't, darlin', why are you sitting in my living room telling me about it?" he asked, reasonably, eyebrows raised in amusement.

"This isn't funny!" Avery was furious.

"No, it isn't. That's certainly something we can agree on."

"I've made such a mess," Avery whispered.

"Something else we can agree on. You know I'll want a paternity test."

Avery's mouth opened and quickly closed as she bit down on her unspoken protest.

"I'm sorry to be insulting, but you owe me that," Andrew pointed out. "You did sleep with me on the first date, so you don't have a leg to stand on."

"I don't—! I wouldn't—!" she sputtered.

"Yet, you did. Fact. I'm not accusing you of anything, but I think it's important for legal, medical, and psychological reasons to ascertain that I *am* the father."

Standing abruptly, he strode to his desk, booted up his computer, and brought up a search engine.

"How do you determine paternity before a baby is born?" he typed into the search bar. His back was to Avery as he read the factual information aloud.

"A non-invasive prenatal paternity test can be performed as early as the seventh week of pregnancy. A simple blood draw from the mother analyzes free-floating fetal DNA from the mother's plasma. DNA is collected from the possible father using a cheek swab. The prenatal paternity test results are generally returned in about one week."

Andrew turned to Avery. "Simple as that. One week. I'm assuming I'm the father. Where do we go from here?"

She stared at him, mute.

"Avery? Where do you want to go from here?"

Finding her voice, she said, "I told you."

Keeping his voice steady, Andrew said, "I'm not sure I find that acceptable. You're telling me you have no intention of telling this child—*our child*—who his father is. And raising him—or her—with no contact from me. Is that correct? Why are you even here?"

When Avery didn't answer, Andrew's voice took on a harsh tone.

"Oh, I get it. This is about child support. Of course, it is."

"NO!" Avery shouted. "This is not about child support! I said I don't want or expect anything from you."

"So, why are you telling me? Apparently, I don't

get any input if you have your way. Your body, your choice. I get it. But what if I *want* this baby?"

"You—you want a baby?" Avery stared at Andrew uncomprehendingly. She shook her head from side to side as if to clear her ears.

"Well, no, not especially. Not a baby, any baby, for the sake of having a baby. But this is different. This is real."

"I don't understand."

"With two parents, you could finish law school if you want. Take a leave of absence and go back next year after the baby's born. When's it due? Let me think; you would have gotten pregnant the night you did moot court, so beginning of April. April, May, June, July...October, November, December. Sometime right around Christmas. And second semester starts when?"

Ignoring the question, Avery whispered, "And where will you be? Don't you have a visiting professorship, just for a year?"

"You have to be out of the dorm when the semester ends, right?" Andrew considered the logistics. "You could move in with me, or you could visit your parents for a month or two, as long as it's safe for you to fly back, and then move in with me. I'm working on a new book, and it's set in Boston, so I'm going to stay on and spend the summer writing. You could take a leave of absence, have the baby in December and then spend the spring semester bonding. Next summer, you could take a refresher and start your coursework again next fall."

Avery stared at him, her mind racing.

"I'm sure it won't be hard for me to secure a job at one of the colleges or universities in the area," Andrew said. "Although, truth to tell, the royalties from book sales support me handsomely. I don't actually need to work, and I do it because I love teaching."

Chapter Four

That summer, so long ago, Lauren dropped Avery off at Logan International, and she'd flown to London to spend two months with her parents.

"Your young man called while you were out," Carmeline Beall told her daughter two days after she arrived. "He said he hadn't heard from you and wanted to make sure you arrived safely. I have his number if you want to call him back." Avery thanked her mother and took the proffered slip of paper, but she had no intention of calling Andrew. Her emotions were in turmoil and she wanted nothing more in the foreseeable future than to eat, sleep, and take long solitary walks.

But Andrew was persistent and after he'd made several more fruitless overtures, Avery relented and took his call. Surprising herself, she was glad to hear a familiar voice and talk to someone who understood her situation far better than most. At first, the conversations were sporadic but became more frequent as the weeks passed.

By the end of her stay, Avery found herself

looking forward to Andrew's calls, sharing the minutiae of his day, becoming increasingly more enmeshed with the life in Boston that awaited her.

Andrew was solicitous of her health and interested in the progress of her pregnancy. Avery wondered if she had misjudged him and made a concerted effort to forge a meaningful relationship.

When she returned at the beginning of August, Andrew was waiting at the gate in Arrivals. He scanned Avery's face, trying to assess her mood. She met his eyes and smiled. She was almost five months along, unmistakably gravid, but she looked well with thick, shiny hair and a glowing complexion.

"How was your flight? How are you feeling?" he asked.

"I slept through the entire flight," she confessed. "But I'll be glad to get into my own bed. Your bed, I mean." She turned scarlet with mortification as she realized what she'd just said.

"The bed, I mean. The b-bed at your condo," she stuttered in embarrassment.

Andrew put his arm around her shoulders and propelled her toward baggage claim.

"I know what you mean," he assured her. "I don't think you have to worry about your virtue. That horse is out of the barn." A laugh exploded from him, and Avery couldn't help but respond. They laughed so hard, tears streaming from their eyes, that they had to stop, letting the throngs surge past them on either side.

The next morning, the mood was serious as Avery picked up the small black jeweler's box that sat beside her place at the breakfast table. Andrew watched her somberly as she slowly lifted the lid.

"Oh!" she gasped. "Oh, my God! It's *huge*! It's gorgeous!"

Andrew grinned. "It is, isn't it? I just sold the movie rights to <u>Margin Of Error</u>.

He slid the six-carat stone onto Avery's ring finger

"Avery, will you be my wife?" he asked softly.

She closed her eyes. Tears slipped through her lashes and trembled there.

Andrew gently wiped them away with the tip of a finger and waited for her to speak. *Is she overcome with joy? Is she trying to figure out how to say no? Or is she just overwhelmed with jet lag and exhaustion?*

Avery raised her head and looked deep into Andrew's eyes, searching.

"I will," she finally whispered, nodding. "Yes." Tilting her chin up, she gently pressed her lips to his. Andrew gathered her in his arms, holding her close, deepening the kiss, the tip of his tongue teasing hers.

Avery Beall and Andrew Markham were married in an elegant evening wedding on the first Saturday in November, with both sets of parents in attendance. Avery's cousin, Hailey, served as maid of honor; her law school classmates Lauren and Alina were bridesmaids. After considering a dozen of Boston's most desirable and dramatic wedding venues, including the iconic Boston Public Library and venerable Old South Meeting House, the couple settled on the Harvard Club with its rich oak paneling and silver chandeliers. Both Andrew and his father had graduated from Harvard, and Avery would be a graduate of Harvard Law herself in a few short years. The Harvard Club held special meaning both for the groom and for his bride.

"Too bad you can't go to Paris for a honeymoon," Hailey commented as she handed Avery her exquisite arrangement of dahlias, chrysanthemums, chocolate cosmos, ranunculus, fresh greenery, and seasonal berries. Tied with a trailing velvet ribbon and cascading down the front of Avery's empire-waisted, long-sleeved, scoop-necked off-white velvet gown, the bouquet minimized but could not conceal the fact that she was within a month of her due date.

"Yeah," Avery agreed wistfully. "But it's pretty cold in Paris. Maybe we'll go in the spring when the baby's old enough to travel. I'm going to breastfeed so I wouldn't be able to leave her." Avery's lips curled into a smile, and her eyes were dreamy as she thought of her unborn daughter. "I don't think I'd want to leave her. I love her so much already!"

"I love *you*, Avery. I wish only good things for you." Hailey kissed her cousin on the cheek before leaving to take her place at the altar. As the processional swelled, Palmer Beall stepped forward to walk his daughter down the aisle.

Four months later, the couple had settled into married life, with Andrew finishing the school year and Avery treasuring this time out of time when baby Olivia was the center of her universe. Andrew had submitted applications for two visiting professorships at area colleges for the following year and had just inked a contract for a two-book deal over the next two years. Avery was planning to interview a part-time caregiver for Olivia so she could take a six-week refresher course during the summer before starting at Harvard Law in September as a 2L.

Then the letter arrived, the letter that changed everything.

"You're awfully quiet," Avery observed as she and Andrew shared a bottle of wine over dinner. Andrew had bathed his infant daughter, a routine he followed at the end of his workday, while Avery finished preparing their evening meal. After she was fed, Olivia would nod off and sleep until her ten o'clock feeding, so Andrew and Avery had several hours each evening to spend quietly together.

Andrew looked up, his expression inscrutable.

"I got a letter today," he began but stopped abruptly. When he didn't explain, Avery frowned, her expression quizzical.

"From whom?" she asked.

"It took me by surprise," Andrew said. "It's nothing I applied for. It's an offer from a university in Virginia for a Writer-In-Residence. The stipend is generous, and there's a housing allowance, office space and support staff, plus a platform to promote my work in addition to teaching. It's quite an honor."

Avery's eyes widened as she realized the import of his words, as the reality sunk in.

"Andrew," she whispered, the blood draining from her face. "What about Harvard Law? I have two more years." Tears shimmered in her eyes.

"It's asking a lot, I know. But I have an established career, and you're still a student. There are some fine universities in Virginia; I'm sure you wouldn't have any trouble getting accepted. You could finish your law degree there. That's not an issue."

"It's an issue for me!" Her voice rose. "I busted my ass to get into Harvard, and I busted it during the hardest year of my life. You have no idea how hard it was! A law degree from any other school won't ever be the same as a law degree from Harvard."

Andrew rose and moved around the table, pulling out a chair next to Avery and taking her icy hands in his.

"You're right. But one of us is going to have to make a sacrifice. I'll turn it down if Harvard means that much to you." Avery's head snapped up, and she searched his face.

"Really? You'd turn it down?"

"Avery, you're my wife, the mother of my child. I want you to be happy."

In that moment, Avery realized how deeply she

loved Andrew Markham. And she knew she'd already made her decision.

Olivia usually woke at six, wailing with hunger and the discomfort of a sodden diaper. But Olivia was still sleeping peacefully the next morning, so Andrew all but tiptoed from the room, allowing Avery a few more minutes of the rest her body craved.

"I withdrew from Harvard Law this morning," she told him as they sat down to dinner that evening. Andrew had just picked up his fork, but it fell from his fingers with a clatter.

"What? You withdrew? Oh, baby, I thought we were going to talk about this."

"There's nothing to discuss. I read the letter you got. You can't turn down an opportunity like that. And I'm kidding myself if I think I can get through two more years at HLS, even if we had the best caregiver in the world. I did some research online today, and, with my background in criminal justice and a year of legal studies, an ideal fit for me would be as a private investigator."

Andrew looked alarmed, and he started to protest.

"I know what you're going to say, that it's too dangerous. But wait, let me finish. I'd only have to complete a sixty-hour course, and Virginia doesn't even require that candidates pass an exam. I've already been fingerprinted, and I've been the subject of an exhaustive background investigation as part of my application for the FBI's summer honors internship. I would have to be bonded. But I could do strictly administrative work like finding missing children and missing persons or skip tracing, supplier-, vendor-, and employee-screening programs, or working for an insurance company to uncover insurance fraud. Or investigate medical malpractice claims. I wouldn't have to do surveillance or be licensed to carry a firearm."

Andrew looked thoughtful. "You may be on to something," he said slowly. "You certainly have the educational credentials, with a bachelor's degree in criminal justice and a year of law school."

"I could work from home, for the most part," Avery enthused. "I don't want Olivia parked in daycare."

Andrew pulled Avery in for a long hug, and he kissed the top of her head. "You're a good sport, Avery. A lot of women would be resentful or bitter."

"I might be if it was just the two of us, and I had to sacrifice my career. But I had no idea how deeply I would be committed to family once we had Olivia." She grinned crookedly. "I guess I'm taking lemons and making lemonade."

Present Day

On the night of Andrew's funeral, after all their friends and Andrew's colleagues had left, Avery stood in front of the bureau in the bedroom they'd shared for almost thirty years. Her reflection in the mirror showed a drawn and pale woman with deep shadows beneath her eyes. She stared down at her left hand and, tugging gently, slowly drew the diamond ring from her finger. The elegant emerald cut was simple enough to suit Avery's style, but the extravagant and ostentatious size had always embarrassed her. Although it was insured for its full value, she had always worried about wearing an item of jewelry so appealing to burglars and muggers.

But the ring seemed to be a symbol for Andrew, just as the silver Porsche had been, just as his handmade shoes and bespoke sportcoats were. Those material goods were the outward manifestation of Andrew's success, far more than the prestigious position he held or the literary acclaim he'd earned. Avery learned later that the Porsche was a lease, the first of many.

"You should sell it," Hailey told Avery in a low voice that afternoon, gesturing toward Avery's left hand. The two women stood together in the cemetery. "You've never liked it. If you're not going to continue wearing it, why keep it, why hide it away in a safe deposit box where it won't do anyone any good?"

Avery did not respond, and Hailey did not press. But that night in the privacy of her bedroom, Avery slid the diamond into the little velvet box it came in. Someday soon, she *would* sell it. For her, it symbolized the pain she'd endured for almost thirty years, the bone-deep pain, a sorrow that never left her, although she'd hidden it well.

Avery equated the ring with the reason Andrew

had offered to marry her, with the child who would bind their union. The child who did not live to her first birthday. What Avery cherished was her wedding band and the memories of her marriage. She and Andrew had had twenty-nine good years.

Now, she turned the band around and around on her finger as she stared at the map of the United States. It glinted in the overhead light as she reached out and traced the borders of the state of Iowa with her forefinger. She was no longer married to Andrew, and she could no longer remain in the house provided for the head of the Writers Project.

"Andrew's successor won't be here until the end of July," Wendell Murray, the University's President, told Avery kindly. "I'm sure you'll need some time to sort through An—your things and make arrangements for somewhere to live. But take your time; there's no rush."

"Will you be staying in the area?" Leah Murray inquired.

"I—. I'm not sure," Avery replied hesitantly. It was apparent to both Murrays that the question caught Avery off guard. She'd been sleepwalking through the days, numb with grief, and hadn't given any thought to the fact that she'd need to vacate her home.

A month after the funeral, Avery had sublet a condo in a high-rise building only a few blocks from campus. It was only for six months, but that suited her as it would give her time to consider her options. She was familiar with the area, yet it was a complete change of scenery from the gracious stately home she'd lived in for almost three decades, and it was completely furnished. If she were to buy a home in Iowa City, it would be small, and she would need to downsize considerably. With that in mind, she placed ads in the local paper and the campus newspaper, quickly selling all but a few cherished pieces of furniture and most of her household goods. A moving van would arrive in a few more days, taking most of her belongings to a rented storage unit.

Andrew had carried a significant life insurance policy, and the royalties from his books and movies should provide well for her for the rest of her life. Although it was comforting to know she was financially secure, Avery found her future bleak. *Three more decades. I could have three more decades to fill. Or more.*

She'd lost fifteen pounds since the afternoon she'd gotten the phone call, telling her that Andrew had collapsed on his way to his office after one of his graduate seminars three days into the second semester. It had been a foreboding dark day as the sky lowered and snow threatened. Andrew was wearing the tweed bucket hat Avery had given him for Christmas with his long woolen topcoat. His new cashmere scarf, also a Christmas present, was wrapped around his neck and up over the lower part of his face, shielding him from the icy wind that blew across the quadrangle. Students walking between classes did not recognize him, saw only a man falter, stagger, and fall. Medics had arrived within minutes, an ambulance transporting him only a few blocks to the university hospital's emergency room.

In fact, Andrew was dead before he even hit the pavement, but it wasn't until Avery rushed into the ER, wild-eyed and frantic, that a staff social worker gently conveyed the information that she was Andrew Markham's widow.

Avery hadn't felt so bereft, so numb, so hollowed out, since the months following Olivia's death twenty-nine years earlier. It was Avery who discovered her darling six-and-a-half-month-old daughter, cold, stiff, and blue, face down in her crib. Andrew was on a ten-city book tour, cut short abruptly in Milwaukee, but he was there to shepherd his grief-stricken wife through the grueling investigation that ensued. There was no evidence of parental abuse or neglect, no underlying genetic or physiological findings to explain the premature death of a seemingly normal, healthy baby.

Avery was questioned repeatedly about the baby's bedtime routine. She had breastfed the infant at ten pm as she habitually did, sitting in the big rocker in the corner of her dimly lit bedroom. She had placed the child on her back, carefully, as she always had, in the crib next to the rocking chair. Both Avery and Andrew were knowledgeable about SIDS, sudden infant death syndrome. One of the features that attracted them to the house in Virginia was the huge master bedroom that could accommodate both their king-sized bed and the infant's crib.

The small room directly across the hall doubled as Avery's home office and Olivia's nursery, where she lay in her playpen or rocked contentedly in her swing chair while Avery studied, where she was bathed and changed. When Olivia was old enough that the danger of SIDS had passed and when she was weaned, Avery and Andrew would relocate the crib to the nursery. By that time, Avery would have completed the requirements for her private investigator's license and would begin working part-time, with Olivia in daycare a few days each week.

But that day never came. Avery was prostrate with grief, insisting that they cremate Olivia's tiny body so she could take the ashes with her, wherever she was, for the rest of her life. Andrew watched helplessly as his wife dragged through the endless days, eating almost nothing, seeing no reason to dress or undertake the normal activities involved in getting established in a new community. The Markhams had only been in Virginia for six weeks when the tragedy occurred, so Avery had no friends to comfort her or support her.

Andrew himself didn't have the luxury of giving in to his grief; he had commitments he had to honor and professional responsibilities he had to undertake. While he was preparing lectures for the upcoming semester and outlining his new novel in response to his agent's persistence, Avery's loss was so profound it became clear she was not healing as the months passed. The door to the nursery remained closed, and Avery could not bear to sleep in the room where Olivia's crib had once stood. She and Andrew slept, alone together, in what would have been a guest room if they had entertained guests.

Andrew's mother and father and Avery's flew in as soon as they learned of Olivia's passing. The house could easily have accommodated both sets of grandparents, but they stayed at a nearby hotel to give the grief-stricken parents privacy and time together. It was Hailey who brought Avery's condition to Andrew's attention months later during a brief visit.

"My God, Andrew. She's a walking skeleton! She won't eat. She doesn't want to get dressed or leave the house, and she barely says two words. Her unhappiness breaks my heart. I don't know what I can do to help her."

"It's more than unhappiness," Andrew acknowledged sadly. "She's despondent. I'd hoped that you, more than anyone, could get through to her. I certainly can't. I feel so guilty because my life appears so normal, but she barely acknowledges my presence or absence."

"Have you considered professional help, a therapist? Or, what about a support group? You could go together. There are so many couples who've lost a child to SIDS. Maybe it would help to connect with others who've had a similar experience, who have the same feelings."

"I've suggested that, believe me. I'd do *anything*, try anything. But she just stares at me like she doesn't comprehend the words. I can't exactly drag her out the door. I don't know how to help her, and I'm starting to fear for her health. She can't afford to lose any more weight, that's for sure."

"You're going to have to think of something," Hailey counseled. "What about taking a trip? Maybe she'd benefit from a complete change of scenery. You have a few weeks before the semester starts, don't you? Even a long weekend away might help."

Chapter Five

But a long weekend away didn't help. Avery was apathetic when Andrew suggested it. With air miles accrued from his book tours, he proposed San Francisco, Seattle, or Vancouver. When she expressed no interest in a trip, Andrew booked a flight to Portland and arranged for a rental car and luxury accommodations in Vancouver.

"We have to leave very early in the morning," Andrew told his wife. He looked around the bedroom they shared, searching for a suitcase or any evidence she'd begun to pack. He glanced into the bathroom and was dismayed to see her toiletries and toothbrush still in their usual place.

"Avery? Shall I get your suitcase?"

Avery closed her eyes as if the thought of packing pained her.

"Sweetheart?" he prompted. "Are you tired? I can help you pack."

When she failed to respond, Andrew resolutely began opening drawers, placing underwear, two nightgowns, and a few teeshirts on the bed. Opening her closet and perusing the racks, it occurred to him that Avery's clothes would hang on her now. It also occurred to him that perhaps her clothes were too much a reminder of better times, too distressing to wear in her current frame of mind.

I'll just pack a few basics, and we can shop when we get there. Avery loved clothes and had always enjoyed shopping, so that activity might provide some pleasure.

But Avery barely spoke on the drive to the airport and seemed almost unaware of her surroundings as they boarded a shuttle from the parking area to the terminal and passed through the departure lounge to their gate. Once they boarded, she sank into her seat and immediately put her head back, closed her eyes, and fell into a deep, medicated sleep, rousing only when the aircraft began its descent hours later.

On their first day in the city, Andrew booked a manicure, a pedicure, a facial, and a massage for his wife at the hotel's spa. While she was occupied, he asked the concierge to recommend a hair salon and direct him toward an area with upscale clothing shops. On her better days, Avery dragged a brush through her hair and scraped it back into an unflattering ponytail. She hadn't applied makeup since Olivia's death, and it was everyone's considered opinion that her spirits might begin to lift if she looked better. To that end, Andrew also arranged for a session with a makeup artist at the same salon that expertly cut his wife's hair.

When Avery emerged two hours later, Andrew hardly recognized her. The transformation was complete; her hair was styled in flattering layers that effortlessly framed her face, her complexion glowed, and her makeup was subtle but effective. Shopping came next, where a saleswoman guided them through choices that included delicate lingerie, as well as shoes and bags to complement the tailored and tasteful clothing Andrew selected. He'd hoped Avery would show some interest in shopping, but she just shrugged as each article of clothing was presented.

"You look stunning," Andrew told Avery that evening as they settled themselves in the back seat of the taxi he'd summoned. He intended to have a cocktail before dinner and order a nice bottle of wine with dinner, so he'd opted not to drive their rental car in an unfamiliar city. There were so many wonderful restaurants to choose from that it seemed a shame to have only a few days in the city. But the evening, and the trip itself, was not the uplifting experience Andrew intended. Instead, Avery picked listlessly at her food and seemed apathetic despite her husband's concerted efforts to enjoy a mini-vacation. When Avery got into bed the first night and turned her back, it was clear that this would not be a romantic getaway.

"How'd it go?" Hailey asked when Andrew phoned her from his office upon their return.

"Like pulling teeth. I'd almost have to say it was a total disaster," Andrew admitted. Hailey could hear the despair in his tone. "We shopped and ate and did some sightseeing, but it's like she's sleepwalking. She's profoundly depressed, and nothing I say or do gets through to her. We haven't made love in months, not since—well, you know."

"You've done all you can," Hailey commiserated. "I can't tell you how worried I am. She needs professional help, and you may have to make some hard decisions."

"I'm going to insist she see a therapist regularly, two or three times a week. Or daily, if it comes to that, if it helps."

Hailey's silence spoke volumes.

"You could start there, but it may not be enough," she finally said.

"Are you suggesting—*inpatient?* Is that what you're saying?"

"Maybe. But even that may not be enough. It may just be too hard to live in the house where Olivia died."

"Oh, God." Hailey watched on Facetime as Andrew's face twisted with anguish, and he raked his fingers through his hair. "We should move! I'll call a realtor tomorrow and start looking at houses."

"It still won't be easy to live in the same town where Avery took Olivia with her to the pediatrician or to do errands. Everywhere Avery goes, she'll be reminded of her loss."

"So are you suggesting we—*what?*—move away?"

"I'm not sure I'm suggesting it. I thought we were putting our heads together, trying to figure out how to help Avery. But now that the idea is on the table, maybe that *would* be for the best."

None of the positions Andrew considered over the next few months held any appeal. Instead, he questioned whether he needed to find a job or whether the revenue from his career as a writer could sustain them through old age. He had just engaged the services of a financial advisor when he learned from a colleague that a search committee was identifying candidates for a position as the director of the Writers' Project in Iowa.

"If it were just the two of us, we'd be comfortable," Andrew told Hailey six weeks later. "But I'm assuming we'll need to educate future children."

"Does Avery want more children? Are you sure of that?" Hailey inquired gently.

Andrew drew in a deep shocked breath, a gasp. "Why would you even ask that? Of course, we want more children! Olivia's death was tragic, but we're not the only parents to lose a child to SIDS. A good therapist will help Avery come to terms with her loss—*our loss*—and after a time, we'll be ready to start again."

"You and Avery aren't—*intimate*—are you? Your sex life is none of my business, of course, and please don't think I'm prying, but my guess is that Avery has an aversion to sex at present. I'm no therapist, but I'm guessing that, deep down, she's afraid of getting pregnant."

After a long silence, Hailey spoke again. "We haven't discussed it, so I really have no idea how Avery feels. I'm just guessing. But I'd say that if your romantic getaway wasn't very romantic, you need to consider that possibility."

"I want her to start therapy immediately," Andrew said. "I can live without sex for as long as it takes, but I don't want her suffering in silence. I loved Olivia as much as Avery, but it must be so much harder when you've nurtured and sheltered a baby inside your own body."

"You're a good man, Andrew Markham. Avery is lucky to have you."

His candidacy for the director of such a prestigious program would be a long shot, Andrew thought, but he tendered his name. He was immensely gratified to receive a letter a few weeks later advising him that he'd made the initial cut. Within another few months, the head of the search committee phoned, inviting Andrew to come to Iowa for an interview. He wasn't sure how Avery would react, and he wanted to wait and see if he was offered the position before introducing such a momentous possibility.

When he told her he'd be away for three days, she nodded noncommittally and asked no questions. Andrew's agent and his publicist often scheduled one-

or two-city book signings, and it was not unusual for him to take short trips.

"It went well," he told Hailey as soon as he returned. "It's a beautiful campus, and there's always a lot of energy in a college town. I got the two-dollar tour and met everyone in the department. The position includes housing, and it's a lovely stately home on campus. I only saw the exterior, but I think Avery would love it!"

When the search committee narrowed their choice to their top three candidates two months later, Andrew was invited back for an in-depth interview. Three weeks after that, the position was his if he chose to accept.

"Avery? Sweetheart? I have something to tell you, and we need to discuss it." Avery sat dutifully, waiting for her husband to impart his news, whatever it was.

"Iowa?" she asked as if she had never heard the word, as if she had no idea where Iowa was. But she seemed receptive to leaving Virginia, and that was all the encouragement Andrew needed.

He listed the house fully furnished the next day, and it was under contract in less than a month. He intended to take nothing, not a frying pan, dustpan, bath towel, or bowl, from the life they were leaving behind. He wanted Avery to choose new furniture, rugs, and lamps once they arrived in Iowa and purchase new bedding, new linens, new small appliances, and everything the new house would need for their new beginning.

He booked a two-week stay in a residence hotel near campus. While he threw himself wholeheartedly into his new job, Avery rose to the task of furnishing and outfitting their new home and overseeing deliveries.

When they'd been there a month, the university president held a reception to welcome the Markhams and introduce them to department heads, faculty members, and their wives.

"Where are you from originally?" several people asked Avery."

"My family is in Connecticut, where I grew up. But I lived in Boston for several years when I went to college there."

"Do you have children?" several of the wives asked, and Avery responded simply, "No. No, we don't." Her therapist had practiced this scenario with her until she could respond smoothly, providing no details.

The years passed, and there were no further pregnancies, no more offspring. The Markhams had an active social life, but their circle of friends did not include young families with children. Whether by design or happenstance, Avery and Andrew gravitated toward professional couples like themselves. To all outward appearances, they were childless by choice, and there was no overt speculation as to whether Avery might be barren or Andrew sterile. They were affectionate in public and resumed a loving relationship in private soon after arriving in Iowa.

On the first of her annual visits to Iowa, Hailey sat with Avery in an alcove with a small table and two antique straight-back chairs, overlooking a perennial garden. The table was set with a lovely lace tablecloth and an antique tea service in delicate bone china.

"Good?" Avery asked as her cousin sampled a chocolate-filled croissant.

"Mmmm," Hailey moaned, her mouth full of the confection. She chewed slowly, and swallowed. "I can't believe you learned to make these. Are you sure you didn't smuggle them in from some little bakery just off campus?"

"All mine." Avery laughed. "Once you master the basic croissant dough, you can stuff them with anything sweet or savory—chocolate, Brie and fruit, or ham and cheese, chicken salad. Andrew and I have scrambled egg, sausage, and cheese breakfast croissants on Sunday mornings. They're so easy and so versatile. By the time you leave a week from now, you'll be sick of croissants, I promise you that.

Hailey gave her cousin a mock side eye. "So, you didn't just stick some stuff in a crescent roll?"

"I did not!" Avery protested. "I practiced until I mastered making the dough and, believe me, I've had a few disasters. I learned to put the yeast on one side of the bowl and the sugar and salt on the other side of the bowl before mixing. If you put salt or sugar directly onto the yeast, it can negatively affect the rising process or even kill the yeast altogether."

Hailey rolled her eyes again. "Well, *who knew?*" Then her smirk faded and she told Avery, "You know, Iowa has been good for you. When you were so depressed in Virginia and we were so worried about you, I told Andrew I thought you needed complete change of scenery. After you'd been here a few months, he called me and said, 'You were so right. You know her so well. She loves the house and has done wonders with the décor. She has such good taste.' "

"You can thank my mother for that." Avery laughed. "And yours."

Hailey nodded in agreement, smiling fondly at the memories of her mother and her aunt instructing the two young girls.

"Andrew hated the thought of me working as a private investigator but I couldn't just sit in this house being a faculty wife, once we'd gotten it furnished and decorated," Avery confided.

"As soon as we were settled, and there's nothing more I needed to do, I looked into the requirements for licensure in Iowa and, I'm here to tell ya', it's pathetic. Iowa doesn't require education or investigative experience. Do you believe that? You apply for a business license as a PI, and, voilá, you are a licensed Iowa PI business. You don't even need a private investigator course or official state private investigator training to work as a private detective here."

"It's like that in a surprising number of states," Hailey agreed.

"Andrew was not in favor of his wife 'running around as a private detective.' He said he'd watched too much television, and it just seemed like I'd be in harm's way too much of the time. I teased him and said I thought he'd written too many crime novels where his private detectives are in harm's way most of the time. But, he was really upset. He still insists he's the reason I'm not an attorney. I chose to drop out of Harvard Law, but he says he'll always know I gave up my career aspirations because he was offered the Writer-In-Residence gig in Virginia."

"Gave them up willingly," Hailey chided. "Andrew can't beat himself up forever. You were a new mother with a husband whose academic career was taking off like a rocket. And with one year of Harvard Law under your belt, you certainly had a preview of coming attractions," she pointed out. "You knew how difficult the second year would be with a newborn and the third year with a toddler. All other considerations aside. Well, it obviously worked out. Literally, because you're working as a PI now."

"Andrew says I gave up Harvard Law and he can't stand in my way again. I loved my criminal justice courses, and I had no doubt I'd be an excellent investigator. He and I had this conversation a long time ago. I told him I could do skip traces or search for missing children or missing persons, or do pre-employment background checks. Nothing dangerous. We compromised before it became a sore subject. So, I got an Iowa business license and I expected to work out of a home office. But Andrew thought I should rent office space. There's so much room in this house, he insisted I have an office here as well, to work from home on days when the weather's inclement. He said we haven't been through an Iowa winter yet, and, listening to other people tell stories about blizzards, he's probably right about that."

Within a year, Avery had a thriving practice and all the work she could handle. She was self-employed, freelancing for several large firms in Des Moines, Cedar Rapids, Davenport, and Sioux City. It was win/win as Avery was busy and fulfilled, Andrew did not worry about his wife's safety, and the firms' operatives were freed up for riskier work in the field, conducting surveillance and process serving, personal delivery of summons, and subpoenas.

"Avery," Andrew said one glorious fall afternoon. "I have a proposal for you." They'd gone for a Sunday afternoon outing to a local orchard where they picked apples. When their wooden basket was full, tantalizing aromas led them toward the barn where oven-hot apple turnovers were served with cider straight from the press.

"You sound so serious."

"It's something I've been thinking about for a while. I want to create a new series with a new character."

"So, what's the proposal?"

"I want to write one book a year, set in a different foreign country. I think the main character is going to be a consultant, a specialist in human trafficking. I'd like to visit a different country every summer. We could spend a couple of months traveling around, getting a feel for various settings. You could write a weekly blog and post it to my website, promoting the new book and engaging readers. We could write the outline together at the end of the summer."

"What a great idea! I love it!" Avery's enthusiasm was contagious, and Andrew reached for her hand.

"You really think so? You like it?"

She nodded, admiration for her husband apparent when she said, "You're so talented."

"You are too, Avery. I need to hire a researcher full-time, and there's no one I'd want more than you. You have the perfect skillset. You're familiar with investigative practices and legal issues, you have an exceptional ability to absorb and organize material, and you're quite a competent writer yourself."

Avery's smile dimmed slightly. "Quit my job, you mean? Is that what you're asking? To help you with your books?" Her voice rose. "To work for you?" She looked away.

"Yes. That's precisely what I'm proposing. To work with me. You already have a wonderful home office, and I'd pay you more than you make now. Plus a percentage of the royalties. I need you, Avery."

Andrew tugged her hand, turning her to face him. "I want you, Avery. Just you, no one else. As my partner." An idea occurred to him.

"Forget it. You won't work for me, and I won't pay you. You'll be my co-author with your name on the cover and full credit. This will be our creation." His mouth quirked, and his eyes danced. "We can take turns writing chapters. The story will be full of twists and turns that neither of us saw coming because we won't know where the other one takes it. I've always wanted to do that!"

Avery's mouth opened in surprise, but Andrew continued speaking.

"That gives me another idea. What a fun course that would be for my creative writing students. To work in teams. It hasn't been done before, and it should be really popular. It's something different."

Chapter Six

Now, almost three decades and twenty-three books later, Hailey asked, "What will you do now? Will you continue writing crime novels?" The cousins had been talking on the phone for over an hour and had yet to discuss The Elephant In The Room.

Avery gasped, and her cousin continued, "Well, you could, couldn't you? I mean, you've collaborated for so long, you could probably do it in your sleep! You understand the process, and you've got the writing style down pat. All you need is a plot."

"N-n-no," Avery stuttered, her voice barely audible. "No," she said more forcefully. "No, I really can't."

Hailey waited a moment to see if Avery would elaborate. Then, when the silence stretched, she asked gently, "Can't or won't?"

Avery drew a deep breath, but her voice was steady when she replied. "Won't, I guess. Andrew's publisher asked me the same thing. The truth of the matter is that I could, but I don't want to. That was something Andrew and I did together. We took a trip every summer to get a feel for the setting—I've been to so many different countries all over the world—and I have so many memories of Andrew. It would feel dishonest to continue without him."

"You two parlayed that concept into a money-making machine, that's for sure." Hailey's tone was warm with the admiration she felt for her cousin. "I always envied you. Well, not envied; that's the wrong word. You know what I mean. You two had something special."

"And that's why I can't do it alone. What we *had* and what we *did* was special. But it's over. Andrew dovetailed our collaboration into the most popular course ever taught at the Writers' Project! Students loved the idea of learning to collaborate, and there was always a waiting list to get into that class."

So, have you given any thought to what you're going to do? Now that you've moved out of the house and probate is wrapping up? Will you go back to work as a private investigator? It must be hard to fill up the days, living in a condo. I don't know what I'd *do* without my gardens."

"The condo is a sublet. It gave me somewhere to land when I had to vacate the house. I knew it intellectually, but it just never occurred to me daily that my living quarters were tied to Andrew's job. If I stayed here, I'd probably buy a little house close to the university, but, honestly, I don't see myself staying. Nothing is holding me here, and there are too many memories."

"You have friends there."

"A few. But most of them were Andrew's colleagues or wives of his colleagues. So, I feel like a square peg in a round hole, to use a well-worn cliché."

"Come here," Hailey said.

"There? To Greenwich?" Avery's voice rose. "Oh, I don't think I could do that. It would feel like going backward."

"No, silly. I meant come for a few weeks. Think of it as a transition from where you are to where you're going. I've missed you, and we could have so much fun! There are so many great restaurants and shopping—well, I don't have to tell you how good the shopping is. We could even go to the beach a time or two. I'm sure you don't get much beach time out there in flyover country."

Avery snorted.

"I know, I know. 'Today's tan is tomorrow's wrinkle.' I've seen that on a teeshirt. We don't have to lay in the sun; we could just bring late-afternoon appetizers and a cocktail and take a walk on the beach. Doesn't that sound good?"

"It does, actually," Avery concurred. "I would love to walk on the beach. I can feel the water on my bare feet now."

"So, you'll come?"

"For a little while. It will give me a chance to run into the city to see my folks."

"I always imagined them retiring right here, not in

New York. Ugh!"

"They don't spend the whole year in New York. They were in Portugal for almost six months last winter. I think it suits them to split their time like that."

"Their co-op is almost as big as the house in Connecticut." Hailey laughed.

"I thought Connecticut had seen *your* backside when you went off to school on the west coast," Avery said.

"Me, too," Hailey agreed. "What are the odds of my going to school in California and falling in love with Jayson Betancourt from *Wilton, Connecticut*?"

"And ending up living a few miles from your parents. Don't leave that out."

"The apple didn't fall far from the tree," Hailey admitted. "We're such a stereotype with a husband who commutes into the city, a wife who lunches and supervises the housekeeper and the gardeners, and kiddos in private school."

"At least Jay isn't a hedge fund manager. And he doesn't take the train into Grand Central."

"I'd probably see him more if he were a hedge fund manager! His driver picks him up before dawn. And he doesn't get home until late. Either he's away on special assignment, or there's breaking news—"

"Goes with the territory! He's the most famous broadcast journalist in America," Avery pointed out. "He loves it. He thrives on it."

"And the money's not bad," Hailey joked. "So,

you'll come? How soon? How long can you stay?"

"I'm going to drive," Avery said. "It will take me a few days to get there. I'll put my stuff in storage here, and then I'll send for it once I find a place to settle down."

"Where will that be? You must have given it some thought. You must have some sort of a plan."

"I don't have a plan. Well, not a definitive plan. I've spent a lot of time online, looking at maps of the country and rolling the names of towns around on my tongue. I'm kind of thinking I'd like to drive up Route 100."

"In *Vermont*?"

"Why not Vermont? It's gorgeous!"

Avery and Hailey spoke on the phone almost daily as Avery tied up loose ends. She didn't want any reminders of her life with her late husband and all but reinvented herself. With a large contingent of students living off-campus, a few ads produced a steady stream of eager buyers, and the furniture, rugs, lamps, and small appliances she and Andrew had chosen to furnish their home were soon sold.

"My memories are in my heart," she told Hailey sadly. "It's just too hard to see everything we had together. I start to cry, and I can't stop. I've cried until my eyes swelled shut. Finally, I had to buy one of those blue gel eye mask things you put in the freezer. I can't keep doing that to myself."

Avery brought most of her clothes to Dress For

Success, the elegant, beautifully tailored garments Andrew had delighted in selecting for her. The thought that her lovely clothes would empower women to dress for interviews and work thrilled her. Perusing the empty cloth-covered hangers on the rod in her closet, she put them into a bag and took them too. Davenport was only an hour away, and she loaded her Prius with bags and boxes, leaving early one morning and arriving minutes before the posted hours for making donations.

Next, she made an appointment with a day spa in Des Moines and drove the hour and forty-five minutes in the opposite direction for a full day of self-indulgence. She chose the most expensive option for skincare, the revitalizing and rejuvenation she needed most for her muddy, sallow complexion. She luxuriated as her hands and feet were coated with wax and slid into warm mitts to soften and slough off the roughened skin on her neglected extremities before her manicure and pedicure. She relaxed more than she had in the six months following Andrew's death with an herbal body wrap and a hot-stone massage. Then she was turned over to the hairstylist, who lifted Avery's long hair and clucked with disapproval.

"I'm Keely. What happened here?" she scolded.

"My hair has always been a vibrant red," Avery told her. "My husband—my late husband—loved the color and wouldn't let me cut it. He had a thing for long hair."

Avery's expression was pained. "But since he died—." Her voice trailed off, and she swallowed hard, forcing herself to continue. "The color is so faded now. One day it was bright and healthy, and overnight, it got so drab. I want to cut it all off."

Keely looked horrified. "Oh, don't do that! When you go through menopause, your metabolism changes and your hair may not grow the way it always has. Once you cut it, you may never have long hair again. I've seen it happen too many times, women who come in here wanting something different, a cute short cut, thinking they'll just grow it out if they change their minds." She shook her head emphatically.

"I have an idea for you," Keely recommended. "If you try to maintain red, you'll have obvious roots as you get older and your hair goes gray. You'll end up coloring it every few weeks to maintain a vibrant red. So why not get ahead of it and go silver but keep it long? It will be *so* dramatic!"

Avery was shocked. "I'm a widow. I already feel bad enough; I don't want to look like an old lady!"

The stylist laughed. "Oh, you won't, trust me. Here, let me show you some pictures of what I have in mind. Your red is almost a strawberry blonde which is a plus, but this isn't something we can do in one session. We'll apply bleach and toner today to transition to light blonde then, in another session, we'll transition to silver. It takes time, but it's totally worth it."

Avery still looked doubtful.

"Don't cut it! The juxtaposition of your uncommonly long hair and the silver color will be stunning. I promise!"

Avery flipped through a few pages and held up the brochure.

"Like this? Will it end up looking like this? I like it."

"After you go blonde today, you'll need an appointment about six weeks out."

Avery's face fell. "I can't. I'm leaving. Moving."

"Oh." Keely's face clouded. "How soon are you leaving?"

"Um. Pretty soon. I'm moving to Vermont, but first, I'm going to stay with my cousin in Connecticut for a few weeks."

Keely raised her brows.

"Where in Connecticut? How far is your cousin from New York City? There are some top-notch salons in New York."

"My parents live in the city, and I'll be visiting them for a few days too."

"There you go. Problem solved." Keely's smile was encouraging.

"Let's do it!" Avery decided. "You've convinced me."

An hour and a half later, Avery was stunned by her reflection in the mirror.

"It's so different. I feel so peculiar."

"Well, sure. It always takes some getting used to

when you make a big change. But that's what you said you wanted, something different. For the new you." Keely winked playfully.

There was a message from Jayson on the answering machine when Avery walked in late that afternoon. She'd picked up takeout on the way home, intending to have an early dinner while she watched the news, then take a long shower and crawl into bed. Hailey always phoned, never her husband, and Avery hoped he wasn't calling with bad news. She dumped her bags on the counter, pulled her cell out of her pocket, and speed-dialed her cousin.

"Hailey? Jayson left a message on my machine, asking me to call him. Is something wrong? Are you okay? Are the kids okay?"

"Everyone's fine," Hailey quickly assured her. "He wanted to talk to you about your car, that's all."

Avery was stunned. "My car? What *about* my car?"

"He's right here. We've got a dinner thing tonight, and we're about to walk out the door, but you have to catch him when you can. Hold on."

"Avery." Jay's voice was smooth and self-assured, and he came right to the point. "Listen, I don't think it's wise for you to drive cross country by yourself."

Avery started to protest, but Jay silenced her.

"Wait; hear me out. I suggest you fly from Des Moines to Hartford. There are flights closer to Iowa City, from Davenport, or even Cedar Rapids, but you don't want to fly on a feeder if you can avoid it. My advice is to book with a major carrier from a major airport. You'll want to spend the night at an airport hotel, but there's a flight out of Des Moines at a pretty reasonable hour, about 8 am, with one stop. The layover in Minneapolis is only about an hour and a half."

"What about my—?"

"Your car? I suggest you sell your Prius there. Post it on the faculty bulletin board, and I'll bet someone will snap it up within a day or two. If you're hell-bent on living in Vermont, I'm not sure the Prius is the right choice for secondary roads in snow. If you absolutely don't want to part with it, you could fly and ship the car here. Look online; you'll find any number of reputable companies that can put your vehicle on a transporter and have it here in two or three days. But I recommend you sell it there and buy something here."

"I read that Subarus are very popular in New England," Avery said. "The Prius has front-wheel drive, but I'd feel more secure with all-wheel drive and better ground clearance. You might be right. Let me think about that."

"I'll go with you if you want to look at cars locally," Jay offered. "There are several Subaru dealers within a reasonable distance." He chuckled. "I'm kind of a local celebrity. I have no doubt any one of them would fall all over themselves to give us a good deal."

"Thank you, Jay. I appreciate you thinking of me and offering to help."

"Any time. Gotta' run. See you soon."

"So? What's the story, morning glory?" Hailey asked the next morning. "I think Jay is right. I'd worry about you every minute and every mile between there and here. Make it easy on yourself and just get on a plane."

"It's tempting," Avery admitted. "I might just do that. I'm mentally wrung out, making decisions and tying up so many loose ends."

"To say nothing of packing up a house you've lived in for—what?—thirty years?"

"Not quite. I was twenty-four when Andrew took the job here, and I'm fifty-one now, so we lived in the house for twenty-seven years."

"That's a long time by anyone's standards. It's shocking how much *stuff* people accumulate."

Avery groaned. "Tell me about it! I've sold, donated, and given away a boatload. I'm down to the bare essentials now. I want to travel light and then start over with things that won't have memories attached. It's not like I'm trying to erase those years; it's just that it's so painful to have them in front of me every minute."

"Kind of like a snake shedding its skin and slithering away," Hailey teased to lighten the moment.

"Just like," Avery chortled. "I didn't have to go

dragging through probate for months and months, but there's *so* much paperwork. And we didn't even own property."

"You're financially secure," Hailey pointed out. "You'll be able to buy a house if you want, once you decide where you want to settle. Vermont surprises me, though; you've never expressed interest until now."

"I did some skiing in Vermont when I was an undergraduate, and I loved it. Killington once or twice. Okemo several times."

"What about Stowe?"

"Too far. There were quite a few ski areas within a couple of hours of Boston, but my friends and I mostly went to Cannon or Waterville Valley in New Hampshire."

"So, is that the draw? Skiing?"

"Some. Fall foliage. Covered bridges. Pretty little towns. I just want to drive around until I find someplace that appeals. I'll probably stay in bed-and breakfasts or Airbnb for a night or several nights. Then, if there's somewhere I want to stay longer, I'll look for a rental."

"Do you know anyone in Vermont?"

"Not a soul. That's part of the appeal."

"You and Andrew never went to Vermont together?"

Avery shook her head.

"Avery?"

"Oh, sorry." She laughed. "I was shaking my head

'no.' But you didn't see that."

"You should have switched to Facetime."

"To answer your question, I wouldn't have gone to a dog fight with Andrew when I first met him. Then I was so sick with morning sickness, the only place I went was into the bathroom. I was struggling to get through 1L. And then he got the position in Virginia. Next thing I knew, we were packing up and heading south. I always thought we'd get to Vermont someday, on vacation or something. I thought we'd do a lot of things together." Her voice quavered. "I thought we had so much time."

"I know," Hailey murmured. "You just have to put one foot in front of the other. You'll feel better once you get here. I can't wait to see you!"

Chapter Seven

Avery strode through the East Concourse once she'd landed at Bradley International. She was one of the first passengers to disembark, having paid a surcharge to book an aisle seat in First Class for that very reason.

Hailey sat in her car, listening to her audiobook in the cell phone waiting lot until Avery called to tell her she was standing on the curb at Domestic Arrivals.

"That's it?" Hailey gestured to Avery's roller bag. "That's all you've got?"

Avery groaned. "I don't do baggage claim. Nuh-uh, no way, José."

A scowling security guard motioned Hailey away from the curb as traffic backed up. She waved to let him know that she'd be moving momentarily. She reached for the handle and quickly stowed Avery's carry-on in the rear of her Tesla.

Avery whistled. "Wow! New car? I'm impressed."

"You know Jay. He's a car nut. It's clear that Washington is rapidly phasing out gas and diesel engines, and there are more and more charging stations, so he got on the waiting list for a Model Y as soon as he read that Tesla was making an SUV. It seats seven, and there's a ton of cargo space. There was quite a wait, but we love it."

"So, you *both* have Teslas?"

"Jay's is a Model S. It's the ultimate luxury car. I told you, he's a car nut! We have his-and-hers wall charging stations in the garage. I chose this classic white with a black interior but wait 'til you see his. It's the brightest red you've ever seen."

"I hope he doesn't try to talk me into getting one," Avery teased. "I feel like the Country Mouse after so many years in the corn capital of the United States."

"Speaking of the country, the traffic is so heavy on I-95 that I take Route 15 to New Haven and get on and off I-91 there. It's longer but much more scenic and less hectic." Hailey explained their route.

"Sound good to me," Avery concurred. "I was just thinking how built-up Connecticut has gotten. I remember flying into Bradley and looking down at all the tobacco netting. Some was white, and some yellow."

"Those days are long gone," Hailey said. "The tobacco industry is gutted, and most of the land sold to developers. You know how that goes."

"Yeah. It's called progress. I sure hope Vermont is still unspoiled."

Hailey slanted a look at her cousin but didn't comment.

"How long can you stay?" Hailey asked instead.

"As long as it takes to transition my hair. Seriously. I had an appointment with a stylist in Des Moines, and she convinced me to color my hair silver. It had to go from strawberry blonde to light blonde first, so it's only halfway there. I need an appointment at a salon here or in the city in about a month."

"Since when was your hair strawberry blonde? It's always been such a bright red."

"Since it got stressed, and it faded. I'm not kidding; the color just leached out of it. I looked like a hag," Avery complained.

Hailey reached over and squeezed Avery's hand. "Oh, honey, I'm sorry. Maybe I'll go silver, too. What d'ya' think? We could make appointments together."

Avery's smile was genuine. "Don't even think about it. Your hair is perfect just the way it is."

"You have no idea how expensive and time-consuming it is to get this artlessly casual look." Hailey laughed. "The style is called a beachy wave, and the twenty-shades-of-blonde that look like I've just been out in the sun, sailing, or playing tennis, is achieved through a process called balayage. I'm the epitome of the high-maintenance woman."

"Well, Jay can afford it. You look fabulous, and I am so glad to see you!"

"Are you ready to go car shopping tomorrow, Avery?" Jay asked at dinner one Friday night about a week after she arrived in Connecticut.

"I've been looking online, Jay, and I don't think I'm going to be doing much shopping. I'm pretty sure a Subaru Outback is exactly what I'll need. The safety record is excellent, and it has all-wheel drive, plenty of headroom and legroom, generous cargo space, CarPlay, and collision-avoidance features. I'm pretty impressed."

"There are some comparable alternatives, and most cars have similar features. I think you should test drive several vehicles before you decide. I have all day; we can make the rounds of the various dealerships," Jay offered.

"Subaru seems to have good ground clearance and a low center of gravity," Avery persisted. "I know several people who have them, and they swear by them."

"I'm not trying to talk you out of it. I just think you should take your time and see what the possibilities are before you commit."

"You're not trying to talk me into a Tesla, are you?" she teased.

Jay's expression turned serious as he spoke. "The day is coming—and soon —when all vehicles will be electric. I've been buying Tesla shares and also shares in an electric-charging company. I think it's the future, and I'm taking the long view. "

"That could be," Avery said. "But I have grave concerns about mining nickel and cobalt for the batteries in third-world countries, and how people will get rid of old batteries. I'd hate to think we're solving one problem and creating another." Seeing that Jay was about to defend his position, she added quickly, "There are two sides to every story and I don't want to argue. It's just that I'm not sure where I'll end up, and I'm leery of having an electric car when I don't know how accessible charging stations will be."

"You could lease a car," Hailey pointed out. "That way, you won't be stuck owning one. The technology is changing so fast, who knows what features will be available four years from now? Plus, you can always buy the vehicle when the lease is up."

"You're intent on moving to Vermont?" Jay asked, frowning. "Winters are harsh, and property taxes are high."

"No place is perfect, "Avery retorted. "I hate to sound snobbish, but the places where property taxes are low don't appeal to me. And everyplace seems to have a detriment weather-wise; some places are too hot or too humid, or they're at risk for tornadoes or hurricanes."

"Wildfires and mudslides," Hailey added.

"Exactly! Vermont isn't at risk for any of those things, not really, and there are no water moccasins, copperheads, rattlesnakes, brown recluse spiders, or scorpions."

"No alligators. No fire ants," Hailey said.

"So high taxes and long, cold winters," Avery concluded. "But Vermont is gorgeous. I just feel drawn to it."

"I love Vermont," Hailey said. "I'll come and visit you."

"So, what's your plan, Avery?" Jay asked. "Do you have one?"

Avery stared at him for a long moment before she asked, "Do I need one?"

"This has been such a relaxing visit," Avery told Hailey two weeks later. "I hate to leave, but my mom called this morning. She has a hole in her calendar, so I told her I'd take the train in on Wednesday and stay through the weekend."

"Why don't you catch a ride in with Jay? His driver can drop you at your parents' place. He always leaves early, but he doesn't have a set time to be in the studio, so he could go in a little later. I'm sure he'd be happy to accommodate you. I'll ask him."

"I wouldn't think of it," Avery protested. "I don't mind taking the train."

"Granted, the train between Greenwich and Grand Central is either express, one-stop- or two-stop but, still, why put yourself through that? If it doesn't work out for you to go in with Jay, I'll run you into town. It's only about thirty miles."

Avery rolled her eyes and groaned. "It's a long thirty miles!" She smiled. "But I appreciate the offer."

"Not negotiable," Hailey insisted. "One or the other."

"I have an idea. Let's compromise. I'll pay for an

Uber Wednesday morning. We can go to lunch with my mom and do some shopping. Then you can catch a ride home with Jay."

Hailey grinned. "That's an offer I can't refuse. I don't see my aunt and uncle nearly often enough. I'd love a day in the city."

"I haven't made a hair appointment because I wasn't sure when I could do it. I imagine the best salons are booked way in advance, but I'm sure my mother will have a few ideas. I'm hoping to get in somewhere Thursday or Friday. Or I could get a trim and color when I get back here."

"And then you'll be ready to go, with a new car and new hair." Hailey's voice was flat.

"You were hoping I'd decide to stay in Connecticut," Avery guessed.

"I was," Hailey admitted sadly. "I've missed you, and we've had such a good time. I thought you might not see the need to go anywhere."

"Hailey." Avery met her cousin's eyes. "This is *your* life. It was your parents' life and my parents' life, but it was never my life. The life I had, the one I loved and was comfortable in, is gone. I need to find something to take its place."

"You can't find that here? Are you sure?"

"It crossed my mind. It's beautiful here and peaceful, but it's the kind of beauty and peace that you buy. Homes and neighborhoods like this are enclaves. I can't explain it. It's a wonderful life for you, for your husband, who has a highly paid career in the city, for your kids. It's a wonderful life for your dog! I just don't see *myself* living in a New York City bedroom community."

"But you don't even know where you see yourself!"

"I'll know once I get there," Avery insisted. "I'm ready to get going."

"When will you leave?"

"I don't know. I'll get back from New York on Sunday. Don't even ask how. You watch, my dad will insist on sending me in a town car."

Hailey laughed. "That sounds like Palmer Beall, all right. So sit back and enjoy the ride; no point in arguing."

"I thought I'd stay here another day or two and then take off, maybe Wednesday or Thursday of next week."

On Monday afternoon, Avery was sorting her clothes in the laundry room. Hailey stood in the doorway, leaning against the door frame.

"Avery, can I run something by you?" she asked.

Avery looked up. "Sure."

"I wonder if you could do me a favor?"

"Of course! You've been a wonderful hostess for the past month. I would love an opportunity to do something for you. What is it?"

"It's a big ask."

Avery grinned. "Ask away."

"I volunteer as a pet transporter—"

"Really?" Avery interrupted. "I didn't know that."

"I've been doing it for the past couple of years. There's a whole network of volunteers who each drive animals a few hours to help place them in forever homes. I've made a few trips to Massachusetts with dogs and one to upstate New York."

Avery raised her eyebrows. "I've read about people doing that and private pilots flying animals places to relocate them. Good for you!"

"I got a call yesterday asking if I could transport a Siamese kitten to Vermont. It's only three or four hours, I think. I could do it, and I would do it, but—"

"But I'm going to Vermont, right?"

Hailey nodded.

"This is a purebred Siamese kitten?" Avery asked in disbelief. "Why would the shelter be involved?"

"It's a long story."

Avery closed the lid and selected the water temperature before starting her load of laundry. "I'm listening."

"Okay. There's a woman in Bridgeport, a young woman who works as a paralegal. She just got assigned to a high-profile case, and she's going to be working insane hours. It's going to be months before the case goes to trial, and the trial could drag out for weeks."

"What does that have to do with the kitten?" Avery frowned.

"I'm getting to that. The woman's roommate has a Siamese cat, and she thought she could make extra money by taking it to a stud to be bred, and selling kittens. Unfortunately, the last pregnancy was a miscarriage, and then the subsequent litter produced only one kitten. The money-making venture didn't pan out, and she got involved with some guy who hates cats. So—big surprise—she took off and left this woman stuck with the cat and the kitten. Plus, she stiffed her for the month's rent. The woman likes the adult cat and agrees to keep it, but not the kitten. Apparently, the roommate's sister in Vermont is willing to take it if the woman would drive it up there to her."

"But the woman can't because of her work schedule. I get that, but how did *you* get involved?"

"The woman—I hate to keep calling her that, but I don't even know her name—doesn't have time to deal with it, so she called a shelter in Bridgeport to see if they could help her. They called me to see if I could get the kitten and drive it to Vermont," Hailey explained.

"What would be Plan B?" Avery asked.

"I guess she'd surrender the kitten. It's weaned and litter trained. I think it's about four months old. The shelter is strictly no-kill, and they sure wouldn't have any trouble adopting it out."

"So, why doesn't she just do that? Don't answer; I know why. Because there's someone who's driving to Vermont this very week." Avery pursed her lips and stifled a sigh. "Do you know where in Vermont?"

"Newfane. I've never heard of it, but I looked on a

map. If you're going to start out on Route 100, it's just a little bit out of your way."

"Let's go look at the directions in Mapquest," Avery suggested. "I've never heard of Newfane either."

The next evening, Avery pointed to a car just pulling out of a metered parking space on the outskirts of Bridgeport, and Hailey guided her Tesla smoothly into it.

She thumbed her key fob as the cousins got out, and the car's lights flashed once as it emitted a chirp.

"It should be okay here," Hailey said. "We're not going to be long, and I can keep an eye on it. Starbucks is right over there. She gestured diagonally across the street.

Avery suggested they meet the woman with the kitten—who they now knew as Brittany—in a safe location near her apartment. As they approached the café, a young woman seated at an outdoor table near the entrance waved and pulled out two chairs for them.

"You must be the transporters. Thank you *so* much for doing this," she gushed.

"It's not a problem," Avery assured her. "It's a lucky coincidence that I'm headed to Vermont tomorrow. I'll be happy to deliver the kitten to your roommate's sister. You texted me the address, and now I just need the crate and the kitten's things."

Brittany's face clouded. "Um," she said slowly. "I

don't have a crate. It's in this box." She lifted a small box from the fourth chair and placed it on the table. Avery and Hailey heard piteous mewing coming from inside and frantic scrabbling on the cardboard.

"Wait! *What?* The kitten's not in a crate?" Hailey demanded just as Avery asked in bewilderment, "What about a litterbox?"

"Don't yell at *me*," Brittany said defensively. "This isn't even my deal."

"Okay, fine. No problem," Hailey said. She picked up the box. "We're all set."

Neither woman spoke until they reached the car. Hailey placed the box on the back seat.

She depressed the home button on her phone and queried, "Siri?'

"I'm listening."

"What's the nearest pet store?"

"Here's what I found on the internet," the virtual assistant responded.

"We'll just get a crate, a litterbox, litter, food and water bowls," Hailey told Avery. "Can you think of anything else?"

"I'll put an old teeshirt or something in the crate tonight so the kitten will have familiar smells when it gets where it's going. Poor thing."

"What a dumbass," Hailey commented derisively. "I wouldn't want Brittany on my team if I were a trial attorney."

"You won't believe this!" Avery blurted the

following afternoon when the call connected, and Hailey answered her cell.

"Uh-oh. I take it the delivery didn't go well. What happened?"

"Well, I didn't have any trouble finding the house, but it's no place for a tiny terrified kitten, and I couldn't leave it there," Avery exclaimed. Then she went on to explain what she found when she arrived at her destination.

"The sister seemed nice enough, but her life is in total chaos. She has three children under five, her husband was laid off from his job last week, and there are two big dogs. In addition, the mother-in-law just had her foot amputated because she has diabetes, and she's losing her eyesight, so Shelley more than has her hands full. She's already at the end of her rope; she doesn't need one more thing to take care of."

Hailey gasped. "Oh, you're *kidding*? So, now what? I thought about taking the kitten myself," she said. "I love Siamese. Baz is a good boy, but Malinois have such a high prey drive I'd be afraid he'd go after a cat.

"I guess I could find a vet," Avery said. "There must be one around here. Maybe they could place it."

Later that afternoon, Avery saw an attractive sign advertising a bed-and-breakfast. She turned into the driveway and pulled around back to the parking area.

"One person? For how many nights?" the owner asked when Avery rang the bell and entered the foyer.

There was a small reception desk cleverly tucked under the stairs.

"It's just me," Avery replied. "I'd only need to spend one night."

"I'm Denise Sanders. Dee." The proprietor held out her hand, and Avery shook it.

"I have two vacancies. Would you like to see them?"

Before Avery could reply, the woman strode briskly up the stairs, talking over her shoulder. "We have four rooms, and all have an en suite bath." She unlocked the second door on the left and pushed it open.

"Queen bed," she stated. "There's this, or one with a king."

"Do you take animals?" Avery asked.

The owner turned, her expression dismayed. "I'm sorry; we don't. Are you traveling with a dog?"

"No. Um. No, it's not a dog. I have a kitten. She's in a crate. I put something in it for litter; she wouldn't have to get out. Or—could I give you a damage deposit?"

"It's not that. It's the dander. So many people are allergic. I'm sorry."

"I understand. Can you recommend somewhere nearby that does take pets?"

"Come into the living room and sit down. Let me make a few phone calls. I won't be long. Can I get you something to drink?"

"That's very kind, but I'm fine, thanks. I have

water in the car."

Ten minutes later, Dee shook her head, her expression rueful. "Every place I tried is full. Vermont is a tourist draw, and people either have a reservation, or they get off the road by mid-afternoon and find lodging as a walk-in."

"I'm planning to drive up Route 100," Avery said. "What's the next big town?"

"Oh, gosh. I'm not sure you'd find anything going that way. You'd probably have to go to Brattleboro. It's only about twenty minutes away, but it's in the exact wrong direction."

Avery closed her eyes, her expression pained. *Could this day get more screwed up?*

"Where are you headed?" Dee asked. "You must be planning to visit someone if you've got a cat with you."

"No. Not exactly. My cousin volunteers as an animal transporter. The rescue people asked her to take this kitten to a home here in Newfane. Since I was headed up Route 100, this wasn't much out of the way, so I agreed to do it instead." She grimaced. "But it didn't work out. You know how that goes; no good deed goes unpunished."

"So, it's not really your kitten?"

"Well, it is now, I guess. I thought maybe a vet could place it, so I took it to Davenport Veterinary Clinic."

"Who did you see?" Dee's smile was wide. "Kyle Davenport graduated from Tufts a few years ago and went into practice with his dad, Clay Davenport."

"I didn't actually see a vet," Avery admitted. "I explained what I wanted to the receptionist but, while I waited, I changed my mind. I might need this kitty as much as she needs me. I don't want her to go to just anybody. She's so beautiful and so sweet. And she's so scared. It just didn't seem fair to leave her there."

Dee met Avery's eyes. "I'll tell you what. My daughter's at UVM, up in Burlington. She's a sophomore. She had a summer job there, and now classes have started, so her room has been empty. I don't rent it out." She laughed. "It looks just like the day she went off to college. If you can stand it, you're welcome to it." She laughed again. "In fact, I should probably pay you!" she joked.

Avery opened a small can of kitten food and left her new pet in the crate to eat in peace while she went to find a take-out dinner for herself. When she returned, the kitten's dish was licked clean, and she was curled into a tight ball, fast asleep.

Sated after enjoying some surprisingly good Chinese, Avery stepped into the bathroom. *Oh, that feels so good.* The water pressure was excellent, and Avery bowed her head, letting the water beat down on the tight muscles in her neck and shoulders. She'd been looking forward to a hot shower for hours. *What a day!*

Chapter Eight

There was a TV in Shelley's room, so Avery slipped into her pajamas and sat in bed, watching the news and the weather. She flipped through a few channels with the remote she'd found on the dresser, but nothing piqued her interest. Finally, she opened a map of Vermont on her tablet and selected the southern part of the state, enlarging the image, trying to decide where the road would take her the next morning.

She'd go north on Route 30, she decided, and pick up Route 100 again. It was only a short distance to Weston, about a forty-five-minute drive, and she wanted to spend a little time looking around in the famed Vermont Country Store. Then she'd drive another hour or so, and spend a night or two in Ludlow, perhaps renting a condo through one of the real estate offices located at the base of Okemo Mountain in order to explore the local area. She remembered liking Ludlow when she'd skied there years before, and she wondered how much the town had changed in the intervening years.

Avery yawned, suddenly too tired to keep her eyes open. Turning off the bedside lamp, she was asleep in seconds. But not for long. Startled, she was disoriented by unfamiliar surroundings and an unfamiliar sound. She turned the light on again and, kneeling, peered into the crate.

The kitten's eyes were squeezed shut, and its mouth wide open, emitting an anguished wail of loneliness and despair. *Oh, kitty, I know just how you feel.* She picked the kitten up and snuggled it against her chest, where it began to purr and knead.

Fifteen minutes later, the kitten, now named Anya, slept contentedly, safe and warm under the covers, pressed against Avery's torso, each drawing comfort from the other.

"The eggs are from my own chickens," Dee said the next morning as she placed a plate with silver-dollar-sized pancakes, two sausage links, and a serving of fluffy scrambled eggs in front of Avery. "They're free-range during the day, but they spend the night in the henhouse for their safety."

"What would harm them during the night?"

"Fox. Coyote. Maybe a fisher."

"What kind of chickens are they?" Avery asked.

"White ones. I bought chicks at the feed store, and they didn't specify. You'd expect white chickens to lay white eggs, but, curiously, their eggs are brown."

"Probably Leghorns," Avery surmised. "And that is about the extent of my knowledge concerning poultry."

"How far will you go today?" Dee asked.

"Not very far." Avery laughed. "Just up the road. Weston. I've seen the Vermont Country Store catalog, but I'd like to look around in the store itself. They have so many practical gadgets you just don't see anywhere else."

"You'll love it!" Dee exclaimed. "I do half my Christmas shopping there."

"I want to get a gift for my cousin in Connecticut. I just spent a month with her."

"She'd probably appreciate Vermont maple syrup. You can get it there, and they'll ship, of course."

"Then I'm going to go on a little farther, to Ludlow. I may try to rent a condo and stay a few nights so I can explore the area."

"Don't miss Woodstock," Dee advised. "It was voted 'Prettiest Small Town in America' some years ago, and now it's a tourist mecca. It's like a movie set, with little bistros and boutiques. And the general store in the center of town is an absolute delight. It's very upscale, and you might find a great gift there for your cousin. They sell maple syrup, too. I love the rectangular cans with a Vermont sugaring scene on them."

"I'm looking for a town to settle in," Avery confided. "My husband passed away earlier this year, and I need a complete change of scenery."

"I'm so sorry. Where were you living?"

"I grew up in Connecticut, and I went to college

in Boston, but I've lived in Iowa for the last thirty years. My husband was a writer, and he was head of the Writer's Project at the university. The position included a beautiful stately home on campus, but I had to vacate so his successor could move in. So, it seemed like an ideal time to make a clean break."

"What did he write? I love to read. Would I have heard of him?"

"He wrote mysteries—crime novels. Andrew Markham."

"Oh, my God!" Dee's voice rose. "I love his books! I've read them all." Then her mouth fell open in surprise as she realized who her overnight guest was.

"Wait! You're *Avery* Markham! I've seen your name on book covers. So, you're a writer too."

"I'm a private investigator by profession. I worked as Andrew's researcher for years, and then I became his co-author."

"Will you keep on writing? There's not much industry in this state, and it's hard to find employment in small towns because locals seem to be hired through word of mouth before jobs are even advertised. A lot of people who move here are self-employed, or they telecommute."

"I get asked that a lot lately." Avery shook her head. "I don't think I can. Well, I'm sure I *can*, but Andrew and I had such synergy that I don't think I have the will to continue without him. I'll have income from royalties, but I don't know how much or for how long. Once I get settled somewhere, I'll just look for a little job that will pay for groceries and keep me occupied."

"I hope you'll keep in touch," Dee said sincerely. "I'd like to know where you end up. If it's somewhere nearby, come back to see me some time."

"How do you like Ludlow?" Hailey asked that night when Avery called her.

"I like it. It's an old mill town that's become gentrified. But it's very attractive, and there's some interesting architecture. Looks like there are quite a few nice restaurants and some cute places that just serve breakfast and lunch. I spent quite a bit of time at the Vermont Country Store earlier today, and I didn't get to Ludlow until late afternoon. There are real estate offices on every block—sometimes more than one—so I didn't have any trouble renting a condo. It's the shoulder season, between summer and foliage, so the prices are reduced. I'm going to spend two nights here so I can get a feel for the town and scope out the area."

"What about clothing shops?" Hailey asked. "The weather is gorgeous now, but it will start getting pretty nippy in the early morning and the evening. You should start picking up a few things and building your winter wardrobe. Since Ludlow is a ski town, you might find some sweaters or jackets there, maybe even on sale before they bring in this year's inventory.

"You won't *believe* what I found yesterday at the Vermont Country Store. You'll never guess," Avery told Hailey. "Tigress!"

"Tigress cologne? Are you kidding? We used to love that stuff. I haven't thought about it in years. Decades! I thought it had vanished off the face of the earth."

"I got us each a bottle. It smells as good now as it did then, and, boy, did it bring back memories. And you wouldn't believe the mens' colognes from back in the day. Do you remember English Leather? British Sterling? St John's Bay Rum?"

Hailey laughed. "You must feel like a time traveler!"

"Something like that. Here I am, looking for a small town from a simpler time. I like Ludlow, but I don't think this is it. I'm afraid it'll be thronged with Connecticut and Massachusetts and New York license plates half the year. The realtor I talked to yesterday told me Okemo was a family-owned ski area until recently, but Vail Resorts bought it for something like seventy-five million dollars."

"So, what's next?"

"A few more miles. The owner of the B&B I stayed at last night told me not to miss Woodstock. I called the Chamber of Commerce to ask about a B&B or Airbnb where I could bring Anya, and I found out that the Woodstock Inn has pet-friendly rooms. There's a hefty fee, but I don't want to try to sneak her in somewhere.

Hailey snorted. "I met a couple in an elevator once who snuck their dog into the hotel. A Great Dane, can you imagine? I mean, that's not some teacup poodle you can stick in your shoulder bag."

"I bought Anya a little collar and a cat backpack today. It looks like a regular backpack, but one side is a clear plastic bubble with air holes. I don't want to leave her in a hotel room all day, so I'll have a room-service breakfast and ask one of the restaurants at the inn to pack a lunch for me. Then, once the maid service has come and gone, I'll put her back in the room for a few hours to use the catbox and take a nap while I cruise the shops."

"That's what you named her? Anya? Sound like you're managing to travel with her well enough."

"She's good company. I had no idea Siamese were so affectionate and so vocal. She's quite a talker."

"I've known a few. They're very people-oriented."

"I Googled Woodstock, and there's a gorgeous town green," Avery continued excitedly. "There's a covered bridge right in the center of town and five hundred acres that Laurance Rockefeller donated to the town for recreational purposes. Did you know he spent summers there and was one of the town's benefactors? The Rockefeller mansion is open for tours now that he and his wife have passed on."

"There's a ski area near there," Hailey said. "I can't remember the name, but I read once that it's the site of the first rope tow."

"I wish Andrew and I had been able to spend

some time in Vermont. It's just so beautiful." A sob caught in Avery's throat, and scalding tears stung her eyes. "I can't believe I'm never going to see him again. I miss him so much."

Hailey's own throat was tight as she attempted to comfort her cousin. "It's going to take time. You have to keep yourself busy."

"I'm so lonely," Avery whispered. "I feel so alone." The tears were now streaming down her cheeks.

"You have us. You can turn right around and come back, you know. Tomorrow, next week, next month. Our door is always open."

"Thank you, Hailey. I don't know what I'd do without you. But I'll be better in the morning. I want to do this; I don't want to go backward. I'm looking forward to seeing Woodstock."

"Send pictures," Hailey demanded. "It sounds wonderful. Maybe I'll surprise Jay with a weekend getaway there for our anniversary in April."

"So, how was it?" Hailey asked two days later.

"Pictures don't do it justice. It probably *is* the prettiest small town in America."

"Is there a 'but?'"

"Yes and no. No, not really. I put Anya in her backpack and hiked up Mt. Tom, although hiked is probably a misnomer because the path is actually a carriage road. It's uphill the whole way but not steep. There's a circular lake at the top called 'The Pogue,' and it's lovely. I walked partway around and then up to the bluff overlooking the town.

"Really? You were looking down on the town?"

"There's a wooden frame up here on the bluff with lights on it. Apparently, you can see the star way up above the town at Christmas time as you're driving in on Route 4. That's what someone in one of the shops told me."

"It sounds fabulous!" Hailey said.

"You know how the Rockefeller family donated land in Maine that became Acadia National Park, and it has carriage roads all through it? They must have sent one of their crews over here to create similar carriage roads. There are hitching posts used to tie up the carriage horses that brought families up on Sunday afternoons for picnics, and there are stone watering troughs. This is a national park now as well."

"It sounds like a fascinating town."

"It is! The whole downtown is a historic district with wrought-iron railings around the town green and lamp posts that look like old gas lamps. Everything has to be approved by the planning board, the signage, and certain colors. It's just gorgeous."

"But?"

"I don't know. Have you ever eaten something that's too rich? You know how you can only eat a little of it? That's how this feels. You have to drive ten miles to West Lebanon, New Hampshire, to a supermarket or big-box stores and franchises because

Woodstock is too perfect for the stuff you need to sustain life. You know what I mean?"

"So, what's next?"

"Keep going. I'm not saying this isn't where I'll end up. But I want to see more of the state before I commit."

"I thought you were planning to rent? That's not much of a commitment. You can always pick up and move."

"I could," Avery said slowly. "I'm not ruling that out. But it's harder to wrench yourself away once things begin to feel familiar and you've made a few acquaintances. I'd rather find a place that feels right and settle in."

"So you'll continue up Route 100?"

"I want to see the whole state. I think I'm going to take a look at Rutland and then go up through the Champlain Valley to Middlebury and on up to Burlington. I might like living in a college town, so I may spend a night in Middlebury and a few nights in Burlington. Then, from Burlington, I can explore the northwest corner of the state."

What about Bennington?" Hailey asked. "That's a well-known college town."

Avery sighed. "It's in southern Vermont. By going up Route 100 and then to Newfane, I missed Bennington on the west side of the state and Brattleboro on the east side. I want to see the state capital, so I'm going to take I-89 southeast to Montpelier when I leave Burlington and, from there, go up Route 2 to St. Johnsbury. That's called 'The Northeast Kingdom.' Isn't that a cool name?"

"I've heard of that. Going to be mighty chilly up there by the Canadian border in the winter. My teeth are chattering just thinking about it," Hailey teased.

"Well, if I wanted to wear shorts all winter, I'd be moving to Florida, now, wouldn't I?" Avery shot back.

"Proceed," Hailey ordered, ignoring Avery's rhetorical question.

"I've been studying the map. From St. J, I guess I'll take Route 5 all the way down to Brattleboro. It parallels the interstate, but if I take I-91, I'll miss all the small towns that Route 5 passes through. Then Route 9 east-west to Bennington. After that, I'll have to backtrack a little to pick up Route 100 again, but I want to drive back up through Ludlow and Woodstock to see what my second impressions are because they're both candidates."

"I'm exhausted just thinking about all that driving," Hailey said. "Better you than me, Cuz."

"I love it!" Avery exclaimed. "There are so many pretty little towns, but I keep wondering what's around the next bend."

"How's your kitty?"

The corners of Avery's mouth turned up in a spontaneous grin, and her voice was soft as she replied, "Adopting her is the best thing that could have happened. You have no idea what good company she is."

"She must be a good traveler."

"I was afraid she'd yowl the whole time, but she just curls up and goes to sleep. She seems quite contented."

"Is her crate on the passenger seat where she can see you?"

"Yes." Avery laughed with pure pleasure. "I put her crate on the seat, facing me. When she gets bigger and I can buy a harness that fits her, I'll teach her to ride in a car seat, up high where she can look out the window. I saw one for small dogs that would be perfect for her. She's very smart."

"She sounds like good company. You needed her, and she needed you. I hope you get everything you need in Vermont," Hailey added, her tone serious.

"Me, too," Avery agreed. "I know what I need, and right now, I'm looking for what I want."

Eight days later, Avery's journey came to an end. She spent another night in Ludlow and one more in Woodstock. She'd started getting 'fanny fatigue' from doing so much driving, and the novelty of being on the road had worn off. Avery found herself yearning for a place to call home.

She wasn't surprised to have slept so deeply and so long when she spent another night at the Woodstock Inn. That had happened the first time she'd stayed there, slipping into bed and falling asleep almost at once. This time, she'd intended to get an early start and thought she'd wake at her usual time, but it was almost mid-morning when she put her overnight bag into the car and checked out. The café would close in another fifteen minutes, so she quickly filled her travel mug while she waited for a breakfast sandwich.

Then, with Anya in her backpack, Avery strolled across the town green, dry leaves crunching underfoot. She sat on a bench, appreciatively sipping her coffee, black and hot, just the way she liked it. She bit into her sandwich, melted cheese oozing into her mouth, and chewed thoughtfully.

"What do you think, Kitty? Is this it?" Although no dialogue was forthcoming, Avery had developed the habit of addressing her cat.

"Me, either. This is such a beautiful town, but I just don't feel drawn to it. I can't put my finger on it. So, we'll continue up Route 100 through the middle of the state and see what lies around the next bend."

Chapter Nine

Avery's Outback had a half tank of gas, and she knew she should make time to top up in Woodstock, but she was eager to get going. She settled Anya's crate on the passenger's seat. The sun poured in, and the kitten basked in the warmth, stretching, yawning, and curling into a ball, asleep before Avery even circled the green and followed Route 4 west out of town.

Just past Killington, she picked up Route 100 and saw on her GPS display that she'd pass through several small towns. She planned to fill up in Westfield, a larger town less than a half-hour ahead. But even the smallest towns in Vermont seemed to have a general store, so Avery decided to stop in the next one she came to and refill her travel mug with a second cup of coffee. *I might as well get gas at the same time.*

Back in the car, she addressed Anya. "Well, Kitty, no gas pump, but we could have stocked up on nightcrawlers if we wanted to go fishing. And the pizza smelled good, but it's a little too early for lunch.

So, we'll see what the next town has to offer."

Avery consulted her GPS and learned that Winslowe had both a country store with a deli and a gas station.

After continuing up Route 100 for about ten miles, Avery saw a directional sign for the Winslowe covered bridge and turned right onto Covered Bridge Road. The weathered wooden bridge spanning the Mad River was shorter and simpler than the one she'd admired in Woodstock, but it, too, had a set of thick planks, four boards wide for each set of tires, laid at right angles to the structure's wooden floor. *Welcome to Winslowe*, Avery thought, grinning. She'd yet to see what the town offered, but already she had a good feeling.

Turning left on Main Street, Avery passed a post office and the volunteer fire department. Anya was wide awake, and she seemed restless. "I'll bet you need to use the cat box," Avery observed. "Just give me a minute."

Just ahead, she saw an attractive, two-story white frame building with a hanging sign advertising it as the town's general store. Although the early-fall day was warm, not hot, Avery knew how quickly a vehicle could heat up, and she needed to get her kitten situated comfortably so she could go inside. It was just about noon, and the sun was directly overhead, but she found a satisfactory place to park. She pulled her car up into the deep shade afforded by a large tree and cracked the windows. She got Anya's cat box from the cargo hatch, put it in the passenger footwell, and then snapped the lid off a small plastic container of kibble and poured water from a thermos into a shallow bowl. "I'll get something to go," she told the cat, "and I'll be back in a few minutes."

Stepping into the store's interior, Avery glanced around, awed by various sections and the number of goods offered for sale. There was a bakery section with numerous desserts and homemade bread, a liquor section with local craft beer, spirits from a local distillery, and wine from a local vineyard. The artisanal cheese selection was exceptional, with milk sourced from a local creamery and goat milk from a local herd. The varieties of homemade fudge made Avery's mouth water. But the deli was clearly the heart of the store. The array of made-from-scratch soups and side dishes, the salads and the thick sandwiches, took Avery's breath away. Daily specials were scrawled on a chalkboard, each more tempting than the one before.

"Have you decided?" A man's deep voice broke into her reverie, and Avery swiveled toward him. He was slender, of medium height, with his dark hair mostly hidden under a baseball cap. He wore a dark green teeshirt with jeans and the ties of his dark-green cotton apron wrapped around his narrow waist. Avery noticed that the hat, the tee, and the apron all bore the store's logo.

His mouth quirked up in a bemused smile, and his eyes were warm, but he glanced over Avery's shoulder to assess the number of customers waiting in line behind her. He looked behind him and turned abruptly, crossing the space to the open back door and sighing heavily. Smoke from the grill drifted toward diners seated at the picnic tables on the deck, and several attempted to fan it away with paper plates or napkins.

He turned back to Avery and apologized, "Sorry. I'll be right with you." She watched as he got a small caged fan from a storeroom and set it in the doorway. As soon as he turned it on, the smoke blew in the opposite direction. Striding to the grill, he snatched up a metal spatula and deftly flipped half a dozen burgers.

Returning to the counter, he raised his eyebrows, and Avery was ready with her order. "Everything looks so good. It was hard to decide, but I'd like the roast beef with Boursin."

"Sounds good! I'll have the same," said the man standing behind Avery. "You're sure slammed, Todd. Where's Emmie?" Since he spoke so familiarly, Avery figured he was a regular, probably local.

"Same deal every year," Todd replied, shaking his head. "Summer help goes back to school, and we're always short-handed in September and October. Emmie has a doctor's appointment in Burlington, and we were so busy all summer she's already rescheduled twice. How about you get back here and give me a hand?" he teased.

"Would if I could, buddy, but I gotta get back to

work."

Todd turned his back and reached for two hard rolls. Splitting them expertly, he smoothed horseradish aioli on each of the four halves.

"I've already wasted half my lunch break on the phone, trying to get Travis added to my car insurance," the man said. "Kid passed his driver's test last week, but he can't use our vehicles until he's insured. You know how that goes; you spend fifteen minutes on hold while they keep telling you to remain on the line because your call is so friggin' important to them." He snorted with derision.

Todd called over his shoulder, "You want that to go, right, Kenny?"

"Yep. I'll just grab a bag of chips and a soda."

"What about you, miss? Here or to go?

"I'll just take it out on the deck."

Todd arranged Avery's sandwich on a heavy oval disposable plate with a spear of pickle and a portion of crisp golden potato chips, dusted with coarse grains of sea salt. "The pickle and the chips are both homemade," he told her. "We try to do everything from scratch."

"Is it okay if I get my cat out of the car and bring her with me? I see some dogs out on the deck. She'll be in a backpack so, most likely, no one will even notice her."

"*A cat?* Seriously?"

"A kitten," Avery told him. "She's a bluepoint Siamese."

"Well, sure, I guess." He shrugged. "That's a first!"

Just as Avery came down the wooden stairs to the lower level, a family was finishing their meal at the far end of the deck. The man shook his soda, then tipped it up and swallowed the last mouthful before tossing the can into a nearby trash receptacle. The kids, two girls and a boy, scrambled out from their seats on the picnic benches, and, as they stood, the woman motioned to the table, indicating that they should gather the detritus from their lunch and dispose of it.

Avery hesitated at the bottom of the stairs, and the woman called, "This table is free if you're waiting for one."

Spotting Anya, one of the girls asked, "Is that a *cat*?"

"It sure is," Avery replied. "Her name is Anya. She's a bluepoint Siamese."

"She rides in that backpack? Doesn't she try to get out?" the boy inquired.

"She sleeps a lot," Avery told him. "When she's awake, she's happy just to be with me. Siamese are very outgoing, and they like to be included."

As the family left, one of the girls turned and gave Avery a little wave, grinning shyly.

Todd appeared in the back door and perused the deck, ensuring that all was in order. Walking to the railing, he took in the scene below. A few minutes later, he emerged and closed the distance to Avery's table in a few long strides.

"Looks like you enjoyed your lunch," he observed.

"Every bite," she assured him. "The sandwich was delicious, and the pickle was perfect. The chips were perfect, too. I'm stuffed!"

"What," he teased. "No room for dessert? All bakery items are homemade. If you can't eat it now, you should get something to take with you."

"Actually, I'm thinking I might stay over. I have a guidebook that says there's a 'must-see' waterfall not far away."

"Where'd you come from?" Todd asked, then continued before she could reply. "If you came up Route 100, you missed it. It's just south of town a few miles. There's a sign for the parking area."

"I must have seen the sign, but I didn't pay any attention to it. I was looking for the turnoff for the covered bridge. I just read about the waterfall while I was sitting here." She held up the guidebook.

"It's quite the tourist attraction. It's one of the best swimmin' holes around. All the locals go there and most of the visitors."

Avery wrinkled her nose.

"It's pretty crowded all summer, families and kids. Y'know? And it'll be mobbed during leaf-peeping season. But, right now, this is what we call the 'shoulder season.' Kids are back in school, and the foliage hasn't turned yet. You should be okay. You'll love it."

Avery nodded.

"So, you looking for a place to stay?" He gestured vaguely behind him. "Inn's right over there. You must have seen it when you drove in. Price-y, but nice. There's a restaurant, too, so you can count on a nice dinner."

"Do they take animals?" Avery wondered.

"Cats, you mean? That I don't know. They advertise a few pet-friendly rooms, but I don't know if they mean just dogs. You could ask. I know they charge extra for a cleaning fee or a damage fee, maybe. I could call and ask. Why don't you and—your friend..."

"Anya," Avery interjected.

"Why don't you and Anya take a little trip to the falls? Stop back by, and I'll have an answer for you. You can have something from the bakery case and a glass of hot spiced cider then."

"Well, that sounds appealing. You certainly know how to upsell a simple sandwich." Avery laughed, feeling genuinely happy for the first time in a long time. Apart from her cousin, she hadn't had more than fleeting contact with anyone and hadn't realized how lonely she was.

Later that afternoon, Avery set Anya's catbox down on the bathroom floor in one of the inn's pet-friendly rooms. She unrolled the top of a bag and poured in a few inches of litter. She ran some water into Anya's bowl and filled her food dish with a handful of kibble.

After washing her own face and hands, she told the kitten, "You're all set. Make yourself at home, and I'll be back in a little while."

Avery was very pleased with the inn's accommodations and decided to pamper herself with a three-night stay after her weeks on the road. She walked the short distance to the general store and saw Todd ringing up a teeshirt sale. She gestured toward the stairs and the door marked CLOTHING THIS WAY. Catching her intent, Todd shook his head and slashed his hand across his throat.

When the customer left, Avery asked, "Is the upstairs closed?" Todd said nothing for a long moment, then sighed heavily. "Do you know how many times a day I get asked that question?" He sounded exasperated. "*Yes*, it's closed. *Again.*"

Avery was perplexed and waited for him to explain. Holding a clear glass mug under the spigot, Todd filled it with steaming amber cider, redolent with cinnamon, and slid the mug across the counter toward Avery. "On the house," he told her. "Welcome to Winslowe." He gestured toward the bakery case and asked, "What would you like to go with that?"

"They used to hold community dances up there, once upon a time," Todd said. "Now it's a clothing boutique, but, for the last several years, there've been a succession of managers. It seems like it's closed more than it's open. Right now, it's closed. Again."

Wearily, he massaged his forehead.

"Did you have much damage from the hurricane?" Avery asked, tactfully changing the subject. "I saw on the news that there was a lot of flooding in New England."

"That was awful," Todd said. "The rain was relentless, and the flash flooding was catastrophic all over the state. I've lived here all my life, and I've never seen the river that high. The water just lifted houses off their foundations and uprooted trees, and swept it all downstream. Several bridges were damaged or destroyed. Ours was closed because floodwaters undermined the bridge and the riverbanks were dangerously eroded. Where were you?"

"Iowa," Avery told him. "My late husband was a college professor. He was head of The Writers' Project for twenty years."

"You're a widow," Todd stated. "Is that where you're from? Do you have family there?"

"No," Avery said, shaking her head slowly. "I grew up in Connecticut and went to college in Massachusetts. My cousin still lives in Connecticut, and my folks have an apartment in the City now that my dad's retired."

Todd didn't need to ask what city.

"So, you think you might stick around here?" he inquired. "It's a great little town," he said enthusiastically. "You can get anything you need or want in Burlington, and there's great skiing just up the road. And there are always great places to eat and cute shops near a ski area."

"I love to ski," Avery said enthusiastically. "Although I guess I'm what you'd call an advanced beginner."

"You've heard of or read about Mad River Glen?" Todd asked. "It's famous or—more accurately—infamous." Avery shook her head.

"You will, soon enough." Todd grinned. "There are a few beginner-friendly trails, but it's known for its challenging terrain." Disappearing into the kitchen for a minute, he re-emerged, holding a red-and-white bumper sticker. "MAD RIVER GLEN: SKI IT IF YOU CAN," it read.

Avery burst out laughing. "I don't think I'm quite ready for that, but I love this place already."

The Glen has thirty-six hundred feet of elevation, with a vertical drop of two thousand feet. It's the highest ridge in the Green Mountains, so it gets a lot of snow, plus picking up precipitation from Lake Champlain. There's some snow-making and grooming, but the trails are narrow and depend more on natural snowfall," Todd told her.

"Wow. That's different."

"That's not the only way it's different," Todd stated. "It almost went under, but a group of die-hard skiers bought it and formed a cooperative. You can buy a share and have a say in its management. That really sets it apart from the corporations that have bought up most of the major ski areas in the country and packaged them as ski resorts. And it's different because it has a single-chair lift. The only other one in the U.S. is in Alaska. You'll see the sign." He laughed. "It says, *'Still Single After All These Years.'* The single chair was built in 1948. It had to be shut down in 2007 because most of the chairs had severe rot and rust. They used the original 1940s plans for the lift to restore the structure, and the whole thing was rebuilt according to the original specs and modified to current safety standards."

Avery frowned. "I'm no business major, but that doesn't sound cost-effective. Why didn't they just tear it down and put in a high-speed double or a triple? Or a quad?"

"Because the shareholders finally voted to restore it. Besides, those runs aren't 'thousand-skier' runs; they're best with a few hundred out there at a time. They raised a shitload of money and took down the old towers. They poured new concrete bases that summer and had the old towers flown by helicopter down to Bath. There's a shipbuilder that had the capability to sandblast, straighten them, and re-paint. Then they were trucked back to Mad River Glen."

Avery nodded knowingly. "The Bath Iron Works. I grew up in New England, remember?"

Todd was still talking about the restoration. "It takes twelve minutes to get from the bottom to the top, but it's worth it."

Avery said, "Maybe I'll take some lessons and get good enough to go there.

"Not this winter," she added quickly.

"Oh, don't be intimidated. The Glen has a ski school, and you'd be fine there. The only place you can buy those bumper stickers is in the base lodge. There's an honor box, and you just donate a dollar. You can even get it as a temporary tattoo if that's more your style." He winked, and Avery blushed, shaking her head in amusement.

"The original ad campaign goes back to the mid-80s," he continued. "It's become such an icon that a marketing strategist would be insane to mess with a good thing. Travelers have taken those bumper stickers to the craziest places all over the world. There's more than one at the top of Mount Kilimanjaro!"

"You must be an experienced skier with all this right out your back door," Avery commented

"I've been on skis since I was old enough to walk," Todd said proudly. "I was a ski racer all through middle school and high school. And I was on the ski team in college, of course."

"Where did you go to college?" Avery asked.

"UVM. Go, Catamounts!" Todd pumped his fist then looked abashed. "Well, that was a lotta' years ago."

"What about your wife?" Avery asked. "How did you meet her?"

"Emmie? I've known her almost all my life. Just kidding. This is a very small town, so we went to the same elementary school, Pre-K through sixth. Winslowe kids go to middle school and high school over in Morsetown. It's about twelve miles up the road."

"Were you high-school sweethearts?" Avery teased.

"Not hardly." Todd grimaced. "We were both ski racers, so we spent a lot of time on busses going to meets. Neither of us had much time for a serious relationship. I dated some, though, and I think she did too. We were just teammates and acquaintances, not even friends, really."

"Did she go to UVM as well?" Avery asked.

"Nope. She was a brainiac. She was in all AP classes, and she was class valedictorian. She went to Mount Holyoke and graduated *magna* with a degree in English."

"What did she do after graduation?"

"She landed a job at the *Boston Globe*, writing features for the Travel section."

"That sounds like a fun job," Avery said. "So, how did you get together?"

"Em was writing a feature on Cabot Creamery and the dairy co-op so she was spending a few days with her folks, doing some research. There was a Nor'easter, and my mom asked if I could plow out their driveway because her dad had just had gall bladder surgery. Mrs. Caldwell invited me in for hot chocolate when I finished, and I ended up staying for supper. Emmie and I just kind of connected. I guess the time was right. We got married two years later."

"Do you have children?"

Todd's smile lit up his face, and his eyes shone. "We do. Eliza is fifteen, and Toby is thirteen. You'll probably meet them if you're going to be around. They're in and out. Emmie is usually here most of the day, too, so come by tomorrow and meet her."

Chapter Ten

. Avery slept late the next morning after the best night's rest she'd had in a long time. She might have slept longer, but Anya was awake and ready for her breakfast. Since Avery was in a room where pets were permitted, she did not relegate the kitten to her crate. Anya had expressed a preference for snuggling against Avery's torso, and Avery always felt comforted by the presence of another body, however small.

Now, Anya tapped Avery's face with her tiny paw and, when that didn't elicit a response, she thrust both paws into Avery's hair. Avery opened one eye and squinted into the kitten's face, inches from her own. Having achieved the desired result, Anya began to dig furiously at the covers, determined to rouse her companion.

The kitten's antics never failed to amuse Avery, and she threw off the luxurious bedding, swinging her feet over the edge of the bed and feeling for her slippers. A glance at her phone, still on the charger, confirmed that she'd missed the full complimentary breakfast by minutes. Her stomach rumbled at the thought of food. Still, she assumed the staff would be efficiently switching from breakfast to the lunch service, and she'd have to seek sustenance elsewhere.

Dropping a handful of kibble into the kitten's bowl, she decided to forego a shower for the moment and dash across the street to fill her travel mug and order a breakfast sandwich to go. She could bring it back to the room and dress for the day at her leisure, then she and Anya would head out so the cleaning staff could come in.

"I'll be right back," Avery told the kitten. She pulled on the clothes she'd worn the day before, tucked her hair under the newly purchased baseball cap she'd gotten in Woodstock, and hastily brushed her teeth. "I'll floss later," she informed Anya.

Hanging the DO NOT DISTURB sign on the door, she jogged down the inn's front stairs, across the street, and up the steps of the general store. She filled her travel mug from the array of self-service carafes and took a restorative sip of hot, black coffee before approaching the deli counter.

An attractive woman wearing the store's logo teeshirt and apron smiled at Avery and asked in a low, melodious voice, "What would you like?"

"I hope I'm not too late to get a breakfast sandwich. I'm staying at the inn, and I think I've just gotten the best night's sleep I've ever had. I slept right through breakfast, and now I'm starving."

"Not at all. We serve breakfast until eleven, so

you got here with time to spare."

"Are you Emmie?" Avery asked.

"I am." She reached over the counter and held out her hand. "Emerson Clayton. Are you the woman with the cat?" Avery nodded. "Todd told me about your kitten in a backpack."

"I spent a month with my cousin in Connecticut," Avery explained. "She volunteers as an animal transporter, and she needed to take a Siamese kitten to Vermont. I was planning to drive up Route 100, so Newfane wasn't far out of the way, and I agreed to deliver her. The problem was that it didn't work out, and I couldn't leave her there, so I took her to a local vet to see if they could place her in a good home. At the last minute, I decided to keep her myself. Not that I have a good home to offer." She grimaced ruefully. "I'm homeless at the moment."

Emmie waited for a further explanation, but Avery didn't elaborate, embarrassed that she'd confided in a total stranger.

"Your new friend was in this morning. The woman with the cat," Emmie told Todd when he came in about fifteen minutes later. "You just missed her."

"Early lunch?" Todd asked, glancing out the back door to see if Avery might have taken a sandwich onto the deck.

"No, late breakfast. Avery said she slept so well last night, she missed breakfast at the inn. I made her an egg sandwich on a croissant, and she took it back to her room. Pets are allowed, and Avery wanted to get going before the cleaning crew came. She said she'll put the kitten in her backpack, and they'll spend the day exploring. She seems quite taken with Winslowe."

"Do you think she's serious about staying a while?" Todd wondered. "If she is, she probably needs to find a rental. I don't imagine she'll want to shell out for more than a couple of nights at the inn."

"Two couples with kids came in while she was here," Emmie said. "They needed nine brown-bag lunches to take to the falls, so I didn't have more than a few minutes to talk to Avery. I suggested she stop in at Apex Realty and ask for Daisha. She keeps her ear to the ground and knows every possibility within twenty miles."

"Here comes the noon stampede." Todd laughed. "It's so much easier to crank out one lunch after another with all the prep done—tomatoes sliced, cheeses sliced, the soup on simmer. I don't know how we're going to manage for a month during foliage with you out of commission. I wish you could have shoulder surgery during our slow season."

"What are you talking about, Todd Clayton?" Emmie demanded, her expression incredulous. "We don't *have* a slow season anymore."

Todd shook his head. " 'Be careful what you wish for,' that's for sure. We'll have to talk about this later when we have a break, but you'll be laid up for a month, and we're going to have to get some temporary help," he said in a low voice. Both Todd and Emmie greeted their customers with welcoming smiles and took their orders, and the afternoon sped by with a flurry of activity.

When the store was empty at last, Emmie sagged onto a stool behind the counter. She pulled a round brown plastic container from her apron pocket, placed her palm over the cap, and gave it a practiced twist.

"Your shoulder must be killing you," Todd said. "It's only been a couple of hours since your last pain pill. Why don't you just go home and take it easy? It can be pretty slow once the breakfast and lunch rush is over, so I can get through the next few hours by myself. If you want to help, see if you can think of someone we could hire for about six weeks. Having someone come in early to cook sausages and bacon, then get the soup started and slice meat, cheese, and veggies would be an enormous help. Put the word out; someone will know someone; you know how that goes. We'll get it figured out."

Emmie slid off her stool. "Thanks." She smiled thinly, but she was obviously in pain.

Avery came in just before five and perused a shelf of homemade jams, jellies, and fruit butters while she waited for Todd's customers to leave.

"Hey," he greeted her. "Are you just getting back? You must have gone all the way to Montreal," he teased.

"I didn't actually go far," Avery told him. "I found a fabulous glass gallery, and I was there for almost two hours. I spent some time with my cousin in Connecticut this summer, and I wanted to get her a special gift. Well, look no further!" She laughed. "It was difficult to pick something out because there were so many extraordinary pieces. I loved them all!"

Todd whistled. "You must have melted the numbers right off your credit card. I know exactly the place you're talking about. Their work is museum-quality, and they can command stratospheric prices."

"Yeah." Avery wrinkled her nose and nodded. "This hasn't been a cheap stop, between the inn and the glass gallery. I found a cute place for lunch in Westfield, so Anya and I sat on the patio, and then we cruised a few of the boutiques. I saw a lot of things I'd love to buy, but I don't want to start dragging stuff around until I know where I'm going to be living."

"So, you and Anya did lunch and went shopping," Todd teased. "Sounds like you need some people girlfriends."

Avery looked around. "I met Emmie this morning, and I think we might become friends if I stay. She's not here?"

"She had an MRI in Burlington yesterday. She hurt her shoulder a few months ago when she was helping a friend move into an apartment. They were trying to wrangle a couch up a narrow flight of stairs. Emmie was on the downhill side, and she had to lift the couch over her head. They had to turn it sideways to get it through a doorway, and the friend lost her grip for a moment, so Emmie's arm got quite a wrench. She's lucky she didn't fall down the stairs."

"Why didn't they get a couple of guys to do it?" Avery asked.

"Well, duh." Todd sounded exasperated. "That was *my* first question. I told her she should have called me, but she said Jana's boyfriend broke up with her, and he kicked her out. She wanted to get her stuff out of his place before he had the locks changed, so she and Emmie just went ahead and did it before he got home."

"Oh, that's too bad," Avery commiserated. "That shoulder must be painful. I noticed this morning she was holding her arm close to her side and sort of favoring it, but I thought maybe she'd whacked her funny bone or something."

Todd puffed out one cheek and blew a stream of air out one side of his mouth in a universal symbol of disgust. "Emmie researched shoulder injuries online and self-diagnosed with frozen shoulder. The pain kept getting worse, and she was having trouble sleeping because she couldn't get comfortable. Her friends suggested chiropractic or told her she should get it injected with cortisone, but we were slammed all summer, so she kept popping over-the-counter pain relievers and anti-inflammatories and icing it at home. She has some green gel that she smears on her shoulder when she comes to work that seems to help some. I can visualize the tube on our bathroom vanity, but I can't remember the name of it."

"I've heard of frozen shoulder, but I don't know anything about it," Avery admitted.

"The pain finally got so bad she went to an orthopedic guy, and he ordered an x-ray and then an MRI. Turns out she has a torn rotator cuff," Todd said. "It will have to be surgically repaired, and the recovery time is four to six weeks, plus physical therapy." He groaned. "This just couldn't come at a worse time. We have a couple of college kids working here during the summer, but they both went back to school. We had another kid lined up, but he got a better offer and quit before he'd even started." He rolled his eyes.

"Who will take care of Emmie after her surgery if you're here all day?" Avery wondered. "You and she both have family in Winslowe; isn't that what you told me?"

"Her sister lives in Truro, on the Cape, but she's coming to stay for two weeks. The surgery is arthroscopic and outpatient, but apparently, the surgeon makes several incisions, and there are stitches. It's not major surgery, but it's not exactly minor. Emmie's mom and my mom will take care of meals and laundry and house cleaning, and they'll drive her to doctor's appointments and rehab."

"I was about to ask if I could help," Avery said. "But it sounds like you've got it covered."

So don't plan on a Ladies' Day Out with Emmie any time soon," Todd joked. "You'll have to make do with your cat for a while."

"We did okay today," Avery told him. "Anya curls up in her backpack and watches the world go by. She's so quiet that most people don't even notice her. "

Todd grimaced, shaking his head. "My cat wouldn't put up with that for one second. It's an ordeal taking him to the vet. He always screams his head off and messes in his crate.

"Where's Anya now?" he asked.

"Across the street," Avery told him. "Sound asleep."

"Are you having dinner at the inn?" Todd asked. "There's a tavern in the basement that serves casual pub food. You can get a burger or fish and chips, stuff like that."

"I saw a Thai restaurant advertised that I'd love to try. It's at the ski area, and I rented a condo there for a month, so I might do that next week once I get settled. For tonight, pub food sounds good. I haven't had fish and chips in quite a while. I hope they have malt vinegar."

"I'm sure they do," Todd said. "But save a little piece of fish for your friend." He winked at Avery. "So, you rented a condo? When do you move in?"

"The day after tomorrow. It's furnished, and all I have is my clothes, so moving's no big deal. It will give me a little time to look around and find something long-term. The condo is booked starting November first, so I'll have to be out in a month

139

regardless. They may have another unit I could move into, but I don't want to play 'Musical Chairs' all winter."

"You should put up a few fliers in the area," Todd suggested. "We can post one here. Everybody in town comes in sooner or later, so you're bound to turn up a few possibilities. You're welcome to use the office computer here to type up something and then print a bunch of copies to take around. You know how to rotate the text so you can put your phone number on the bottom? Copy and paste it vertically all across the bottom of the page and then cut strips so people can tear them off if they want to get in touch with you."

"I have a laptop," Avery told him. "I can do that tonight after dinner."

"Email it to me when it's done and come back in the morning. I'll leave a note for Emmie to print about twenty copies. She'll be in early to start food prep. I eat with the kids and get them off to school. Then I stay until closing, and she goes home to oversee supper and homework. She's teaching Eliza to cook, so we've had a few interesting meals lately."

"Hey. I heard you rented a condo on the mountain," Emmie said the next morning. "Todd told me you'll be moving tomorrow. We'll miss you."

Avery laughed. "I'm not going far, and it's only for a month. I hope to find a more permanent place to rent for six months or a year here in Winslowe."

"I printed your fliers when I came in this

morning," Emmie said. "Let me get them. I'll tape one to the front of the register so no one will miss it when they come in here."

A minute later, she handed a large manila envelope to Avery. "The fliers are in there, and there's a box of push pins and a roll of tape."

"Emmie, thank you. That's very thoughtful."

Avery had lingered over her breakfast at the inn and walked across to the store when she was pretty sure the morning rush was over.

"Todd will be in any minute," Emmie told Avery. "There's usually a little lull between breakfast and lunch, so I thought you might have a cup of coffee with me. If you have time?"

"I have all day." Avery laughed. "Anya and I are going to spend it putting up fliers."

"Where is she?" Emmie asked.

"She's in her crate in the car. It's cool enough. It's parked in the shade, and I won't be long. I don't like leaving her in the room when the maids come in."

"I'd love to see her," Emmie said. "I'll walk out with you when you leave."

She led Avery over to the carafes and told her to take her pick. "As my guest."

The two women situated themselves at a small table, and Emmie's questions tumbled out. "So, you moved here without knowing *anyone?* You don't have family in Vermont? You didn't go to school here?"

Avery held up her arms, palms out.

"I'm not trying to pry," Emmie protested. "I'm just curious. I mean, why Vermont? And why Winslowe?"

"I can't answer that," Avery said. "I don't have an answer. My husband died in January, and I just couldn't stay where I was. I needed a complete change of scenery."

"Todd told me you're a widow. I'm so sorry." Emmie reached across the table and laid her hand on Avery's, communicating her sympathy. "Was he ill?"

Avery shook her head. "No. He was an English professor, head of The Writers Project at the university in Iowa. He was walking across campus after a class, and he dropped dead from a heart attack. He was only fifty-eight."

"How awful!"

"It *was* awful," Avery said. "We lived in a beautiful house on campus, but, of course, the university hired Andrew's successor, and I had to move out so his family could move in and get settled before the school year started. The house went with the position."

"So, you lost your husband and your home all at once. You poor thing," Emmie said. Her expression was subdued, and her eyes sad, but she smiled when she said, "I hope you find a place to live and decide to stay in Winslowe. This is a great town, and you'll find the people are very supportive. Neighbors help neighbors."

"That's very appealing." Avery smiled back.

"That's how Todd and I got together," Emmie offered. "Sort of. I've known him since kindergarten, so I saw him all the time at school. And then we were both on the ski team in high school, but he had a girlfriend, Lisa Jacobsen. I was busy trying to keep my grades up. All my classes were advanced placement, so I had tons of homework and papers to write. Then we both went off to college. After college, I worked in Boston, but I was in Vermont on assignment, staying with my folks. My dad had just had abdominal surgery, and we had a big Nor'easter, so Todd's mom sent him over to plow us out. My mom asked him in for hot chocolate, and she invited him to stay for supper. I guess the time was right because we sort of connected." She grinned. "And the rest is history!"

"What's the story with the clothing store upstairs?" Avery asked. "Todd says it keeps opening and closing. I asked him about it, but he seemed exasperated and didn't really explain. Do you know when it will be open?"

Emmie snorted. "Maybe never! I should take the hanging sign off the front porch. Women keep coming in, thinking they're going to go upstairs to look at clothes, and they get aggravated when we tell them it's closed. As if it's our fault."

"Whoa!" Avery said. "Sounds like a sore subject."

"The owner's an asshole. He's impossible, and he can't keep a manager. Most of them don't give any notice. He pisses them off, and they say, 'I'm outta' here.' "

"I didn't bring many clothes with me," Avery told Emmie. "I donated almost everything to Dress For Success before I left Iowa. Partly because I didn't want to schlep them, but mostly because I didn't want to be reminded of what I wore on various occasions with Andrew. So, now I need to buy some warm clothes before it starts getting cold. I'm guessing clothes in the ski shops or the boutiques on the mountain will be expensive. Can you recommend a few places I might look?"

"You'll have to meet my friend Marley," Emmie exclaimed. "She loves to shop, and she knows every store within a hundred-mile radius."

Chapter Eleven

Four days later, Avery drove into the center of Winslowe. It was only a few miles from her condo and less than a ten-minute drive. She noticed that the traffic volume was heavier on Route 100 as she waited to cross, and she was shocked by how congested Main Street had become, so different from only a few days before. She'd chosen to arrive in late morning, expecting the breakfast rush at the general store to have subsided and hoping to find Emmie free for a few minutes. But vehicles were parked helter-skelter, and the store was mobbed.

Emmie caught her eye over the heads of a Japanese couple at the counter and grinned. Avery decided her best opportunity to have a few words with Emmie was to get in line for lunch but, by the time she reached the counter, Emmie was nowhere in sight, and Todd was serving customers.

"Eliza forgot her duffle this morning, and her lacrosse gear is in it," he explained. "She called almost an hour ago, frantic, and this is the first chance Emmie has had to break away long enough to run home to get it and take it to school. This is a *crisis*, of course—he rolled his eyes and heaved a sigh— because all Liza's gear is in it. She can't play without her chest guard, her goggles, and her cleats."

"Oh, no!" Avery exclaimed.

"No kidding," Todd's tone was sarcastic. "Look at this place!"

"Call Emmie and tell her to get the bag and come straight back here," Avery said decisively. "I'll take it. Lacrosse practice isn't until after school, right? So, there's plenty of time. I have all afternoon."

Todd stared at her. "Really? You'd do that? You're a lifesaver. We'll take you up on that offer. Lunch is on us; what would you like?"

Avery made her selection, and while Todd ladled soup onto a styrofoam cup and arranged half a sandwich on the paper plate, she noticed a large glass jar on the counter next to the register. There was a picture of a dog and a hand-lettered sign that read DONATIONS FOR ROADIE. Avery saw that there were a number of ten-and-twenty-dollar bills in it.

"Who's Roadie?" she asked when Todd returned. "That jar wasn't there before, was it?"

Todd's expression hardened. His mouth was a grim line, and he murmured through stiff lips, "Tell you later."

Avery sat on a stool at a long counter against the wall and ate a spoonful of her soup. It was thick and creamy with chunks of potato, transparent slivers of onion, and crisp bacon bits. The panini sandwich with smoked turkey breast encrusted with coarse black-pepper, melted swiss cheese, and a lettuce leaf on French bread was the perfect complement. Just as she finished, Emmie rushed through the front door and came straight over to her.

"I can't thank you enough. You have literally saved the day." She set a large duffle in what Avery assumed were the school colors on the stool next to her. "You can put the address in your GPS. It should only take you about twenty minutes unless you get stuck behind an RV or something. It's that time of year, which is something you'll learn quickly enough. Route 100 will be clogged with recreational vehicles, camper vans, and tag-along camping trailers for about the next month. It's great for the economy, so I'm not knocking it, but sometimes it's a real pain in the ass if you're in a hurry and you can't pass. Anyway, just take it into the office when you get there; they're expecting it, and they'll get it to Eliza."

Todd beckoned Emmie, and she held up a finger to indicate she'd be a moment. She held out her phone to Avery.

"Put your contact info in my phone. I'll call you later."

Neither spoke as Avery hurriedly tapped the keys to enter her name and number. She unclipped her car keys from the leash inside her tote, slung it over her shoulder, and picked up Eliza's bag with the same hand. With the other, she carried her litter to the counter and deposited it in the trash receptacle.

Emmie looked up and mouthed, "*Thank you!*"

"Do you know someone named Brandi Tyler?" Avery asked that evening when Emmie phoned. "I met her this afternoon. She says she knows you."

"Gosh, yes. I've known her *forever*. She lived two houses down from me when we were kids." Emmie laughed. "She was 'Barbara Ann' back in the day. She came home from Sarah Lawrence for Thanksgiving her freshman year as 'Brandi,' and I hardly recognized her when I passed her on the street. She got her doctorate in clinical psychology at Columbia, got married, and then lived in Manhattan. She and her husband had a Park Avenue practice together for years."

Avery frowned. "But she lives here now?"

"They had a place on the Vineyard. They went there for long weekends and took the month of August off every year. I married Todd and settled down in the same town I grew up in. So we didn't travel in the same circles. Then hubby cheated, got caught, told her he was in love with someone else, and she divorced his ass. She got full custody and moved back home. Her boys are eleven and fourteen. She got a job as the school psychologist, so her schedule would coincide with theirs."

"That's a helluva pay cut," Avery commented.

"Poor, but happy. You know how that goes," Emmie said. "She's been seeing the assistant principal at one of the elementary schools for the last couple of years. They're good together, but he's divorced too, so they agreed to take it slow."

"Yeah, helluva pay cut. I can relate to that," Avery commented. Emmie didn't know much about Avery's current situation, and she waited for the other woman to offer more information. When none was forthcoming, she asked, "Where did you run into Brandi?"

"She was in the office when I dropped off Eliza's lacrosse bag. She asked how I know you, and I told her that I'm new in town, that I'd been staying at the inn for a few days, and had gone into the general store several times."

"She and I are going to listen to some live music on Saturday night," Emmie said. "It's bluegrass, a band from Montpelier. They're really good. A few of us get together about once a month, and Marley will be there, too. Why don't you come?"

Avery was touched by Emmie's invitation. "I love bluegrass! I'd be delighted. Where is it?"

"You won't have to go far. That's one thing about a ski area; they have a lot of activities for the resort guests and not just in the winter."

"I saw a flyer for a wine tasting," Avery said. "I thought I might like to go to that."

"That's an annual event during foliage season. All the area restaurants participate, providing appetizers to go with the various wines. The winery is local, so there's a lot of support. There'll be a chili cook-off in October and Christmas caroling in December. For a town that isn't much more than a wide place in the road, you'll be surprised how much there is to do around here."

On Saturday evening, Avery dressed carefully. Given her vibrant red hair, her palette had always been autumn hues and earth tones, but now with her shoulder-length hair newly silver, she needed a new look to go with her new life.

She enjoyed shopping, but Andrew had had elegant, expensive taste in his own wardrobe and relished buying clothes for his wife. Avery was content to let him choose her outfits, happy to share in his pleasure at seeing her wear items he'd selected. But now, she wanted to put together a small collection of casual attire, different from the dressier clothes she'd needed for the many functions she attended in Iowa with her prominent husband.

A few days earlier, Avery had meandered through nearby Westfield, browsing through some of the shops and just driving around to get a feel for what the area was like and what it might offer. She knew she'd be dressing mainly in jeans and was pleased to find a classic high-waisted, straight-leg style that suited her in one of the boutiques. She bought four pairs, in a dark stonewash, black, wheat, and olive. She also bought several turtleneck sweaters in lightweight wool and, in the men's section of an upscale resale shop called Back On The Rack, she found two jackets that would complement her purchases admirably. One was a Harris tweed, and the other a solid camel color. Avery had blinked when she saw the designer label and the hundred-percent camel hair fabric content. It didn't appear ever to have been worn, and she stroked its softness, hardly believing her good fortune. With her long arms and slender body, Avery found that sportcoats had longer sleeves, and the length hit her at mid-thigh rather than mid-hip the way women's jackets did.

"Avery! You came!" Emmie exclaimed joyfully when Avery joined her group. "Here, sit here. I saved you a seat." Turning to her friends, she introduced them one by one. "Avery, this is Marley Wainwright, and next to her is Merritt St. John. And Jerica Swenson. Sienna Calvert and Krista Boling couldn't make it. Brandi Tyler and Larry Turner are here, but they're sitting over at that big table with a bunch of teachers."

"They won't be sitting for long," Merritt said. "They'll be on the dance floor the minute the band starts playing, and they'll be out there all night. Larry loves to dance."

"He's from out west somewhere," Jerica said, "and—."

"He's from Texas. And, man, can he do the two-step!" Merritt interrupted.

"He's from Wichita, Kansas," Emmie said. "You're confusing that with Wichita Falls, Texas. Not everyone from Texas can do the two-step, you know," she teased.

151

The teasing was good-natured, and Merritt turned to Avery. "Just wait; you'll see."

"Do you get asked to dance?" Avery asked. "Can you all do the two-step?"

"I would if Todd were here, but this is Ladies Night Out," Emmie said. "Guys will come up and ask us to dance, but we usually just get in on some of the line dances once Larry gets 'em going."

Seeing Avery's pained expression, Jerica asked, "Have you ever line danced?"

"You haven't?" Merritt frowned. "Not even the Electric Slide? Jeez, I thought everybody could do that. It's been around forever."

"My husband was an English professor," Avery offered a feeble explanation. "We were more likely to see a play than go to a honky-tonk."

"Was he older than you?" Merritt wondered.

"A few years," Avery admitted. "But I have a confession to make. I love classic country and bluegrass, so I ordered a pair of western boots online when Emmie invited me to join you tonight. I love them but—." She grimaced. "They need some serious breaking in. I got a blister just walking over here."

"You *live* here? On the mountain?" Merritt asked.

"Do you own a condo?" Jerica asked, the two women talking over each other.

"No," Avery told them. "I'm new in town. I stayed at the inn for a few nights, and now I've got a condo rental for a month. I have to be out on November first. It gives me time to look around for something long-term."

"What's long-term?" Merritt asked.

"Are you planning to stay in the area?" Jerica asked at the same time. They both laughed.

"Yes, she is," Emmie announced. "Right here in Winslowe. So keep your ears to the ground and let her know if you hear of anything."

Each woman took out her cell phone and, as Avery recited her number, they each entered her contact information.

Four days later when she was at Apex Realty in Westfield meeting with Daisha Weaver, Avery's cell vibrated, and she pulled it out of her jacket pocket. Emmie's name came up on caller ID. She knew it was rude to accept a call when you were with someone, but Emmie wouldn't be calling to chat.

"I'm sorry," she said, "I need to take this. I won't be long."

"No problem," Daisha Weaver told her. "Take your time. I'll check my email."

"Emmie, hi." Avery kept her voice low.

"Hey. Are you busy? Am I catching you at a good time?"

"I'm in Westfield right now," Avery said. "I'll probably be a couple of hours. Is there something you need?"

"Well." Emmie hesitated. "I was hoping to see you for a few minutes. I was hoping you could come by the store."

"I should be free by three or three-thirty. Would that work?"

"I'll be gone by then," Emmie said. "I have to pick up Toby after soccer practice. I'll be home by four-thirty. Can you come by my house? I could make us a cup of tea."

"Sure. I'll pick up some scones or something."

"Oh, no. Don't do that. I can grab something from the bakery case here. We get fresh stuff every morning, so if there's only one or two of something left and it's going to be day-old the next day, I'll bring it home for the kids. Toby is a bottomless pit, as you can imagine."

"Okay. I'll see you at four-thirty."

"Do you know where I live?"

"Give me the address," Avery told her. "I'll put it in my GPS."

Three hours later, Emmie set a rattan mat on the table and placed a teapot on it. After pouring tea for herself and Avery, she covered the teapot with a quilted cozy. Avery raised her eyebrows. "I'm impressed."

"I hope you like Earl Grey. It's my favorite. But, if you'd rather, I have teabags. English Breakfast, Irish Breakfast, Constant Comment—."

"This is perfect," Avery said. "Earl Grey is my favorite too. These teacups are so pretty. You hardly ever see teacups like this anymore; most people use mugs now."

"They were my grandmother's," Emmie said.

"The porcelain is so fine it's translucent when you hold it to the light. I loved having tea parties with her when I was a child. She insisted on the proper way to serve tea, with loose leaves in a tea ball. I don't think she ever used a teabag in her life!"

"I'm sorry I couldn't talk when you called," Avery said. "I was at Apex Realty, and Daisha was trying to help me find a place to rent."

Emmie's face lit up. "She's one of my favorite people. If she can't help you, no one can."

"It's not that she can't help me," Avery said slowly. "She had three possibilities, and we went to see them."

"So, did you find something?"

Avery shook her head. "Well, I just started looking, but what I saw was pretty discouraging. I hate to sound like a spoiled brat, but I'm not sure I can face old shag carpet and peeling linoleum—."

"Oh, no," Emmie sympathized. "I think I've got the picture. Let me guess, avocado green and harvest gold?"

"All that, and more." Avery groaned, "Horrid bathrooms, single-pane windows. I know those places have been cleaned, so they're probably as good as they're going to get, but the grime is just ground in, you know. They may be reasonably clean, but they'll never look or feel clean." She shuddered involuntarily. "I don't know what I was expecting. I came from a university town, so there were a lot of sublets and places that were available for periods when professors were teaching in the overseas program or on sabbatical. If you were lucky, you could find a situation house sitting or pet sitting in a beautiful home without even paying rent."

"Keep trying the rental office on the mountain. People's plans change all the time, so you might find something that suddenly comes available. The problem is that we're coming into ski season, so prices will be sky high."

"It's not that I can't afford it. It's that I want to feel settled. The mountain would only work if I could get a rental for six months to a year."

"Things will open up in the spring," Emmie said.

"It's only September." Avery sighed. "That's six months from now. I just didn't think it would be this hard. But, enough about me. What did you want to talk to me about?"

Emmie met Avery's eyes. "I have a big ask. And you don't really even know me. I totally understand if you can't do it or don't want to do it—."

"Emmie! What is it? Just ask me."

"Well, I've got this surgery coming up, and the timing is awful. I feel terrible leaving Todd in the lurch for four to six weeks. I thought it would be easier to find someone to come in first thing to do prep and open up. Everyone I've talked to seems to have their own problems, or their life is just too busy. Anyone with kids is out because they have to get them off to school."

"You're asking if I can come in to help out while

you recuperate. Is that it?"

"Well, yeah. Yes. We'd pay you, of course. Really well. If you can." Emmie bit her lip. "I hate to ask, but I've asked everyone I can think of who might have been able to do it." Her eyes shimmered with tears. "All we wanted was to make a go of it. I just didn't think it would be this hard."

Avery reached across the table and put her hand on Emmie's, the same comforting gesture Emmie made the first time she met Avery and learned she was a recent widow. "I can, and I will. And you're not going to *pay* me! Don't be silly." Emmie's lips parted as her protest formed, but Avery cut her off.

"Listen to me. This is exactly the kind of town I want to settle in. And you're exactly the kind of friend I was hoping to find. Friendships have to start somewhere, so I'll go first, helping you, and we can trade favors back and forth. When I need help one of these days, I'll turn to you. Friendship isn't something you can put a price on, so when Todd insists you'll have to pay me, tell him 'no.' Deal?"

Chapter Twelve

It had rained heavily during the night, and Rhys William's wipers smeared wet leaves back and forth across his windshield. Stopping at the end of his driveway, he slammed his truck into 'park' and wrenched his door open, lifting each blade and scooping a handful of soggy vegetation onto the ground. He should have put the truck into his garage when he got home yesterday evening, but he hadn't. It was a minor annoyance, but he was already in a foul mood when he awoke. Given the nature of the morning's business, his day wasn't about to get better.

The farmhouse looked exactly the same as when he'd last seen it. He made it a point not to come here any more often than necessary, dredging up feelings he preferred to keep repressed and leaving him moody and out of sorts for days after each visit.

A glint in his rearview mirror alerted him to an approaching vehicle. Lifting his chin for a better view, he saw a white Subaru approaching, and he sighed heavily.

His expression was stony and his voice cold as he

greeted the driver with a minimum of conversation and courtesy. "Rhys Williams," he said.

"Mr. Williams, hi. Good morning. Thanks for meeting me. I'm Avery Markham. I left you a voicemail yesterday, and then I got yours. I'm sorry we missed each other." Avery smiled and held out her hand. Ignoring it, Rhys strode across the yard, up the steps, and across the wide porch. Pulling a key from his pocket, he unlocked the door and pushed it open.

"Look around," he instructed and gestured that Avery should precede him. She stepped into a surprisingly modern and upscale kitchen. Although the house had to be at least a hundred years old, perhaps more, it had been painstakingly renovated. Opening a door, she saw a large pantry. A smaller door revealed a utility closet, already housing a Dyson vacuum cleaner and a dustmop as well as a broom and a dustpan. Avery recognized the broom as the same kind sold in the general store and guessed it had been purchased there. Todd was using one, and when she commented on how sturdy it appeared, he explained that top-quality brooms were made from dried sorghum tassels, referred to as 'broomcorn.'

"Mr. Williams?" Avery called, poking her head into what once must have been a parlor but was now a comfortable den with a large-screen TV. "Mr. Williams?" she called again. Receiving no answer, she retraced her steps onto the porch and found her would-be landlord leaning against the railing, perusing something on his cell phone.

Since he hadn't shown any inclination to show her through the house, Avery asked, "Is it okay if I look around?" The look he gave her was so scornful, Avery involuntarily took a step back. She blinked in surprise.

"Fifteen hundred a month; first, last, and security; tenant pays utilities; no pets; minimum six-month lease," he barked.

"Excuse me? I haven't said I'd take it. I haven't even been upstairs."

Without responding, Rhys gestured impatiently, and Avery went back in alone. His attitude was appalling, but that hardly mattered in Avery's situation. Only ten days remained of her tenure on the mountain, and she needed to find suitable housing, or she'd be forced to leave Winslowe. She could undoubtedly rent an apartment in one of the many complexes in and around Burlington, but it was an hour away. In winter driving conditions, Avery probably wouldn't visit Winslowe very often, and it was likely she'd forfeit her budding friendships, so that would be a stopgap at best.

After about twenty minutes, Avery reappeared on the porch.

"I like it very much," she said. "Whoever did the decorating has superb taste. I'd feel right at home here, and I'd like a six-month lease, renewable for another six. I'll need occupancy in ten days. If you have a contract, I'll give you a check that you can hold while you contact my references. And I have a

Siamese kitten. I plan to get her a companion, so I'll need you to write in an addendum allowing two cats." She looked Rhys in the eye as she spoke, and he glared back.

"I said no pets."

"Yes, you did say that," Avery acknowledged. Her tone was cool. "But you have a considerate quiet tenant who will keep your property immaculate and who will pay the full six months rent upfront. I will certainly tender a damage deposit for the kitten."

Turning abruptly, Rhys walked away. At the bottom of the steps, he called over his shoulder, "I have your number. I'll let you know."

"Who the hell does he think he is?" Avery fumed that afternoon as she related the encounter to Todd and Emmie. They exchanged a meaningful look, but neither spoke.

"He was so rude! For no reason! What does he mean, 'he'll let me know?' It's either for rent, or it isn't."

Avery looked from one to the other. "The tension is so thick in here you could cut it with a knife. What's going on? Do you know something I don't know?"

Emmie gestured toward the door to the upstairs. "He's the problem with the clothing boutique. Every woman who comes in here goes upstairs. It's a *gold mine*. Or, it should be. But he's so nasty, no one will work for him for long. Every time someone quits, it's closed again."

"The landlord I just met owns the clothing company here?"

"He owns the building," Todd said resignedly. "He's *our* landlord."

"What? Are you kidding? I thought *you* owned the building."

"We don't," Emmie said, the corners of her mouth turning down. "All we have is a right of first refusal if he ever decides to sell. Not that we could afford it, now or ever."

"What's he like as a landlord?" Avery asked with some trepidation.

"Actually, he's not bad. We work our asses off, and he leaves us alone," Todd told her. "He keeps to himself. The only time he comes in is when something breaks or needs repair, and then it's after hours. Our bookkeeper mails him a check every month, so we don't have much contact with him."

"I told Mr. Williams I'd rent for six months and would pay the entire amount upfront, so I shouldn't have any contact with him either," Avery said. "He said no pets, and I told him he'd have to write an addendum into the rental agreement because I have Anya. And I told him I planned to get a second kitten. So, it's probably out the window. I'm going to go to Burlington tomorrow to look for an apartment with a month-to-month lease. If something comes available around here, I won't be stuck."

"Oh, no!" Emmie said. "The farmhouse would be

so perfect for you."

"You've seen it? You've been in it?"

Todd and Emmie exchanged another look. "Rhys and his wife lived there," Emmie explained. "When she died, he built a new house. I guess he couldn't bear the memories."

"Oh, no. How awful. No wonder he didn't want to go inside. Was she ill? What did she die from?" Avery couldn't contain her curiosity.

"She didn't exactly die," Todd said flatly. "She was killed. By a distracted driver. Some teenage punk texting while driving. He pleaded not guilty, but he was charged with negligent vehicular homicide among other things and convicted on several counts."

Avery's hand flew to her mouth, and her eyes were round with horror.

"He only served two years in jail," Emmie said. Her tone was bitter, but tears stood in her eyes. "It nearly killed Rhys. He's never been the same."

"Did you know her? The wife?"

"She was my best friend," Emmie whispered. "Sloan."

"She decorated the farmhouse," Avery stated. "I think I stuck my foot in my mouth this morning. I told Mr. William whoever decorated it had superb taste. I must have caused him so much pain. He'll never rent to me now."

"She was an interior designer by profession. She gave it up when they moved here."

"Moved here from where?" Avery asked.

"Wilton, Connecticut. She had a lot of wealthy clients, but—," Emmie gestured, one hand palm up and made a face. "Not much call for that here."

"I'll bet my cousin knows her," Avery exclaimed. "She lives in Greenwich, right near Wilton. I'll have to ask."

"Sloan was coming back from a trip to Connecticut when the accident occurred," Todd explained. "Rhys was expecting her home any minute, but he got a call from the Massachusetts State Police. If it had happened here, I don't think he'd have been able to stay. It's hard enough to see those white crosses by the sides of roads without knowing one's for someone you love."

"How awful. I feel terrible."

"Not your fault. You didn't know," Emmie consoled.

Rhys had no one to offer him solace. It had been six years since Sloan's death, six long years, but his pain was as raw and as deep as if the accident had happened just the day before. Blindly, he turned left out of the farmhouse's driveway. His chest hurt; the pressure was almost unbearable, and he felt a wave of nausea.

"It's not a heart attack," Rhys told himself. Dread flooded his body as his panic attack intensified, and he began to hyperventilate, unable to draw a deep breath. Pulling to the side of the road, he scrabbled in the glove box for one of the paper bags he kept there.

Clutching it, he opened the driver's door and retched, but only a thin stream of yellow bile spattered the ground. He dry heaved several times before he could fit the bag over his nose and mouth and begin to breathe in and out, in and out, as he'd been taught.

When the episode was over, Rhys' face was soaked with cold sweat, and he buried his cheeks in the crook of his arm. Leaning his head back against the headrest, he closed his eyes. Panic attacks always left him limp, so he remained there for about fifteen minutes until he felt stronger and then drove slowly home.

Rhys opened the rear door of his truck, and a black-and-tan German Shepherd jumped down. He waited a few minutes until she relieved herself on the lawn, then he went into the house with her on his heels. She flopped down on her bed in the corner of the kitchen, but her eyes were glued to his face as she tried to assess his mood. He shrugged off his jacket, draping it over a chair back. He laid his phone on the table but immediately picked it up again.

I should probably apologize to that woman—what's her name? Evvie? Something like that.

He opened Settings and chose TTY from the Accessibility menu, then selected an option from speed dial. The call was picked up on the third ring, and Rhys forced a cheerful tone.

"Hello, this is Mira. GA," his screen read. Rhys and Mira were used to ending each exchange with the universally accepted letters 'GA,' signaling the other party that it was his turn to go ahead, and 'SK' for Stop Keying.

"Hey, Sweetie," Rhys typed. "Is this a good time? Can you talk for a minute? GA."

"The Governor has a briefing at two o'clock. My colleague was scheduled to sign, but he took a personal day today. What's up? GA."

"I was thinking about you this morning, and I'd like to run down there for a quick visit, just overnight if you're free. GA."

"I would love to see you! Can't you spend the weekend? GA."

The conversation went back and forth easily. When he asked if he should bring the dog, Mira's response was vehement.

"Yes! Bring her. Not negotiable. SK." Rhys laughed aloud when he realized Mira had advised him she'd stopped keying and had essentially hung up on him.

"You up for a road trip, girl?" Rhys asked rhetorically. "I wish we could leave right now, but we'll get an early start in the morning. I'll check the forecast. If it's a nice day, we can pick up some stuff at a deli and have a picnic, the three of us. Someplace we can take a walk, and maybe you'll get a run." The dog's tail thumped rhythmically. She didn't understand a word, but she perceived that Rhys' frame of mind had improved dramatically.

"Sloan Williams?" Hailey recognized the name

instantly when Avery phoned her cousin. "I didn't know her, but I certainly know of her. She was world-class. She had a two-year waiting list. People were willing to wait; she was that good. It was such a shame she was killed. People talked about it for months, and there was a big article in *People,* not just a mention. Apparently, her husband wanted her cremated so he could scatter her ashes, but her parents were devastated, and he escorted her body back to England for the funeral."

"Oh! She was English?"

"Yes. I think she went to university in London, the College of Arts, and got a BA in interior design. And then she got a master's in interior design at the Royal College of Art, also in London. Very posh and prestigious. She was very well trained and very well connected, so you can imagine how successful she was here."

"But you didn't use her for your house?" Avery asked.

Hailey burst out laughing. "If only."

"How'd she end up in Connecticut?" Avery wondered. "Why wouldn't she stay in London?"

"Her husband was American," Hailey explained. "He was in the diplomatic corps."

"The Foreign Service, you mean?" Avery asked.

"I guess he checked all the boxes," Hailey replied. "Undergraduate and graduate degrees from the School of Foreign Service at Georgetown, paid his dues in the early years and served all over the world. I think he was a Special Assistant to the President at one point and might still be an advisor. I think he and Sloan lived in Washington for quite a while when he was at the State Department. They were quite the power couple."

"How did Rhys meet her?"

"In London. He was posted to the embassy in London in some high-level position. I can't think of the name. Oh, I remember; it was in the article. He was Charge D'Affairs for a while when the ambassador left, and a new one hadn't yet arrived. There's an endless round of receptions and dinners, and someone introduced him to Sloan at one function or another."

"Sounds like he was quite a bit older than she was."

"No, they were pretty close in age, I think. He might have been a few years older but not a lot. He was divorced, and Sloan had never been married. She was in her late twenties when she married Rhys, according to the article."

"So, how did they get from D.C. to Wilton, Connecticut, and then on to Vermont?" Avery wondered.

"I think he did something with the United Nations and was spending a lot of time in New York, and then he took a job with a think tank in Connecticut. Sloan's career skyrocketed with the move to Connecticut."

"Where does Vermont come in? Did he retire and move to Vermont?"

"I think they were both consumed by work, and their marriage was suffering. They bought a farm and started going there for long weekends, then he was offered a gig teaching online courses in international studies—something that dovetailed with his foreign service expertise—and they moved to the farm full-time. I'm paraphrasing, but that's essentially what the article said."

The farmhouse is a jewel," Avery enthused. "It looks pretty traditional from the outside, red barn and all, with a few weathered outbuildings, but the inside is a complete surprise—elegant and upscale. Now nothing I look at will be appealing after I saw that. But he—Rhys—was so curt and so rude. We really got off on the wrong foot, so I just need to put it out of my mind and keep looking. He probably won't even have the courtesy to let me know."

"You'll find something," Hailey said. "Don't be discouraged. You can always come back here and look there again in the spring."

Avery snorted. "Are you forgetting about Baz? I don't see him and Anya in the same place at the same time."

"No, I meant you could easily find a condo somewhere around here. It's not exactly high season near the shore during the winter."

"It might come to that—*oh!* I just got a text from Mr. Williams. Rhys. It's an apology, and he's agreed to rent me the farmhouse. And he's agreed to me having two cats. I'll be damned!"

Over a glass of wine at her apartment the following evening, Rhys confided his distress to Mira and told her his boorish behavior chagrined him.

"You did the right thing," she signed.

"You're right, honey," Rhys signed back.

"If she's going to pay the full six months' rent, you shouldn't have much contact with her, if any." Mira's hands flew as they conversed.

Rhys had a cooler he'd plugged into his truck's 12-volt outlet, and he stopped at his favorite deli in Brattleboro just before I-91 crossed into Massachusetts. He put various finger foods for the picnic lunch he planned and two slices of the darkest, most decadent devil's food cake he'd ever seen into his basket. He added a selection of breakfast pastries, picked out a few scrumptious-looking desserts, as well as components for the evening's dinner. He'd caught Mira by surprise with his suggestion of an impromptu visit, and he didn't want her to stress over meals and groceries. He enjoyed collecting treats she'd enjoy, and he looked forward to sharing them with her.

Mira lived alone and kept very much to herself. She shrank from contact with the speaking world, but he knew she was comfortable with him and would allow him to take her to dinner on Saturday evening.

Mira was not congenitally mute, but she hadn't uttered a syllable since the first time Rhys had seen her, shoulders hunched, arms wrapped around herself, head down, and unable to make eye contact. She was only four, had been orphaned in a country ravaged by war. She'd witnessed horrors no child should ever have to endure, including the execution of her parents and two siblings in her presence. She'd narrowly escaped death herself, trapped under the bodies of neighbors who'd been forced from their homes and gunned down in the village square. An American journalist moved heaven and earth to spirit the traumatized child to safety in France, but that was as far as he could get her.

Rhys had served a stint as Acting Deputy Chief of Mission in Beirut, and he and Sloan had only been married two months when he had dinner in a Paris suburb at the home of a former colleague from his posting to Lebanon. Sébastien Paquet, his wife, and four offspring lived in leafy green Sévres, eleven minutes on the N train from Gare Montparnasse near Rhys' hotel. Rhys had visited several times when he had occasion to be in Paris, but this time, there was a difference. The Paquets were fostering a special needs child awaiting placement.

"I call her Mira," Vérène Paquet explained.

"She's undocumented. She can't be repatriated in her condition. Her native country doesn't have the resources to meet her needs," Sébastien burst out. "You'll see what I mean when the kids come to the dinner table," Sébastien cautioned Rhys. "It will be a miracle if a suitable placement can be found for her here."

"It's a miracle she survived," Vérène said. "For now, we're just trying to show her she's in a safe place. Over time, she may open up and start to trust, but we don't know how long she'll be with us or where she will go from here."

"Mira may be from northern Iraq, although Syria is a possibility," Sébastien told Rhys. "So many in that region were displaced; with so little information, it's impossible to know in what country she was born. I'm guessing she's Kurdish. If she spoke, her language would most likely be Kurmanji. Perhaps Arabic."

"She has been with us only a short time," Vérène said. "We have no idea how long it will be before permanent placement is found. She does not appear to be injured or to suffer throat pain, and she responds nonverbally to auditory stimuli, so we don't think she has hearing problems. A French child of this age would be evaluated for developmental delays, but that is hardly the case here. All we can do for now is to provide security and kindness."

"She doesn't let that doll out of her sight," Rhys commented. "I wonder if she's ever had one before."

"My friend Tatienne brought the doll," Vérène said. "She shopped for one with dark hair and dark eyes, one that looked most similar to Mira, that she could relate to."

"That was very thoughtful," Rhys said. "It obviously provides great comfort."

Chapter Thirteen

Rhys knew what Sloan would say when he told her about his visit with the Paquets and described Mira's situation.

He had no children from his first marriage and hoped to start a family with Sloan. He and Sloan had never discussed how many children they'd eventually want, but he was sure she'd like more than one. Sloan grew up an only child and had always longed for brothers and sisters.

"My heart is breaking," Rhys told Sloan that evening in a phone call. "The child sleeps on a cot in a room with the two Paquet girls, but it's quite crowded. Sébastien and Vérène would petition for placement, but they would have to move; there's just no room here for five children. Vérène has taken a leave of absence from her job, but that's temporary. Sébastien makes good money in the private sector but, with four children of their own, he and Vérène need the income from two salaries. I don't think it's going to be easy to place such a damaged and needy child."

"Rhys," Sloan began when she called back an hour later, but her husband interrupted before she could finish her sentence.

"Are you thinking what I'm thinking?" he asked. He and Sloan were soulmates, always in tune with the other. He knew his wife would need a little time to ponder the matter, but he'd been expecting her to call back. Rhys and Sloan talked late into the night and again the following morning.

"I don't know if it's even doable," Rhys cautioned. "There will be so much red tape with several countries involved. We'd have to get an undocumented child from a war-torn country in the Middle East presently residing in France to the United Kingdom for adoption by a U.S citizen."

"But you have contacts and channels available to you that most people don't, "Sloan pointed out. "At least England is part of the European Union; that should help somewhat, I should think."

"An adoption process could drag on for quite some time. Maybe even years. I'll make some phone calls," Rhys promised. "But don't get your hopes up."

Over the next several months, the consul in Paris undertook personally to expedite the Williams' petition for custody of the child known only as 'Mira.' Rhys did not know her, but she was a friend of a friend and a mother herself. Finally, the day came when the Paquets bade a tearful farewell to the young girl they'd come to cherish.

"This is the best possible outcome," Vérène told Sloan as tears streamed down the faces of both women. Both Sébastien and Rhys blinked back tears themselves as the driver opened the rear doors of the embassy vehicle that would transport the little family through the chunnel and escort them home to London.

A year later, Rhys was reassigned to Washington, where his diplomatic career flourished with one high-level position after another for the next sixteen years. Sloan and her partner opened an American office, and their interior design services were much in demand on both sides of the Atlantic. Mira was enrolled in a day school for the hearing impaired on the campus of Gallaudet University, and she, too, remained there until she graduated with a bachelor's degree in interpretation.

The Williams family moved to Connecticut when Rhys was offered a position with a think tank. Mira lived at home and worked as a researcher for her dad's company.

"It's time for Mira to leave the nest," Rhys told Sloan after a year. "She has the skills she needs to get a good job and the confidence now to live independently."

Mira was not unemployed for long; she almost immediately secured a coveted position as a sign-language interpreter for the governor of Connecticut and rented a light-filled apartment in a new building popular with young professionals.

Mira had been seeing a therapist for almost two decades but could not be persuaded to wear any colors other than black or gray.

"I hate that," Sloan told her husband. "It's as if she feels she doesn't deserve something pretty."

"Or she doesn't want to draw attention to herself," Rhys suggested.

**

Nothing had changed in ten years, Rhys noted now as he heard Mira's key in the lock, and she entered the apartment, dropping her shoulder bag and briefcase on the kitchen counter and throwing herself into his arms for a long hug.

Holding her at arm's length, Rhys swiftly assessed her appearance. She'd drawn her long, dark hair into a sleek chignon, and she wore a well-cut black wool blazer with a thin black turtleneck and narrow black gabardine trousers. Her outfit was something Sloan might have worn, but his late wife would have added classic hoop earrings or oversize studs, an interesting chunky necklace or attractive scarf, and several bangle bracelets. Mira, as always, was unadorned, and she wore no makeup.

Rhys and Sloan had thought Mira would make friends with others her age who lived in the same building or would become friendly with colleagues from work, but she received or made no phone calls during his visit. With him, she was relaxed, but she seemed to remain aloof from all others, never allowing anyone the opportunity to get to know her, rebuffing all overtures.

On Friday evening, they feasted on the goodies Rhys had picked up at the deli in Brattleboro, and on Saturday morning, Mira made a fantastic western omelet.

"The farmer's market closes after Columbus Day weekend," Mira signed, putting away the unused half of an onion and red and green peppers. "I'll miss it." After breakfast, they packed the cooler with sandwiches and cheese, fruit, cookies, drinks, and a few dog treats and headed out. Bella tugged at her leash, sensing an outing.

Rhys set the cooler on the back seat of his Silverado and plugged it into the truck's rear auxiliary power outlet while Mira opened the opposite door so Bella could hop in.

There were a number of people enjoying the beach on such a fine day, some walking, some jogging, some flying kites, some sitting and reading, some with metal detectors, so Rhys and his daughter started out with the dog on a long retractable leash. This was one of their favorite activities. Bella charged the incoming waves, barking excitedly and trying to bite them.

Rhys pointed, and Mira surreptitiously picked up a stout stick, holding it close to her leg as they walked so as not to draw Bella's attention to it. As soon as they'd gone far enough that they were nearly alone, they'd let Bella off-leash and throw the stick into the water for her.

By the time they returned to the parking lot several hours later, they were sunburned and windburned, salty, sandy, and tired. Bella's tongue lolled and, as soon as Rhys chirped the doors open with his key fob, Mira retrieved her bowl and poured clear, cold water from a thermos for the thirsty animal.

"Let me take you out for a nice dinner," Rhys signed when they reached Mira's apartment. She hesitated only a moment before signing back, "I'd like that."

While she showered, Rhys booted up Mira's computer and searched for local eateries, wondering if there was something new she'd like to try. When he suggested an upscale restaurant that had recently opened, Mira wrinkled her nose and shook her head.

Have you been there?" Rhys signed.

"No," Mira signed. "But I overheard people from work talking about it. They said there was no parking lot, so they had to walk pretty far after they found a parking space, and they complained that it was crowded and very noisy."

"There's a menu online that looks good," Rhys persisted. "You don't want to give it a try and see for yourself?"

"They said the food was good, and they might give it another try on a weeknight. Let's go someplace casual." After some discussion, they agreed to go to a pub nearby with an excellent craft beer selection and share bar snacks.

Mira plaited her still-damp hair into one thick braid that hung halfway down her back, and in snug black jeans, a black turtleneck sweater, and a black leather vest, she got many envious looks from women and admiring glances from the men in the restaurant.

Mira seemed unaware of the stares. Rhys wore faded blue jeans with a turtleneck, a tweed jacket, and highly polished but well-worn western boots. It didn't escape his notice that they looked like exactly what they were; a beautiful young woman in the company of an older man.

"You realize these people assume I'm your sugar daddy?" Rhys teased Mira.

"Well, aren't you?" she signed and winked at him. Then her expression sobered, and she signed, "You're so good to me." Mira's eyes filled with tears, and Rhys knew she was still grieving for her adoptive mother.

He reached over and covered her small hand with his. "I know, sweetie. I miss her too. Every minute of every day."

"Do you think you'll ever remarry?" Rhys was startled by Mira's question but kept his expression neutral.

"I don't see that happening. Sloan was the love of my life."

"I don't want you to be alone," Mira told him. "There are lots of nice women. You could find

179

someone if you let yourself."

Rhys met Mira's eyes and held her gaze. "I don't want you to be alone either," he signed. "You've grown into a beautiful, talented, independent woman, and you have so much to offer. Do you think *you'll* ever marry?"

Mira laughed spontaneously, a pretty tinkling sound. "I will if you will," she joked.

On Sunday morning, Mira insisted on taking Rhys out for breakfast, and they went to a nearby café they frequented whenever he visited. They both ordered their favorite fluffy Belgian waffles with whipped cream and strawberries. And they both saved a piece of bacon for Bella, which Mira wrapped in a napkin and tucked into her shoulder bag.

Mira had researched dog-friendly state parks nearby, and she suggested taking Bella for a hike before Rhys got on the road.

"We can walk off our breakfast," she signed. "It's such a gorgeous day, and she'll be in the truck for several hours, driving back to Vermont. She'll have to be leashed, but some's better than none, right? There are scenic overlooks, and the website says there's a food truck in the parking area on weekends, so we can grab a burger before you head out."

She held out a shopping bag, paw-printed tissue paper protruding from the opening.

"What's this?" Rhys signed.

"I told you to bring a sweatshirt and hiking boots. I got an outfit for Bella. Sort of." She grinned expectantly as Rhys drew an object from the bag. "It's from Bark Avenue," she signed, taking the item from him and dropping it over Bella's back.

"It's a backpack for dogs. I thought she could carry our water bottles. There's a fold-up bowl in the bag for her. I should've given it to her *yesterday*."

Rhys and Mira sat on a bench in the shade three hours later, their lunch spread out on the seat between them. Rhys took a bite of his fat, juicy burger, but Mira's was untouched, still in its wrapper, as she tore off pieces of the bunless patty she'd insisted they get for Bella. Bella's eyes were intent on Mira's hands, and Mira admonished her before she could get grabby. She patted her chest, drawing the dog's attention, and wagged a finger warningly.

Bella gently took each piece as it was offered, licking grease from Mira's fingers. Mira giggled, and Rhy's heart squeezed with love for his daughter. They'd had such a good time together, and it pleased him immensely to see her so vivacious and happy. But he wondered if she'd ever break her silence. He wished yet again that Sloan was alive and wondered if she would have been able to penetrate the wall Mira had erected around herself, segregating and suppressing memories too painful to bear. He knew Mira loved him with her whole heart, but he felt that Sloan's empathy and her kindness touched Mira in ways he himself could not express.

Mira had never mentioned her sojourn with the Paquet family or asked questions about her early years. But Rhys kept in touch with Sébastien and Vérène, sending pictures and updating them on Mira's accomplishments over the years.

The weekend went by too quickly. Rhys was absorbed in an audiobook on the drive north, a technothriller he'd had on reserve for almost six months. He'd gotten an email telling him it was available for download the day before he left for Vermont. The book was a bestseller by a popular author, and he'd been looking forward to listening to it, but now he was especially grateful to have his mind occupied as he drove up I-91 and passed through Massachusetts. He sighed heavily as he crossed the state line in Vermont and saw the sign welcoming him to The Green Mountain State.

"Shit," he muttered, acknowledging he'd have to call Avery Markham and make arrangements for her occupancy of the farmhouse he'd once lived in with Sloan. Bella had been asleep, stretched full length on the back seat with the cooler on the passenger seat next to Rhys. At his tone, she lifted her head and whined.

"Sorry, girl," he apologized. "I was just thinking aloud. I'm going to have to deal with that damned woman tomorrow, and I'm not looking forward to it. I was a complete ass."

On Monday morning, Rhys drank a cup of coffee while he watched the morning news, then resolutely tapped out Avery's number. He was surprised when the call went to voicemail.

She answered when he tried again an hour later. There was a lot of clattering and background noise with a hum of conversation. Rhys was annoyed when Avery asked, "Who is this?" after he'd identified himself.

"Rhys Williams," he said a second time, trying to keep an edge out of his voice.

"I'm sorry," she apologized. "I can hardly hear you. Hold on just a minute."

Avery stepped out the back door of the general store onto the deserted deck. Sea smoke rose from the river's surface, and she was momentarily transfixed by the beauty of her surroundings.

"Ms. Markham? Are you there?" Avery's phone barked an impatient voice, and she dragged her attention back to the matter at hand.

"I'm sorry," she apologized again. "I stepped outside so I could hear better, and I was admiring the fog coming up off the river."

"It's called 'sea smoke,' Rhys told her. "It's caused by a differential in the air temperature and the water temperature."

"It's beautiful," she said. "I've never seen it before."

"It happens quite often on fall mornings when cold air moves over warm water," he explained.

"Avery?" Todd called through the open door.

"Be right there," she called back.

"Am I keeping you from something?" Rhys asked

with an edge in his voice. He might have been more tolerant of someone else, but this woman irritated him.

"I'm sor—." Avery bit back another apology. *What is there about this man? I just can't say or do anything right.*

"Ms. Markham, I'm calling to see about meeting you at the farmhouse to go over the various systems and familiarize you with the property, have you sign a rental agreement, and give you a set of keys. Would this morning be convenient for you?"

"Um, I'm not sure." Avery took a deep breath, expelled it slowly, and took another. "This afternoon would actually be better for me," she said without offering an explanation. "Would that work for you?"

"Two o'clock," Rhys stipulated and disconnected the call.

"Mr. Williams?" Avery frowned. "Mr. Williams?" *Did he just hang up on me?*

"You okay?" Todd asked when Avery returned.

"That was my landlord. More accurately, my about-to-be-landlord. I'm meeting him at two o'clock to sign a rental contract and take possession."

"You don't look too happy."

"Finding a great place to rent at the last minute is a huge relief, but the landlord is insufferable. He just hung up on me!"

Todd laughed aloud. "You're not the first person to arrive at that conclusion." He pointed at the ceiling and rolled his eyes.

"If it weren't such a wonderful house, I'd keep looking," Avery said. "I'm paying six months upfront, so I won't have to have any contact with him; that's the good news."

Chapter Fourteen

It took no time at all for Avery to move clothes and her few possessions out of the rented condo. She settled easily into the farmhouse, and Anya wasted no time in exploring the various rooms, identifying some favorite spots for catnaps. Over the next week or so, Avery revisited several of the shops in Westfield, picking up items to make the farmhouse feel like her home.

She was habitually an early riser, often awakening before the sun rose, and she usually liked to sit in bed with a cup of coffee and catch up on the weather and the day's news on her tablet. Since she'd offered to help the Claytons while Emmie recuperated from surgery, Avery set her coffeemaker to brew at four o'clock and was out the door with her travel mug by four thirty.

Todd had given her a key so she could let herself into the general store to accept the early-morning delivery of bread, pastries, and baked goods. Next, she assembled the ingredients for the soup *du jour* and got it simmering. Once that task was completed, she sliced meats, cheeses, and tomatoes for lunch prep and tore lettuce leaves into sandwich-sized pieces. Todd arrived about an hour after she did. They worked side-by-side in companionable silence, laying out ingredients for the breakfast rush as customers were usually waiting when Todd unlocked and opened the front door at seven. They'd placed trays of sausage and bacon in the refrigerated deli case and employed Avery's suggestion to put one egg, two eggs, or three eggs into small bowls in the case as well to streamline the actual cooking. As soon as she took an order, Avery handed Todd the components.

"I've gotten used to having you as my *sous chef*," Todd complimented her. "I don't know what we would have done without you!"

"Perfect timing," Avery agreed. "I'm just glad I'm able to help. How's Emmie doing today?"

"Better," Todd told her. "The first few days were rough because she was in a lot of pain, and she couldn't lie down to sleep. It was hard to spend the night sitting in the recliner, but she's better now in bed, propped on pillows. Her mom comes in just before seven to fix breakfast for the kids and get them off to school. Then she makes breakfast for Emmie and helps her eat it, helps her bathe and dress. Dorothy made a list of chores for the kids, and they've been great about pitching in. We decided it would be easier for them to buy lunch at school for a few weeks, and I bring something home from the deli for supper or get take-out from the inn's pub menu.

And neighbors have been very generous, dropping off casseroles or stews almost every day."

"And I'll bet you've called out for pizza a time or two," Avery teased.

The month passed quickly, and Emmie's prediction that working in the store would give Avery the opportunity to meet everyone in town was accurate. Marley Wainwright was a frequent customer, often stopping in for a late lunch as Avery was finishing up so the two women could sit outside and enjoy the October sunshine.

"The chili cookoff is this weekend," Marley told Avery. "It's a 'must-see.' I go every year. I thought you might like to go with me this year."

Avery's face lit up. "I would love to! I've never been to a chili cookoff."

"You've never lived in Vermont," Marley teased. "It's a fall event in half the towns in the state. It's a great fundraiser."

"Is that what it is here, a fundraiser?" Avery asked.

"The ski area sponsors it. They get a lot of local press and goodwill, the winner gets half the proceeds, and the other half goes to our local animal shelter. Bring a couple rolls of quarters. There'll be a big jar at each booth, and you vote by putting a quarter in. Whichever booth has the most quarters in their jar wins. This event rakes in a fortune, in addition to the twenty bucks to get in."

"Speaking of animals, I need to find a good vet. Is there someone you can recommend?"

"Is something wrong with your cat? Is she sick?" Marley bit her lip.

"No!" Avery quickly explained. "No, she's fine. I want to know who I'm going to call if she does get sick. And she'll need routine care. I'm going to have her spayed soon."

"There are a couple of vets in town," Marley told her. "Surprising for such a tiny town, but almost everyone here has animals—dogs, cats, cows, horses, some sheep and goats."

"I'll want to make an appointment with them both, I guess, and decide which is the best fit. Someone told me—probably one of the store's customers—that there's a veterinary practice in an old mill building.

"That's right. That mill has seen a lot of businesses come and go since the textile industry was in its heyday. Here's a piece of trivia: the first patterns for one of the Vermont Castings stoves were made there."

"I have a Vermont Castings!" Avery exclaimed excitedly. "It's beautiful. It's red enamel. It heats the whole downstairs, and the heat rises through the floor registers. Next time I go to Westfield, I'm going to get one of those stovetop steamers to put humidity into the air during the winter when the house is closed up."

"Have you ever had a woodstove?" Marley asked.

"No, but Mr. Williams showed me how to use it

the day he gave me the keys. He said to get the fire started with the stove on updraft and then turn it to sidedraft once the fire was burning well."

Marley grimaced. "I had a wood-burning Vermont Castings for years, but I'd get twenty minutes down the road and couldn't remember if I'd left it on updraft. I've asked a neighbor to go and check for me once too often. When my godmother passed away, she left me a small bequest, and I used it to buy the exact same stove in the propane model. Now, all I have to do is point the remote at it, and there's instant fire."

"Good to know," Avery said thoughtfully. "I'll be extra careful."

"There are some things you'll need if they aren't already there," Marley advised. "See if there's an ash bucket and a shovel. You'll have to clean out the ashes periodically so the stove can draw. I don't miss the mess, but I do miss having an ash bucket. They're sure handy in the winter. I'd just sling a shovelful of ashes under my tires if we had an ice storm and I needed traction or I could sprinkle the walk when it was icy. Just be careful not to dump them on anything wood for days after you pull them from the grate. It's amazing how long live embers can last in the ash."

"You'll want to have a chimfex handy in case you do have a chimney fire. It suffocates the fire within seconds by reducing the oxygen."

"That's right," Avery agreed. "If you don't want a fire to burn, don't give it any oxygen. I remember learning that in about the fourth grade."

"That's not all, " Marley warned. "If you don't burn a fire hot enough, you'll get a buildup of creosote on your glass doors, and then you won't be able to enjoy looking at the flames. You'll have to buy a spray to clean the glass."

"I feel so helpless," Avery said. "When we lived in Iowa, the director of the Writers' Project had the use of a beautiful home on campus. It was one of the perks of the position, and it included maintenance. I never had to worry about lawn mowing or leaf removal. And we had electric heat."

"It'll be winter soon enough," Marley said. "The nights are going to start getting mighty chilly. You'll love that woodstove, and you'll get the hang of using it quick enough. You can call me if you need help," she offered.

"I know who I *won't* call if I need help," Avery muttered, scowling.

Marley picked Avery up at noon on Saturday, and they met her friends at the designated spot.

"Avery, you remember Jerica Swenson from bluegrass night?" Marley made the introductions. "And this is Sienna Calvert, who couldn't make it that night."

"My pleasure," Avery said, smiling. "I've never been to a chili cook-off. This is such fun!"

"I hope you came hungry," Jerica said. "You'll be full by the time we eat our way from one end to the other! My favorite last year was the white chicken chili. I hope that guy is here this year."

"I thought about bringing a pyrex bowl to see if I could persuade him to sell me some for Emmie. She loved it too last year, but she experimented until she got a recipe down pat, and they make it by the gallon at the general store all winter. She's probably sick of it by now," Sienna said.

The women strolled, stopping at each booth for a tiny styrofoam cup of chili.

"I keep thinking each one is the best until I get to the next booth. God, they're all so good. I don't know how they can pick a winner," Avery said.

"Money talks," Marley said, waggling a half-used roll of quarters.

Suddenly, Avery stiffened. She hadn't recognize the man two booths ahead until he half turned and she saw that it was Rhys Williams. He was with a petite dark-haired woman, and he was guiding her with his hand on the small of her back.

"I'm ready for some cold cider," Avery announced, fanning her face. "That last batch was mighty spicy." She turned to head in the opposite direction.

"Good idea," Sienna said. "Let's all go."

"You're awfully quiet," Marley observed an hour later.

"Stuffed," Avery equivocated. She'd been on edge since noticing Rhys in the crowd and had admonished herself. *What do you care? Don't waste your energy even thinking about him.*

"So, what's on your schedule?" Marley asked as she drove Avery home a little later.

"Oh, all kinds of important matters," Avery replied airily. "I'm getting wood this afternoon. The guy said I didn't have to be here when he delivered it. He said he'd dump it right in front of the door, and I left the money in an envelope under the doormat."

"How much?" Marley inquired.

"Three-fifty," Avery told her.

Marley blinked, a startled expression crossing her face, and Avery laughed. "Oh! You meant how much wood did I order, not how much did it cost. A cord. Sorry."

When Marley turned into the farmhouse's driveway, her mouth fell open, and she inadvertently took her foot off the accelerator. The vehicle slowly coasted to a stop, and both women stared.

"What is *that*?" Marley demanded.

"Um. Uh," Avery stuttered, nonplussed. "I don't know, " she wailed. "I told the guy what Todd told me to say. A cord of wood, cut and split."

"Call him!" Marley instructed. "Put him on speaker."

"I brung exactly what you told me," the woodcutter protested. "Lady, you said a cord, cut, unsplit. Most people don't order it that way, but I thought maybe your husband likes to chop his own wood. Sometimes, flatlanders want to, you know, get their hands dirty. Hell if I know."

Marley spoke up. "Is the wood seasoned or green?"

"She didn't ask for seasoned wood. So I brung green."

"Well, I sure hope it's oak and not pine," Marley snapped.

"I screwed up, didn't I?" Avery said in a small voice when the call concluded.

"Let's just say you're having a steep learning curve," Marley consoled. "It's not ideal, but it's not the end of the world. At least that idiot brought your wood in sixteen-inch pieces. That's the standard size for woodstoves."

Avery had another unpleasant surprise the next morning. Todd had told her to take Sunday mornings off now that peak foliage had passed, so she luxuriated in bed with her cup of coffee and read the *New York Times* on her Ipad. She showered and dressed in sweats and a pair of her new thick Ragg socks and went into the kitchen to make herself some breakfast. Glancing out the window, she saw to her horror that it had rained during the night, and then the temperature must have plummeted. The mountain of wood in front of her porch steps was encased in a sheet of glistening ice, frozen solid.

She sank into a kitchen chair and gave in to the feeling of despair that overwhelmed her, tears sliding down her cheeks and all the sadness and loneliness of the past year engulfing her until she broke into sobs. Anya crept into her lap, and Avery cuddled the kitten as Anya kneaded Avery's thigh, oblivious to the unfolding disaster.

"Oh, man!" Marley commiserated an hour later when Avery called her. "That sucks!"

"So, what do I do?" Avery asked.

"At this time of year, you can buy bundles of fireplace wood at convenience stores, gas stations, hardware stores, grocery stores, garden centers, even online," Marley counseled. "They have it at the general store; it's right there on the porch. You probably never noticed. But you don't want to drive anywhere until it melts out some. What about those outbuildings? There might be some tools in one of them. See if you can find a maul—."

"A what?" Avery interrupted.

"A maul. It's got a long straight handle and looks kind of like an ax, but it's got a blunt head. You use it to whack stuff. If you can find a maul, whack a couple pieces loose. Bring them into the house to thaw. Put them on a sheet of plastic; cut a trash bag open, and spread it out. The wood is dirty, and it'll make a mess on your floor as the ice melts.

"You can use it, but wet wood creates lots of smoke and lots of creosote buildup," Marley continued. "And it'll take a Hell of an effort to get a fire going with the wet, green hardwood you just had delivered. You'd want to start your fire with a few pieces of pine and then add the oak once it's nice and hot." She sighed. "I don't suppose you have any kindling?"

The sun came out later that morning, and melting ice dripped off eaves and branches. By early afternoon, Avery felt confident about venturing out, and she bought two bundles of kiln-dried pine firewood at the general store. Todd poured them each a cup of hot chocolate and sat with her at one of the tables since there were no customers at that moment.

"How was the chili cookoff?"

Avery grinned from ear to ear. "I wouldn't have believed there were that many varieties of chili. I was rooting for Great Bowls of Fire."

"I heard that Chili Billy won," Todd said. "Third year in a row. Emmie was sorry to miss it, but Dorothy dropped the kids off there."

Although Avery wondered if Rhys Williams' girlfriend was local, she didn't mention seeing him and didn't ask.

When she got home, Avery saw a large cardboard box on her porch, right outside the front door, where she couldn't miss it. It wasn't there when she left, so someone had obviously stopped by. When she got closer, Avery saw that it was a box of kindling, and the card read, "Warm wishes, Marley."

She immediately tapped out Marley's number and spoke without identifying herself. Her voice was thick with emotion. "Oh, Marley, that's one of the nicest things anyone's ever done for me! What a thoughtful thing for you to do. I'm sorry I missed you. I was at the store buying firewood."

"I can give you a phone number for someone who

can split that wood and stack it at the end of your porch. You can let it sit there, and it'll be dry by this time next year, so you can start the winter with seasoned wood. It's gonna cost you, but then you can order another cord for this winter. You'll have to pay a premium at this late date for seasoned wood, but it's doable and worth every penny. Get it stacked closest to the door."

Avery's breath hitched, and she wondered if she'd still be in the farmhouse in a year or even still in Winslowe.

Two weeks later, Dorothy brought Emmie into the general store on the way home from physical therapy.

"Where's Avery?" Emmie asked.

"She left about fifteen minutes ago," Todd told her. "You just missed her."

"Oh. I thought I could catch her, but I'll call her when I get home. Mom and I wanted to ask if she has any plans for Thanksgiving. We don't want her spending the holiday alone and wondered if she might like to join us for Thanksgiving dinner."

"She didn't mention any plans, but Thanksgiving is three weeks away," Todd said.

"Three weeks is nothing," Dorothy chided. "The grocery store has end caps on every aisle now with stuffing mix and canned cranberry sauce and turkey gravy in jars."

Todd clapped his hands to his cheeks in mock

horror. "Not mixes and cans and jars," he teased. "It wouldn't be nearly as good if every morsel wasn't made from scratch."

"Actually, I think I'll get my pies from you this year, Todd," Dorothy said. "My theory is if I can't do it as well or better, why try? Can I put in an order for one pumpkin, one apple, and one pecan?"

"Sure can. Go for it!" He winked. "What about rolls? The bakery will make them, and you can bake them at home."

Emmie was disappointed when Avery admitted she'd made holiday plans just the night before.

"My cousin, Hailey Betancourt, asked me to come to Connecticut," Avery told Emmie. "But the Betancourts have a high-energy Belgian Malinois, and I'd be afraid he'd go after Anya. That breed has an exceptionally high prey drive. I don't want to leave her, so I could bring her, I guess, and shut her in the bedroom, but she's so people-oriented I know she'd hate that."

"I'm not sure I've ever seen a Belgian Malinois," Emmie said.

"Sure, you have. The army uses them as working dogs," Avery said. "You've seen them lots of times on the news when special forces are air-dropped. The dog is in a sling across the paratrooper's chest.

"Oh. I thought those were just small German Shepherds."

"They're similar in appearance to a German Shepherd, but they have very different temperaments."

"So, you're not going to Connecticut?" Emmie asked.

"No. Not this year, at any rate. I have such a strong urge to nest, to make a home, and settle somewhere. When my husband died, I felt like the earth had fallen out from under my feet. I really want to have my first Vermont Thanksgiving in my own home. More accurately, what passes for my own home at the moment. So I think Hailey and Jayson and the kids are going to come here."

"Jayson Betancourt, oh, my God," Emmie breathed. "He's the Nightly News anchor. We watch him almost every day. Todd records it. Most nights, when the store is open late, he and I eat in front of the TV, long after the kids have eaten, and watch the news. That's your brother-in-law?"

"Yes. Hailey went to Stanford," Avery explained. "That's where she met him. It's just a coincidence that they're both from Connecticut. They got married right after college, but they were in their thirties before they had kids. My niece is seventeen, and my nephew is fifteen. They're both in prep school; Ivy is a senior at Loomis Chafee, and Wes is a sophomore at Deerfield. We haven't got firm plans, but the kids are already watching the long-range forecast, hoping for an early snowfall. If they come here, they'll be on the slopes every minute they can be. Needless to say, they're agitating for Thanksgiving in Vermont."

Chapter Fifteen

"Wow!" Hailey exclaimed, stepping into Avery's kitchen and looking around. "Oh, my God! Is this Anya? She's gotten so big." She scooped the kitten up, and Anya stepped onto her shoulder, purring loudly.

Wes came in next, pulling two roller bags. Ivy followed her brother, pulling her own roller bag and her mother's.

"Where's your dad?" Avery asked.

"He's getting stuff out of the car." Just then, Jay came in, toting two large duffels.

"Just how long are you guys planning to stay, anyway?" Avery joked.

"That's our ski stuff," Wes told her. "Should we put our skis on the porch?"

"This is a really cool house," Ivy said. "You really lucked out. Most rentals are sh—." A stern look from her mother cut the girl off in mid-sentence, and she quickly amended her statement. "Dumps."

"How are things with the landlord?" Hailey asked in a low voice. "Copacetic?"

Avery snorted. "Don't know; don't care."

"Are we upstairs?" Jay asked. "Wes and I'll take these bags up."

"There are three bedrooms upstairs," Avery told him. "There's a large guest room with a king-size bed and an ensuite bathroom, and two more bedrooms with a shared bath. You and Hailey will have the large bedroom with the ensuite, of course."

"What a wonderful house!" Hailey exclaimed, turning to Avery. "Decorated by *Sloan Williams*. It looks like something out of an architecture magazine. Actually, it *was* featured in *Home & Design.* I remember now! They did a kind of 'before-and-after' feature with the farmhouse as it was when the Williamses bought it and when they finished the renovations. I'll have to see if I can find the article online or in an archive somewhere; I'd like to reread it. I'm sure the original farmhouse had small rooms upstairs and one tiny bathroom. I'll bet she knocked out some walls."

"I bought a few things I like, but I haven't had to do much," Avery said. "It's just about perfect, right down to the set of heavy white crockery in the cupboard. That's what I would have chosen for myself, but I didn't have to spend the money. I guess the house has been a fully furnished rental for the past several years."

"Sounds like hubby's never gotten over Sloan's death," Hailey said.

"Lots of people have lost a spouse," Avery

retorted acerbically. "And they don't turn into assholes!"

Hailey gathered her cousin into her arms and said, "The house is wonderful. You're lucky you found such a great place to spend the winter if nothing else."

"Speaking of winter—." Avery gestured toward the window. "Looks like you got here in the nick of time." A few sparse flakes drifted from a leaden sky but gained intensity as the women watched.

"What's the forecast?" Hailey asked. "If it keeps up, we might have a White Thanksgiving, never mind a White Christmas. The kids will be thrilled."

Wes clattered down the stairs and burst into the kitchen. "Mom! It's snowing."

"Indeed it is," Jay said, right behind him. He held up his cell phone. "I just got a weather alert. Fourteen to sixteen inches, more in the higher elevations. Lookin' good, Son." He and Wes high-fived.

"Don't plan on seeing much of those three on Friday and Saturday," Hailey warned Avery.

"What about you? Did you bring skis?"

"Nope. I'd rather spend the time with you. I want to go over to the general store to meet Todd and Emmie, and I'd love to go into Westfield for lunch and some shopping. And that Mad River glass place. I might get a jump on my Christmas shopping. I'd so much rather find gifts myself than buy something online."

"Todd and Emmie invited us to their house for dessert tomorrow," Avery told Hailey. "Emmie thought that would allow time for a big dinner to settle. They'll have three kinds of pie. I'd love for you to meet their family, but I'm not sure we'll be able to go *anywhere* tomorrow unless it's on snowshoes. If it keeps coming down, the roads might not be clear, and I might not be plowed out yet, even if they are. Living here, I've learned to watch the ten-day forecast, so I got a pumpkin pie just in case."

"Tonight, we'll have the lasagna I brought for supper," Hailey said. "It's the kids' favorite."

"Perfect for a snowy evening," Avery agreed. "I've got garlic bread and salad, and I picked up tiramisu at the general store. Wait until you see their dessert case. I may never bake again."

It snowed all day Thursday and, even in the early afternoon, it was a dark day. Hailey, Ivy, and Wes carried in steaming bowls of side dishes as Avery lit candles in the dining room. She closed her eyes for a moment, grateful that she and Andrew had never lived together in this house; she didn't think she could bear to see his place at the head of the table without him in it. Instead, Avery directed Jay to that seat, and he began to carve slices from the perfectly browned bird.

After everyone was sated and helped clear the table, Jay and Wes settled themselves on the couch in the den, glued to the Thanksgiving Day football games. Before they became engrossed, Jay trimmed the carcass for sandwiches later that evening. Blowing snow had drifted across the driveway, and although they heard the town plow rumble by twice, it was clear they wouldn't be going to join the Claytons for pie and coffee.

Avery brought slices of her pie in to the menfolk while she, Hailey, and Ivy took cups of tea and pieces of pie back into the dining room. They shook puzzle pieces from a box and turned them right side up. Hailey studied the picture on the box's lid while Ivy isolated edge pieces and started lining them up. The snow tapered off just before dusk, and headlights raked the windows an hour later.

"Are you expecting company, Avery?" Wes called. "Someone just came up the driveway."

"That's Craig Johnson, my plow guy," Avery called back. "He may come back later for a second pass. You should be fine getting out in the morning."

The Betancourts were up early on Friday morning. Avery found all four in the kitchen when she shuffled in, yawning.

"We made breakfast, Avery," Wes announced proudly.

Hailey poured her cousin a cup of coffee and said, "Sit. It's almost ready." She heaped fluffy scrambled eggs onto one of Avery's white crockery plates and added two strips of crisp bacon. Ivy set a platter of pancakes in the center of the table and pushed the syrup pitcher toward Avery. Wes went around the table, filling everyone's orange juice glasses.

"This is a treat! Thank you. I thought I'd be

making breakfast for you."

"Are you kidding?" Jay teased. "The sun's been up for two hours, and these two have one foot out the door."

"The ski area opens at nine," Wes said. "But they get the lifts running and warmed up at eight-thirty, so they start letting people on at about twenty of."

"And you know this how?" Avery asked.

"We stopped for gas, and almost everybody at the pumps had ski racks. Somebody asked me where we were headed, and he told me. He said they give rides on one of the groomers at sunrise and sunset, but they don't start until next month. How cool is that! I wish we could do it today."

Avery smiled. "You'll have to come back."

After they'd eaten, Ivy started to carry plates to the sink, but Hailey stopped her. "Never mind that, honey. You guys get going. Avery and I will take clean up and run the dishwasher."

Avery glanced out the window at the big thermometer on one of the porch posts. "Brrr. It's eighteen degrees. Better them than me."

"It'll warm up some later in the day," Hailey said. "Supposed to be a high of around thirty today. And, believe me, they have the latest heated gear, so don't feel too sorry for them. All three of them have heated innersoles in their boots. There's a lithium battery that clips onto the back of the boot; they plug them in the night before, and the boots stay hot all the next day. They have heated gloves and heated vests. They even have those heated beanies that they wear under their helmets."

Avery raised her eyebrows. "You must have spent a fortune. Not like the bad old days when skiers heated a sock full of rice in the microwave and put it in their boots while they drove to the ski area. And they layered longjohns, first silk and then cotton thermal."

"*Jay* spent a fortune," Hailey clarified. "You know how he loves gadgets and technology. Forget longjohns! Forget Thinsulate. Those three even have a heated base layer under their snow pants. And all that stuff is Bluetooth-enabled so they can adjust the heat or turn it off and on with their phones."

"What about you? Don't you have all that gear?"

"I do. But I didn't bring ski clothes on this trip. I'd much rather spend my time with you." Hailey shook her head. "We had to rent a big four-wheel-drive SUV as it is, and I don't think we could have fit one more thing in it."

"You must do a lot of skiing to have such expensive equipment," Avery said. "I know you go on a ski vacation out west every year for Christmas, but I didn't realize you were such avid skiers."

"Both kids are on the alpine ski teams at school. Ivy skis at Sundown and Wes at Berkshire East; both areas are about twenty-five miles from their campuses."

"What about coming up here during winter break?" Avery suggested.

"The kids and I could. We would love that! February is sweeps month at the network, and Jay will be consumed with ratings, so he won't be able to get away. But, yeah, hold that thought."

"I did some skiing on weekends in college, but I need to take lessons," Avery said. "It's a way of life here with two ski areas nearby, so I think I'll sign up. I could do a package with rentals, but if I'm going to live here, I'd rather buy equipment and clothes."

"The instructor can recommend the best skis for you, and I'll send you links for the heated clothing."

Hailey wanted to linger over a second cup of coffee, but Avery suggested they drive over to the general store and have one there. They both took showers and, an hour later, stepped outside into brilliant sunshine where melting snow was already dripping from the eaves.

"I'm so glad you could come!" Avery told her cousin. "I've described all this, but now you can see where I live and put faces with names."

Hailey was enthralled with the store. She made a circuit of the interior but continued looking around as she and Avery sat at a table with mugs in front of them. Todd laughed when Hailey kept adding to the pile of purchases she'd set down by the register.

"Looks like you're doing your Christmas shopping," he observed.

"You betcha'," she told him. "I need so many small gifts, and I hate to get what people can buy for themselves at home. This is great!"

"We're headed into Westfield for a day of shopping," Avery told Todd.

"It'll be busy here all day," he said. "Emmie can drive now, so she'll be dropping Liza off to help out. I'll have to pay her an extortionate rate, but she's a hard worker."

"How's Emmie?" Avery inquired. "We're going to go in a few minutes, so we'll probably miss her, but tell her I said, 'Hello.' I'm so glad she's better."

"Almost as good as new," Todd agreed. "She's going to get the turkey soup started. She'll want to stay, but I'll insist that she go on home."

"I was going to boil our turkey carcass for stock and then make soup, but maybe I'll just buy some. Can you set some aside for me, and we'll swing back by to pick it up? I'll get some desserts, too, before they sell out."

"Can do." Todd grinned. "Liza has her learner's permit, and she loves to practice, as you can imagine. I'll let her drive home. We can swing by and drop your stuff off."

"That's out of your way," Avery protested.

"A little. But Eliza will be delighted to add a few more miles."

"I'm not sure what time we'll be back or what time Jay and the kids will be back," Avery fretted. She started to remove a key from her ring, but Todd held up a hand.

"I don't need a key. If you're thinking I'll need to

get into the house to put soup in the fridge, you haven't lived in Vermont long enough. I'll just stick it in a snowbank."

Avery burst out laughing.

"Don't laugh!" Todd feigned hurt feelings. "You'll be doing it, too, soon enough."

"What's upstairs?" Hailey asked, coming up behind Avery.

"Nothing," Todd said.

Hailey frowned. "Nothing? The whole second floor?"

"Avery can fill you in." Todd deftly avoided the sore subject.

Avery pointed out various landmarks as she and Hailey drove to Westfield and attempted to find parking.

"Black Friday." Hailey sighed dramatically. We'll just have to keep circling the block until someone pulls out.

"It's two-hour metered parking," Avery pointed out. "That's the kiss of death. We'll get talking or find something interesting in the shops, and we'll lose track of time, I guarantee it."

"I'll set the alarm on my phone for an hour and forty-five minutes," Hailey offered.

"I'd rather keep cruising the municipal parking lot until someone leaves." Avery was adamant. "Something will open up, and then we won't have to worry about it."

Several hours later, the two women lingered over a cup of tea and a shared dessert. The lunch hour had passed, and the crowd had thinned, so no one was waiting for a table to free up.

"This is so fun." Hailey sighed. "I love having you close enough to visit."

"Do you think you and the kids can come for a week in February?" Avery asked. "I'll be taking lessons, and I think a lot of it will come back to me, so I should be able to keep up with you guys on intermediate trails by then."

"Hold that thought." Hailey smiled conspiratorially and said, "I have something to tell you. I just heard it the other day, and I want to see your face, so I haven't said anything."

Avery waited, but Hailey said nothing, letting the tension build. Finally, she stated, "You won't believe who's single! Someone from Hotchkiss."

Avery demurred, "Well, that doesn't exactly narrow it down. Half of our graduating class is divorced."

"Not someone from our class. Someone a year ahead of us. Male," Hailey teased.

"Oh. Who? Don't keep me in suspense," Avery protested.

"You remember Robyn Brooks? She's in my power yoga class. We walked out to our cars together after class last week, and she told me she was trying to set her friend up with John Zaika. His wife died about six months ago."

"Johnny Zaika! Oh, no, I'm so sorry to hear that. I remember seeing the wedding announcement in *The Hartford Courant,* so they must have been married for about twenty-five years. Were they happy? Six months isn't long to mourn someone you loved for twenty-five years."

"I don't know if they were happy or not," Hailey said. "I just know he and his wife had two daughters. They never divorced, so I assume they were happy. Or relatively happy, at least. He may still be mourning his wife's death, but he owns a chain of drugstores, and Robyn figured he'd be a pretty eligible widower. She wanted to make sure her friend had a shot with him."

"I'm so sorry to hear that," Avery said again.

"Do you ever wonder 'what if?' He asked you out after your sophomore year at Northeastern, remember? That summer? Do you ever wonder what would have happened if you'd gone out with him?"

"He was the road not taken, that's for sure. I almost fell on the floor when he called and asked me out. I had such a crush on him in high school, but he didn't even know I was alive."

"I don't think he dated much at Hotchkiss," Hailey said. "I don't remember him having a girlfriend. I always saw him walking on campus with a load of books or in the library sometimes. I'm not sure he noticed any girls."

"He was so handsome," Avery mused. "I wonder what he looks like now."

"One way to find out. You could call him. His number must be in the alumni directory."

"I could email," Avery countered.

"And if he doesn't reply?" Hailey demanded. "Then what? You could call to offer condolences and keep the conversation going."

"He probably doesn't even remember me," Avery protested.

"Don't be an idiot," Hailey said. "What have you got to lose? This could be a do-over. A second chance. Why *didn't* you go out with him when he asked?"

"I accepted, and it was all I could think about," Avery explained. Her voice dropped to a whisper. "But I chickened out. I called him back and told him I couldn't go, that I was in a relationship with someone, so he wouldn't try to re-schedule. It wasn't true, but I was so afraid he wouldn't like me. I couldn't stand the thought that he might go out with me once and then not ask me out again. It seemed easier just not to take that chance."

Hailey grimaced. "I didn't know that. Do you have any idea how fucked up that is?"

"More tea, ladies?" Both women looked up, startled, when their server approached.

"No, thank you. Just the check," Avery said. Turning to Hailey, she said, "We can probably head back in about an hour since we don't need to swing by the general store to pick up the turkey soup. See why I didn't want to park in a metered space?"

Chapter Sixteen

The seed Hailey planted at Thanksgiving took root in Avery's mind. She found herself reminiscing about her years in prep school and the crush she'd had on John Zaika. *Surely, six months is too soon to start dating.* She remembered how she'd felt in June, barely six months after Andrew's untimely death. She'd been mired in grief throughout the winter and all through spring. If it hadn't been for the imminent arrival of Andrew's successor and her increasingly urgent need to find alternate living accommodations, she doubted she'd have gotten dressed or forced herself to eat.

Hailey had told Avery that John Zaika attended Yale as an undergraduate and gotten his Pharm.D. degree there from Yale's School of Pharmacy. She said he worked for a big-name chain to gain experience and then purchased a small drugstore that was about to go under. Several years later, he purchased another and then a third.

"He owns seven pharmacies; that's what Robyn said," Hailey had told Avery that day at lunch.

"Robyn?" Avery had asked, puzzled.

"Brooks. Robyn Brooks," Hailey reiterated, a touch of impatience in her tone. "She was going on and on about John Zaika's success, what a catch he'd be for her friend once she got her hooks into him."

I might be willing to send him a condolence card, Avery decided. Then she grimaced, thinking back over the conversation she'd had during Hailey's Thanksgiving visit. *But I don't know about getting my hooks into him.*

"What do you think?" Avery asked Marley a week later. Marley invited Avery to dinner, and the two women were sprawled in comfortable club chairs in front of the fire with glasses of wine. "I could buy a card. But I'm not sure he'll even remember me."

"He might. You won't know if you don't make the overture. He sure isn't going to call you up out of the blue thirty-five years later. But if you send him a card, he might respond. I'm glad to see you're thinking of putting yourself back into the social world that includes both sexes. Good for you."

Avery nodded noncommittally.

Do it!" Marley encouraged. "See what happens." She wrinkled her nose. "But don't buy a store card. Figure out what you want to say, and let me make a card for you."

"Now?" Avery was startled.

"No time like the present," Marley grinned. "After we eat. It won't take me twenty minutes. You can mail it tomorrow before you lose your nerve."

"You are so lucky to work from home. Your studio is fabulous," Avery enthused. "Your whole house is fabulous. I love it!"

"Yeah, architect-designed," Marley said, "but then the architect moved out." Her tone was matter-of-fact, with no discernable bitterness.

"Oh. I didn't know you were divorced."

Marley snorted. "I'm not. I've never been married."

"How long did you live together?" Avery asked, eager for the details of her new friend's life.

"Two years. I was crazy about him, but he apparently wasn't into long-term relationships. I didn't even know he was thinking of leaving until he took a job on the west coast. But I got the cabin and the cats. And his office space up in the loft. I think I came out ahead." As she spoke, a marmalade cat leaped into Marley's lap, turned around twice, and curled up. Marley stroked it absently, and loud purring filled the room.

"I love cats," Avery said. "Anya is such good company. I guess I'm good company for her too right now, but if I weren't home all day, I'd have to get her a companion."

"Will you be looking for a job after the holidays?" Marley inquired.

"I don't know," Avery answered truthfully. "I enjoyed helping in the general store, but that was just temporary. I need to get through a winter and see what conditions are like before I commit to commuting. I'm okay financially with my late husband's life insurance, but that's finite. And royalties from his books are iffy. His popularity may wane over time, and that revenue stream could diminish significantly. The novelty of living here hasn't worn off, and I'm not bored yet, but I might need to find a little part-time job just to give me something to do if nothing else."

"How old were you when you got married?" Marley was curious about Avery's background.

"Twenty-two. I got pregnant during my first year at Harvard Law, and we got married a few months later."

"One of your classmates?" Marley probed.

"Not hardly." Avery's smile was wry, but her eyes reflected her sadness. "Andrew had graduated from Harvard years before, and he was already an acclaimed novelist. He'd won several prestigious awards—an Agatha, an Edgar, a Shamus—."

"He obviously wrote mysteries. Very successfully, I'd say," Marley interrupted.

"He'd gotten an award from Mystery Writers of America and a National Book Award for fiction," Avery continued. "He was a visiting professor in the English department, doing a couple of creative writing seminars. He gave lectures in the psych department and even at the med school, describing how he used forensics in formulating his plots."

"Did you take one of his courses?" Marley asked.

Avery shook her head. "I'd seen him around, but I

didn't know who he was. A friend saw his author photo on the back cover of one of his books and recognized him. I actually met him in a bar."

"I've met a lot of men in bars," Marley teased, but then her expression turned serious. "I just never married any of them."

"It was classic," Avery admitted. "I was with a girlfriend, but she went off with some guy. I'd had too much to drink, and I went home with Andrew. Spent the night, didn't know where I was the next morning, did the whole walk of shame thing. Found myself with a bun in the oven."

"You're not the first," Marley said. "But you were married for a long time if he died just this year. What's that, like, twenty-five years?"

"Almost thirty," Avery said. "I'm fifty-one."

"How old is your child?" Marley asked. "He or she must be twenty-eight or twenty-nine."

Marley's hand flew to her mouth, and her eyes widened when she saw the stricken look on Avery's face. "Oh, my God. I'm sorry."

Avery shook her head sadly. "A daughter. She's gone. Her name was Olivia. She died of SIDS."

"Oh, Avery. I'm so sorry. That must have been so hard."

"It was terrible. Beyond terrible. Olivia was six-and-a half-months old. Andrew was away on a book tour. I found her in her crib, dead." Avery spoke in a monotone, relating only the facts.

"Were you in Iowa then?"

Avery shook her head. "Virginia. We had no intention of leaving Boston. I still had two years of law school. But Andrew was offered a university position as Writer-in-Residence in Virginia. He knew how much Harvard meant to me, how hard I'd worked to get into the law school, and how hard I'd worked to stay in—." Avery's voice trailed off, and there was a long silence before she continued. "He offered to turn it down, but I couldn't let him do that. I dropped out, and we moved to Virginia. That's where it happened."

Marley never took her eyes from Avery's face, willing her to go on but unwilling to ask more intrusive questions.

"I was a complete basket case, a total wreck. I couldn't sleep or eat. I didn't care if I lived or died. Nothing Andrew said or did could comfort me. My cousin Hailey suggested to him that living in the house where Olivia died, in the town where I saw her everywhere, was more than I could bear. Andrew applied for the job in Iowa, and when he got it, he listed our house furnished, so we moved away."

Avery saw the unasked question in Marley's eyes. "We never had another child. My husband and I always intended to have several children, but it wasn't meant to be."

"I'm so sorry," Marley said again.

"What about you?" Avery asked, needing to change the subject before her lifelong sorrow engulfed her. "You never married?"

"Two close calls," Marley joked. "I was engaged twice."

Avery raised her eyebrows, clearly interested in Marley's life story, and relieved not to be talking about her own.

"Yep, another woman, both times," Marley said.

"What?" Avery gasped. "You were engaged to two guys who cheated on you before you were even married?"

"Not exactly," Marley clarified. "The first time, it was his *mother*. She was forty when she had him, her only child. We were like two dogs with a bone. I tried to talk to her, explain that once Mike and I were married, we'd be a nuclear family, and she'd be extended family. I told her as gently as I could that there was a place in our lives for her, but there were going to be some changes."

Avery's eyes widened. "I'm guessing that didn't go over well."

"Understatement!" Marley snorted. "She drew herself up to her full height, threw her shoulders back, and looked me right in the eye. 'My son and I are nuclear family and always will be. If you were to die or you and Michael were to divorce, you would be as nothing to us.' That's what she said; I kid you not. Mike insisted it was a misunderstanding, but I could read the handwriting on that wall."

"Couldn't you live somewhere else, nowhere near her?" Avery asked.

"Nope. Distance wouldn't have made any

difference. She'd have been calling him every day, needing his advice or complaining about one thing or another that he couldn't do anything about. She'd have been a constant, albeit unseen, presence, and I'd have gotten more and more resentful. So, no, thank you. I broke it off a week before the wedding when she went to him behind my back, and he took her side."

"I've always thought it's as important to know what you don't want as it is to know what you do want," Avery commented.

"Exactly," Marley agreed. "And I didn't want any more 'mama's boys.' Exit Michael Richardson and enter Christian Richardson, whose mother was on her fourth husband and barely gave her offspring the time of day."

"But?" Avery asked. "There's a but coming, isn't there?"

Marley nodded. "But Chris was divorced, with a ten-year-old daughter who liked having Daddy all to herself. She was possessive, jealous, and threatened. Chris insisted she'd accept me once we were married, but every day was a battle. I could see what the next seven years would be like until she went away to college—*if* she went away to college."

"And no one since then?" Avery asked.

"Oh, there've been plenty of men since then," Marley chortled. "But they have to park their shit at my door. They can stay as long as it's fun and easy, but I don't plan to fall in love ever again. I like my life just fine the way it is." She grinned. "Right now,

I'm sleeping with the bartender from The Slippery Slope. He's fun, and it's easy, but I expect the relationship to last as long as there's snow, and then he'll move on. Which is fine; he's young, and we don't have a lot to talk about, if you know what I mean." She winked. "Not that we do a lot of talking."

"I'm calling to invite you to a get-together at my house on Christmas Eve," Marley said a week later.

Avery was surprised. "You won't be spending Christmas with your boyfriend?"

Marley laughed. "Not hardly. You'd be amazed at how many people have family issues and want to get away at Christmas. The ski area will be full over the holiday. Then it will be berserk the week between Christmas and New Years. Landon will make a small fortune in tips, so I wouldn't be seeing him even if I wanted to. It's fine."

"I would love to," Avery said, a catch in her voice. "This is my first Christmas without Andrew."

"Oh, sweetie. Do you have plans for Christmas Day?"

"I don't," Avery said in a small voice, her pain apparent.

"Well, you certainly can't spend the day alone! Why don't you stay over, and we can do the Jewish thing."

"What Jewish thing?" Avery was perplexed.

"You know!" Marley laughed. "Christmas is a Christian holiday, and Jews don't celebrate it. We celebrate Hannukah, so we go out for Chinese food and a movie on Christmas." She paused. "You look confused. You didn't know I'm Jewish? Well, half Jewish since my dad didn't practice any religion and my mom's family were Reform. Technically, that makes me a Jewess since the lineage is matrilineal. So, you and I could have breakfast on Christmas morning then head for Burlington. Studios always release some blockbuster movie or two on Christmas; we could pick something we both want to see and then get Chinese."

"I'd like that," Avery said slowly, "but I don't want to leave Anya overnight. She'd be confused."

"You could bring her," Marley suggested. "If she gets along with my guys, great, and if she doesn't, we can shut her in your room. We'll drop her off at home before leaving for Burlington, so she'd only be by herself for a few hours."

"Thanks, Marley. I appreciate that. Who else is coming?"

"Merritt, Jerica, Sienna, Krista. Brandi will be with Larry, and Emmie will spend Christmas Eve with family. I thought I'd cook us a leg of lamb as a special treat."

"Oh, that sounds wonderful! You have no idea. What can I bring?"

"How about dessert?"

"I'll get a Christmas pudding."

"I'm glad you said 'get' and not 'make.' Have you ever seen the recipe for one of those things? Gives me the shivers just thinking about it," Marley groaned.

"I'm not a masochist," Avery agreed. "But I will make the hard sauce. It's actually easy."

"So, did you ever hear from the old flame? You sent the card, right?" Marley asked.

"I mailed it, but I haven't heard from him. He probably got a lot of condolence cards and didn't reply to every one. I'm sure he doesn't even remember me."

But John Zaika did remember Avery, and he did respond.

The phone rang one evening a few days before Christmas, but there was only silence on the line when Avery answered it. Frowning, she disconnected. It rang again an hour later, and this time a man's voice asked tentatively, "Is this Avery Beall? Um, no, I'm sorry; I meant Avery Markham."

"This is Avery."

"Um. I'm not sure if you remember me." The caller's voice trailed off, but then he asked, "What am I saying? Of course, you remember me; you just sent me a condolence card. Avery, I'm sorry," he apologized. "Let me start over. Hello, Avery. It's John Zaika, and I'm calling to thank you for the condolence card you sent."

"Well, hello, John. I was hoping to hear from you, but I thought you might email."

"I probably should have. I didn't realize how nervous I'd feel about calling you."

"Was that you who called about an hour ago?" Avery asked.

"It was," John admitted. "I just lost my nerve when you answered the phone. I was married for a long time, and I haven't had much practice with this sort of thing. My wife died six days before our twenty-fifth anniversary. She's been gone six months, and I'm still walking around in a daze."

"I'm glad to hear from you," Avery said warmly. "My cousin, Hailey, visited at Thanksgiving with her family, and she told me you'd recently lost your wife. Hailey still lives in Connecticut, and she keeps up with a lot of people from prep school."

"Hailey Beall," John said. "You two were in the class behind me. How is she?"

"She's great," Avery told him. "She met her husband at Stanford, and, amazingly enough, he's from Wilton. She's Hailey Betancourt now. She has two kids, a boy and a girl. Her son is a sophomore at Deerfield, and her daughter will graduate from Loomis Chafee next May."

"She's not married to Jayson Betancourt, is she? The news anchor?"

"None other," Avery confirmed.

"What about you?" John asked. "You must be in Vermont with an 802 area code. Have you lived there long?"

"Not long at all," Avery said. "I spent a month in Connecticut with Hailey and Jay, and then I moved to Vermont. I've only been here since September."0

"And before that?" John asked.

"I went to Northeastern for undergrad and then got into Harvard Law."

John whistled. "Impressive. So, you're a lawyer?"

"No. I got married after my first year, and we moved to Virginia when my husband was offered a job. Then we moved to Iowa when he took a position as head of the Writers Project at the university. We were there almost thirty years, but he passed away in January. I needed a change of scenery, so here I am."

"He was a writer?" John asked, but then he answered his own question. "He must have been. What did he write?"

"Fiction," Avery replied without elaborating.

"Would I have read any of his work?" John inquired.

"You might have. If you like mysteries."

"Did he use a pseudonym?" John asked.

"No. He used his real name, Andrew Markham."

John laughed. "How funny. My wife loved mysteries. She read all his books and had a whole shelf full. I'm thinking of downsizing, and I just took several boxes of books to donate to the local library. Including his, I'm sorry to say."

Avery and John spent another half hour on the phone once they'd gotten beyond the initial stilted exchanges. As the conversation progressed, they found themselves catching up on each other's lives and reminiscing about former classmates.

225

"I'd like to see you sometime, Avery," John said finally. "Do you ever come to Connecticut to visit Hailey?"

"I haven't yet. I'd probably do that in late spring when I could combine it with a few days in New York to visit my folks. They sold the house in New Canaan when my dad was transferred to his firm's London office years ago, and they bought an apartment on the upper west side when they returned."

"Let me guess," John teased. "In a co-op on Central Park West."

"You got that right." Avery was amused. "They're in the Hotel Des Artistes on west sixty-seventh. The indoor pool was very appealing to my dad. Although they're only there half the year; they winter in Portugal."

"I have to take fifteen credits of continuing education every year, and there are a myriad of streaming and online courses available," John told Avery. "But some are in-person seminars, and I could see what the course offerings might be at the University of Vermont after the first of the year. They're usually held in a hotel conference room so I could fly into Burlington. Perhaps you could join me for dinner one evening."

"I'd like that," Avery said slowly.

When she hung up, Avery was smiling. *Wow, Johnny Zaika. I wonder if we'll even recognize each other.*

Chapter Seventeen

On the Saturday after New Years, Avery, Marley, Emmie, and Sienna were seated on barstools at The Slippery Slope.

"Slow tonight," Emmie remarked as Landon Stokes wiped the condensation from the bar before setting a round of drinks in front of the four women.

"Yeah," he agreed. "Won't be real busy again until winter break in February. Mostly just locals and some folks usin' their condos, or renters in their condos." He gestured with his bar towel, and the women turned in the direction he pointed in.

Brandi Tyler and Larry Turner were seated at a four-top on the far side of the room. Brandi waved enthusiastically and motioned for her friends to join them.

"Go on," Landon said. "I'll bring your drinks over." Marley hesitated, but he told her, "I'll see you later. Probably get out of here around one." She nodded and slid off her stool.

Brandi rounded up two more chairs as her friends crossed the room. Emmie slid into one and patted the chair next to her.

"Sit here, Avery, next to me," she ordered. "So, what's this about you hooking up with an old flame? Tell!"

"What's flaming is Avery's face," Sienna hooted.

Avery shook her head. "Not much to tell, really. It's someone I went to prep school with. He was a year ahead of me at Hotchkiss. I had such a crush on him, but I doubt he even knew I existed. My cousin still lives in Connecticut, and she told me that his wife died recently and suggested I send him a condolence card. I was going to buy one, but Marley offered to make it so I could put my own message on it."

Emmie held Avery's gaze. "So, did you send it? Did you hear from him?"

"A couple of weeks went by, and I didn't think he was going to respond. I was surprised when he called me just before Christmas. We talked for almost an hour."

"Does he live in Connecticut? What does he do for work?" Sienna asked.

"He never left Connecticut. Went to Yale for undergrad and then Yale again for pharmacy school. He owns a local chain of drugstores, seven, I think. He was married for twenty-five years and has two adult daughters. One got married last year, and the other is engaged."

"Do they both live in Connecticut?" Emmie asked.

"That I don't know," Avery replied.

"Are you going to see him?" Emmie asked.

"I don't know that either." Avery laughed. "We might get together when I go to Connecticut to visit Hailey. Or, there's a possibility he could take a Continuing Ed course at UVM. He mentioned having dinner in Burlington one evening if he comes to Vermont."

"Sounds like he's not ready," Marley stated.

"I'm not sure I am either." Avery shook her head. "And I hate the thought that he won't like me. Or that I won't like him. I might be better off just reliving my teenage fantasies."

Larry snorted. "Women! You wouldn't have contacted him at all if you weren't anticipating a response. Why not just call a spade a spade?"

But Avery didn't hear from John, and thoughts of him were driven right out of her mind by Hailey's phone call.

"Avery? Have you got a minute? There's something I want to run by you."

Avery could hear the excitement in her cousin's voice, and her interest was piqued.

"Sure. What's up?"

"You know that space over the general store?"

Avery was confused. "What space?"

"Upstairs," Hailey repeated. "Over the general store."

"*Here?* In Winslowe?"

229

"Well, of course, there. How many general stores do you know of with empty space above them?"

"Okay. What about it?'

"Well, I was thinking. I've been thinking about it since Thanksgiving. Todd took me up there, and I just can't get it out of my mind. There's a lot of square footage just going to waste, and it's a gold mine with so much tourist traffic going through the store downstairs. Todd told me women are constantly asking about the sign that says clothing, and they're disappointed to learn the boutique is closed. So, what if it wasn't closed?"

"What are you talking about?" Avery demanded. "I'm not following this."

"Avery! What if the boutique was open?"

"Well, that'd be great. But I don't see that happening. Both Todd and Emmie have told me that it was Sloan Williams' shop, and her husband can't find a manager to run it the way she did. According to Emmie, no one has Sloan Williams' taste. Also, her husband is impossible. Mrs. Williams must have had impeccable taste because you don't get international acclaim as an interior designer without having great taste. So, that goes without saying. And Mr. Williams is an arrogant asshole. I'm not surprised to hear he's hard on help. I sure wouldn't want to work for him."

"Avery!" Hailey couldn't keep the exasperation out of her voice. "I'm not suggesting you petition him to re-open his late wife's boutique and let you manage it!"

"Well, what *are* you suggesting? What's your point?"

"It's right there, staring you in the face."

"What's staring me in the face?"

"Avery. You may not need the money, but you do need something interesting to occupy your time. You've had a few months to settle in, and the holidays are past, so now's the time to think about what you're going to do."

"That's the first reasonable thing you've said so far. I agree with you there," Avery said.

"Why can't you lease the space over the general store and open your own clothing boutique?" Hailey suggested.

Avery spluttered. "You're joking! Tell me you're joking!" she finally managed.

"I'm not joking," Hailey insisted. "It's brilliant! It's right there staring you in the face."

"So you've said. Several times."

"You don't see it? It's such a great opportunity, and it would be so much fun," Hailey insisted. "Will you at least think about it?"

"Okay. I'll think about it."

"Good," Hailey said.

"I've thought about it," Avery shot back. "For one nanosecond, which is all the time I need to know that I don't want any more to do with Rhys Williams than I'm already stuck with."

"Have you seen him? Or talked to him?" Hailey inquired

"Of course not. That was the whole point of paying six months' rent in advance. I love this house, and I'd like to stay here, so I intend to extend for another six months. My lease is up in March, but I won't be seeing him or talking to him until I absolutely have to."

Hailey sighed. "You're being awfully short-sighted if you ask me."

"I didn't ask you," Avery insisted.

"This is business, Avery. What did he do to you that was so terrible?"

"I'm just not used to being treated with such disdain and disrespect. Once was enough. I'm sure not going to put my head back on the chopping block."

"Okay. If you say so," Hailey conceded. "But the idea certainly has merit. Make a list of the pros and cons. The con is that you don't want to rent space from your landlord. And you don't want to follow in his late wife's footsteps. But the pros are that you like clothes. It would be fun to be part of the general store. It would be a gold mine. The commute isn't bad."

Avery sighed audibly.

"And that's just for starters," Hailey wheedled. "I can think of ten more good reasons why you should give this serious consideration."

Avery's new friends had gathered at the farmhouse for chili and cornbread one evening in mid-January. It was full dark by five o'clock and far earlier than Avery usually ate supper. But she'd quickly learned to consult the hourly forecast to see what road conditions would be like as the evening progressed and the temperature dropped.

When Avery told them about her conversation with her cousin and Hailey's idea, a heated discussion ensued.

"I think your cousin is on to something," Gina Rickman said. She was the newest member of the group, a friend of Merritt's. "I was eager to go upstairs to see the clothing the first time I came to visit, and I was so disappointed that the boutique was closed."

"What a waste!" Emmie added. "It's such a great location. I just don't get it."

"Well, Rhys is a diplomat—was a diplomat—not a businessman," Marley pointed out.

"You don't have to be a businessman to see what's staring you right in the face," Krista stated.

"Those were Hailey's words exactly," Avery said, her voice rising. "She kept insisting a perfect opportunity was *staring me right in the face*."

"Well," Krista summarized, "here we have one party who needs something and another party who has it. If you can come to an agreement, how is that not 'win/win?' "

"That's my whole point," Avery argued heatedly. "Rhys Williams and I don't agree on anything! Why would this be any different?"

"You must have agreed on something, or you wouldn't be living in his farmhouse," Gina said. She withered under Avery's furious glare and held up her hands in mock surrender.

"Sorry, sorry. This is clearly a sore subject, and I don't know enough about it to comment. I should just keep my mouth shut," Gina apologized.

"No," Avery demurred, instantly contrite. "I'm the one who's sorry. I know you're all trying to help. I don't know why I have such a visceral dislike for him. People have been rude to me before, that's for sure. I spent a year at Harvard Law, learning to develop a rhinoceros hide. I can't explain it; he just unnerves me."

Avery's cell vibrated in her pocket two days later, just as she reached for a package of romaine lettuce. Pulling it from her coat pocket, she glanced at Caller ID and set the lettuce back on the shelf. She wheeled her cart off to the side so as not to inconvenience other shoppers.

"Hey, Emmie."

"Hey, Avery. Am I catching you at a good time?"

"Sure. I'm doing some grocery shopping, but I'm not in a hurry. What's up?"

"I won't keep you. I only have a few minutes, myself. I just had an idea I wanted to run by you."

"This sure is my month for people running ideas by me," Avery joked.

"Actually, it's the same one." Emmie laughed.

"Seriously, for business purposes, I'd be delighted to see a clothing boutique re-opened upstairs. And for purely selfish reasons, I would love to see you every day. Your cousin, Hailey, is right: it's such a great concept."

"Except," Avery protested.

"Yes, except," Emmie agreed. "There's a worm in the apple. Listen, he's my landlord too, and no one knows better than I do how hard he is to deal with. So, here's what I'm thinking; maybe you could keep it at arm's length by having the transaction go through Daisha Weaver as the leasing agent. That way, you'd pay the rent to her and report maintenance issues to her. She'd be the one dealing with Rhys, not you. I don't even know if Apex Realty handles commercial property, but I could ask."

"It's a thought," Avery said slowly. "I know the agency handles residential rentals because she showed several prospects to me when I first got here. But I'll call her. You don't have to do that although I appreciate the offer. You have enough to do with the store and kids."

"Oh, good. I'm glad you're willing to look into it, at least."

"I'll call her this afternoon," Avery promised. "If the roads are clear tomorrow and she's free, maybe we can have lunch. There are a couple of cute little places right near her office or, if she can't spare that much time, I could pick up deli sandwiches, and we could have a quick, working lunch in her office.

"Well, Cuz, you'll be happy to know you've got half a dozen people insisting I should swallow my antipathy toward Rhys Williams and pursue the clothing proposal," Avery told Hailey the next night.

"I'm listening," Hailey said.

"I had a few new friends over for chili a couple of nights ago, and, believe me, a boutique was the hot topic of conversation, so to speak. Marley knows I'll be looking for something interesting to do, and Emmie has a vested interest in having it re-open upstairs over her store."

"It wouldn't re-open," Hailey interjected. "It would be different. New. You'd put your stamp on the space, not try to keep someone else's enterprise limping along."

"You're right," Avery conceded. "I didn't even know Sloan, but I can't seem to separate her from the clothing boutique over the general store."

"Neither can her husband, apparently," Hailey said. "From what I could gather, his beef with her successors was that they ordered shipments that wouldn't have been Sloan's taste. With each successive manager, the clothing line got farther and farther from what she would have chosen."

"Well, she isn't here!" Avery burst out. "I don't want to be another one who's trying to compete with a ghost!"

"That's precisely why I think it's imperative you lease the space. Then you'd do your *own* thing."

"It doesn't feel like my own thing. I'm living in *her house*!" Avery wailed.

"The first thing you'd need to do is get a lease signed," Hailey continued, ignoring Avery's outburst. "The second thing is to decide on a clothing line that appeals to you. The third thing is to renovate the space to showcase your collection. And the fourth thing is to have a sale and blow out the current inventory, which looked like a mediocre mishmash from the glance I got," Hailey said. Her tone was decisive, and Avery found herself getting more interested in pursuing it.

"I can address item number one," Avery told Hailey. "Emmie suggested that her friend Daisha Weaver could act as the agent. She's with Apex Realty in Westfield, and I met her when I first arrived. She showed me several rental properties, but none of them were suitable. That's when I rented the condo at the ski area for a month until I could find something more long-term that was decent."

"It's hard to go from living in a gracious home to a hovel," Hailey commiserated. "Most rentals are pretty run down. You are so lucky to have landed where you did; the farmhouse is fabulous."

"See?" Avery sighed. "It's almost a circular argument. We're right back to Mr. Fly In The Ointment."

"So, why don't you call this Daisha?" Hailey asked.

"I did. I talked to her today. I called her this

morning and asked if she was free for lunch, so I drove up to Westfield and met her at a little sandwich shop a few doors down from her office. She doesn't seem to have a problem with Rhys and was perfectly amenable to calling him. She seemed to think he would be willing to do a long-term lease. She says he's not stupid, and he recognizes the location's desirability. What he's been doing hasn't worked, so she thinks he's ready to try something different, even if he doesn't know it yet. She doesn't think he'd initiate any action because it might feel disloyal to his late wife, but he might be willing to consider a proposal."

"Good. If he agrees to lease the space, you're halfway there. Tell the rental agent he'd need to allow some renovation. You could agree in writing to submit a sketch and an estimate plus references for whoever does the work, subject to the leaseholder's approval."

"When did you get an MBA?" Avery asked admiringly. "You've put some thought into this."

"More where that came from," Hailey promised. "I just wish I were closer—I'd want to be your partner."

"You could be," Avery suggested. "We wouldn't have to be equal partners because I'd be doing the day-to-day, but you could take over the administrative side and do merchandising, advertising, stuff like that. If it's successful, maybe you could come up one weekend a month for some hands-on, once Ivy and Wes go off to college."

"Oh, Avery, I would love that! This is really exciting."

"I hate to be a bucket of cold water, but let's see what Mr. Fly In The Ointment has to say before we waste our time."

"Don't call him that," Hailey scolded. "We need him to be part of the solution, not part of the problem."

"What about clothing?" Avery asked. "I hope you've got some bright ideas because I haven't a clue about wholesale clothing. Are there—I don't know—clothing shows shop owners go to?"

"Of course there are," Hailey said. "It'll take a little research, but we can find out just as well as the next guy. But, you know how stores all seem to have the same stuff at the same time? It's as if their buyers all attended the same shows. I'd want something different, something special, more exclusive, you know?"

"I *don't* know," Avery said. "Too bad we can't ask Andrew. He picked out most of my clothes, and they were gorgeous. He loved to shop, and he had an encyclopedic knowledge of fabric and tailoring. I never really paid attention to where he got them from, and I donated them to Dress For Success. I knew I'd continue to mourn as long as there were reminders of a past that's gone."

"I *do* have something in mind," Hailey admitted. "I was thinking more of a franchise, carrying a

239

complete line from one source. Or a couple of sources."

"That would be a lot easier," Avery said. "But who?"

"Have you ever heard of Roundtop Ranchwear?"

"Nooo," Avery drawled. "Should I have?"

"They're in Texas," Hailey said. "The factory and the flagship store. But they have stores throughout the west. We've gone out west to ski every Christmas for the last ten years, and I've seen their stores opening in upscale locations. Jay and the kids are on the mountain every minute of every day, but I need some downtime after a few days, so I usually spend a day shopping wherever we are. There's a Roundtop Ranchwear store in Jackson Hole and one in Park City. The one in Vail opened after we were there, but I got to the Aspen store this year. I could spend a fortune because I always want one of everything."

"What's so special about their clothes?" Avery asked. "And how's it exclusive if the stores are franchises?"

"They're not. They're only in the west, and they're all company stores. The exception is one franchise on Nantucket, and there's a family connection there, I think. There was an article about them in some fashion magazine. Something I picked up in the dentist's office when I was waiting for the kids to have their teeth cleaned."

"We don't have a family connection, so why would they let us open a franchise? I'm confused,"

Avery said. "Unless you know something I don't."

"You know, it *wasn't* a fashion magazine," Hailey said. "It was a business journal, come to think of it. One of the partners is the head designer, and the other has a business degree. They started it from scratch, and it's a runaway success. That's our hook! Vermont has a lot of cachet, largely dependent on tourism. We need to put a prospectus together and convince them we've got location, location, location."

"I'll look at their line, but I'm not sure Ranchwear would work in a part of the country that's synonymous with preppy." Avery equivocated.

"The clothes have a very broad appeal," Hailey insisted. "They're timeless. Great fabrics, simple designs, very well made, very versatile—"

"Okay, okay; send me a link to their website."

"I'm serious, Hailey insisted. "It's called 'ranchwear' and it originates in Texas, but the women who go to Roundtop Ranch to buy show horses live all over the country. You don't think they're going around in prairie skirts and yoked shirts in Grosse Point and Pound Ridge, do you?"

Avery laughed. "Do they have winter clothes? I'm practically layering everything I've got all at once, and we're barely into the coldest part of the winter."

Chapter Eighteen

Four days later, Rhys' phone vibrated, and he withdrew it from his pocket, frowning. He thought the ringer was set to full volume, but with the button located where it was, he sometimes found that the mute feature was engaged. Glancing at the screen, he saw that the green 'accept' circle had a keyboard symbol next to it and knew it was Mira calling. He quickly scrolled to his settings and chose TTY.

"Hey, Dad, have you seen the forecast for this weekend?" Mira typed. "It's not looking good for all of New England. There's a huge Nor'easter headed your way. We'll probably get sleet and freezing rain here, but it's no time to be on the road. GA," she typed to indicate that her father should go ahead.

"I was going to call you later, sweetie," Rhys replied. "I've been watching the forecast, and I was going to suggest we re-schedule, as much as I'd love to see you. GA."

"And as much as I'd love to be tucked up in your cozy cabin in ski country during a snowstorm," Mira typed. "I can almost taste the hot chocolate. GA."

"You may lose power," Rhys cautioned. "I'll worry about you. Can you take tomorrow off and head up here before the storm hits? GA."

"I'll be fine," Mira replied. "I'll be needed to sign all weekend if a state of emergency is declared. I have to go now, as a matter of fact. There'll be frequent updates and warnings for residents. I'm going to sleep in my office. I have a daybed, and the building has a generator, so don't worry about me."

"I love you, sweetie. Be safe and call me as soon as you can. GA," Rhys typed.

"Bye, Dad. I will," she promised. "SK," she typed to indicate she'd stopped keying, and the call was concluded.

Rhys wasn't kidding when he told Mira he'd worry about her. His heart had been in his throat since he'd first seen her in Paris, a traumatized homeless waif. She'd endured so much and was still so broken, mute still after so many years. He and Sloan were so proud of her accomplishments. To her employer and her co-workers, Mira appeared a strong, confident, independent woman but, to him, she seemed fragile. She held herself in reserve, friendly but friends with no one, attractive to men but dating no one.

Rhys thought he was the only person in Mira's life she could relax with, could be herself. He loved her with his whole heart. But he was broken, too. It had been six years since Sloan's tragic death, and he'd never been attracted to another woman, had never flirted, had never entertained the thought of dating.

It occurred to him that he should probably find a therapist and try to come to terms with his grief. He was a very private person by nature, well suited to a diplomatic career requiring an extreme degree of discretion. He wasn't depressed or dour by nature and had never found it difficult to be affable, even outgoing. For so many decades, his postings abroad and in Washington had involved a continuous round of meetings and functions, where he displayed highly polished social skills. To ask anyone, Rhys Williams was well-liked.

Everyone but that dratted woman, what's her name? Evvie? Eva? Ava? Well, who gives a shit what her name is? All that matters to me is that her rent check clears.

Rhys wasn't sure whether to be amused or affronted when Avery insisted on paying for the entire six-month rental in advance. She clearly wanted as little to do with him every month as he did with her.

If he were to do some serious soul-searching, Rhys knew he'd have to admit the idea of another woman in Sloan's house, in her kitchen, was deeply upsetting. He'd been renting the farmhouse for several years, but never to a single woman about Sloan's age. He'd initially registered Avery's attractiveness, although he hadn't given her more than a cursory look. It was the idea of Avery more than the woman herself that provoked him, but her aloofness and near-condescension certainly irked him.

Who does she think she is? It isn't every day you get to rent a beautifully restored and renovated house, decorated and appointed by a world-famous, much-in-demand interior designer. She acts like she's doing me a favor by renting it.

Rhys wondered why he was even thinking about Avery when he needed to do so much preparation for the oncoming storm. He picked up the remote, aimed it at the receiver, and brought up The Weather Channel on his big-screen TV. He stood and watched for a minute as one of the on-air meteorologists presented an update. If, as the man insisted, this storm was comparable to the 2010 blizzard dubbed Snowmageddon, Rhys didn't want to be caught lacking any necessities. It often took days for power to be restored, grocery store shelves to be re-stocked, and the underground tanks at gas stations to be re-filled.

Rhys went outside and manually inspected his standby generator, verifying that the green light was on, indicating that the unit was functioning correctly. It performed a self-diagnostic test weekly and ran for about ten minutes, but he had it serviced professionally every fall and after each period of extended use. He also kept his propane tank topped up. Fortunately, he'd just had a delivery the week before and knew his tank was at maximum capacity, so it was unlikely the generator would run out of fuel before power was restored. And he had a large chest freezer in the basement stocked with meals for just such an eventuality.

"You, too," he told Bella as she followed closely on his heels, cocking her head and peering up at him with a worried expression he found comical. "We have plenty of dog food."

After a while, he opened the truck door and signaled that Bella should jump in. He didn't usually have passengers and kept the rear seat folded flat to accommodate a dog bed. She loved to accompany him on errands, and he wanted to top up with diesel and fill the gas cans he'd placed in the truck bed. He hadn't used his snowmobile yet this winter, and he wanted to make sure it had a full tank of gas as well, just in case.

The first flakes drifted down just past noon. Rhys was glad Mira was not driving from Connecticut to Vermont as much as he would have relished her company.

Perusing the contents of the fridge, he pulled out a foil-wrapped package. It was neatly labeled by the woman he hired to cook and clean. She came every two weeks, bringing casseroles and meals she prepared and assembled at home, stocking his freezer.

"Manicotti. That sounds good," he muttered.

"I should probably defrost some vegetable soup for tomorrow," he told Bella. "And probably some of this cheddar-broccoli. I think we're going to be snowed in for a few days if the forecast is accurate." He glanced out the window. Snow was coming down faster now, obliterating the dirty, compacted snow that already covered the ground.

Rhys spent the afternoon responding to student emails and working on a syllabus for a new course he was outlining. Problems with drought and famine, terrorism, civil war and gang violence, extreme heat and catastrophic flooding in various parts of the world were creating a global migration. Increasingly, those subjects were of particular interest to those majoring in international studies. Rhys was sure his course would fill up fast once it was added to the curriculum.

Rhys was engrossed in his work over the next several hours while Bella dozed on her bed in front of the woodstove, her head resting on the warm slab of fire slate under it. Sleet pelting the windows broke Rhys' concentration, and he glanced outside, shocked to see that it was already full dark. Pushing his chair back, he strode to the window and observed the scene revealed by the sodium light in his backyard. There were already several inches of new accumulation, and a coating of ice would weigh down the electrical lines. If the sleet didn't turn back to snow soon, tree branches would sag under the load, and those that were brittle would break, falling onto the lines and dragging them down. The county road commissioner had crews out all summer, trimming branches overhanging power lines for eventualities just such as this. But every storm created its own set of challenges, depending on conditions, and this one was shaping up to be a doozie!

Just as Rhys had thought, the power was out when he awoke, but his house was fully functioning. His alarm clock projected the time onto the ceiling in large red numerals, and it informed him it was just after seven, an hour later than he usually slept. The room was dim, and a glance outside confirmed that snow fell thickly from the low cloud ceiling.

"Bella. Go out?" he asked rhetorically as she trotted to the door, eager for her early-morning foray.

"Whoa!" Rhys shouted as a gust caught the edge of the door, slamming it back and almost knocking the dog off her feet. She careened into his leg, and Rhys grabbed her collar to steady her. A dusting of snow covered the rug, melting almost instantly in the warmth.

Rhys was no stranger to winter storms, and he'd brought his shovel inside the evening before, anticipating that he might have to shovel a path for Bella if snow had drifted up onto the porch. She whined and pushed the snow with her nose.

Rhys laughed. "Just give me a minute, here," he told her. "Then you go pee, and then I'll make us some scrambled eggs.

Rhys showered and pulled on sweats and a pair of thick socks. He turned The Weather Channel on and watched as he cooked.

"This is not good," he advised Bella. "They're saying the storm is going to stall, and the snow won't taper off until around noon on *Monday!* So, all day today, tonight, all day tomorrow, tomorrow night, and into the following day. That's going to be a shitload of snow; I'm talking feet, not inches. We've already got—what? —about fifteen inches?" Bella tilted her head, listening intently.

After breakfast, Rhys returned to his computer. He had a lot of work to do but found himself ill-at-ease, unable to concentrate. He got a second cup of coffee which he usually enjoyed, but today his stomach felt acidic and unsettled.

"Shit!" he groaned. Bella gave a loud bark, alarmed by his tone. Rhys hadn't realized he'd spoken aloud.

"I'm sorry; it's okay." He stroked Bella's head, and her tail began to wag. Rhys swallowed past the sudden lump in his throat and felt the unexpected sting of tears. He knelt and gathered Sloan's dog in his arms, holding her close, his longing for his dead wife overwhelming.

"You know what I'm going to have to do, don't you?" he whispered. "Her phone is out, her power's out, and she doesn't have any heat except for that little woodstove. What's-her-name."

Bella's eyes were on Rhys' face as he spoke. "You know, what's-her-name? Evvie. Or Eva. She's probably made a bed on the floor in front of the woodstove. She's probably wearing ten layers and planning to eat crackers and cheese for the next three days by flashlight." He sighed. "I'm going to have to go and get her. She's going to have to come here." As he spoke, he gathered his balaclava and battery-powered heated gloves, shrugged into his heated snowmobile suit, pulled on knee-high heated boots, and picked up his helmet.

"You're going to have to stay here, Bella. I'll be back as soon as I can."

The howling of the wind was so loud, Avery didn't hear the snowmobile rumble to a stop at the foot of her steps or see the headlights pierce the gloom as it approached. Opening the bathroom door, she saw her living room bathed in an unearthly blue neon glow. At first, she thought the phenomenon might be St Elmo's fire playing across her ceiling. She'd heard of 'thundersnow' but had never experienced it. Then she heard someone pounding on the front door.

Peering out, she saw a snow machine outlined with light bars that provided the underglow but didn't recognize—couldn't recognize—the person on her doorstep as no part of his face or body was uncovered.

"Evvie!" a hoarse voice shouted, the words whipped away by the ferocious gusts and swirling snow. The pounding continued. "Eva! OPEN UP!"

The only person she could think of who might come to her assistance would be Todd, but surely he was at home, keeping his own family safe. Or maybe this was one of those neighborhood-watch things where an abutter had come to check on her.

She tugged the door handle, and the figure staggered into the room. Lifting his helmet, he rolled a balaclava up onto his forehead.

Rhys Williams! Oh, my God! Of all people!

Without preamble, he said, "It's bad, and it's getting worse. Jesus, it's freezing in here. You'll have to come with me. I have a generator. Get some clothes and toiletries together in a small bag," he ordered.

Making eye contact, he reiterated, "A very small bag! And hurry."

Expecting her to comply, he turned and left, tugging his balaclava down. Even the outlines of buildings were obscured, but Rhys knew every inch of the property and slogged through knee-deep drifts to a small weathered outbuilding. He'd learned his lesson during his first winter in Vermont and had replaced the shed's door with a slider. Unless you had the time or inclination to shovel the area clear in front of pull-open doors, it was far better to have a track-mounted door that would slide open. Sleet had blown sideways, and even the slider was frozen shut. Rhys rammed it with his full body weight and felt it give under the impact of his shoulder. He rammed it again and again until it finally broke free. Dragging the toes of his boot along the edge of the building, he cleared enough free space that the door would slide open. Aiming the beam of his tiny tactical torch into the gloom of the interior, Rhys saw the hump of Sloan's snowmobile under its protective cover in a far corner. He spotted the plastic storage box he was looking for and flipped the lid off. *Don't think about it! Just do what you have to do!* Gritting his teeth, he lifted Sloan's snowmobile suit and saw, to his relief, that her boots, gloves, balaclava, and helmet were all there.

Retracing his steps, he threw open the farmhouse door, strode inside, and unceremoniously dumped the bundle onto a nearby chair. His mouth fell open in shock when he saw Avery rooted to the spot. She hadn't moved since he'd ordered her to pack a bag.

"What the Hell?" he thundered. "Did you not hear me? There's no time to waste! Why are you still standing there?"

"I c-c-can't," she stammered, shaking, her teeth chattering.

"Can't *what?* Are you afraid to ride on a snowmobile? Believe me, lady, that's the least of your problems!"

Avery shook her head and opened the front of her jacket. A tiny head popped out from under several layers. "I c-can't leave Anya."

Sizing up the situation, Rhys went into the first-floor bedroom and yanked a pillowcase off one of Avery's pillows. Holding it out, he said, "Put her in this. She'll be able to breathe. I just need to tie it closed. Do you have a scarf or something?"

Rhys followed Avery's gaze to the row of hooks by the door and saw several long scarves hanging there. Snatching one up, he said again, "Go put your toiletries and a few necessities in a bag. And hurry!"

When she returned, Rhys' suit was partially unzipped, and Anya's little face peered out from the open pillowcase. Avery reached for the kitten, but Rhys handed her the scarf and said, "Tie it closed. She'll have to go with me. You'll be riding pillion, and your front will be pressed against my back; she won't be safe tucked into your suit."

Rhys handed Avery the small snowmobile suit and said, "This belonged to my late wife. Put it on." He pointed to the remaining items. "Boots, balaclava, helmet. Let's go! Let's go!"

Chapter Nineteen

A few days after the storm ended, Marley watched Avery intently, not speaking, awaiting her response. When Avery didn't respond, she asked again, "So, how was it? I can't even imagine!"

The two women sat at Avery's kitchen table, cups of tea and a plate of shortbread cookies in front of them. Strong sunlight glittered on the pristine snow outside, and Avery squinted against the glare.

"Jeez, that's bright," she said. "Be right back."

She stood and tugged on the pull cord that adjusted the wide slats of the wooden blinds at the oversized window over the sink.

"Better?" she asked.

"Much better," Marley agreed. "But you're stalling. Are you going to tell me about it, or what?"

"By 'it,' you mean the two and a half days Daniel spent in the lion's den?" Avery teased.

"If you must know, Rhys was a perfect gentleman and the consummate host. I wondered if it was the same person! He had a freezer full of meals bordering on gourmet. An extensive collection of good liquor and expensive wines. The biggest flat-screen TV I've ever seen. A collection of jigsaw puzzles and board games, as well as an impressive library. Down comforter and flannel sheets in the guest bedroom, and a soaking tub with bubble bath and hard-milled soap in the guest bathroom." Avery ticked off the items on her fingers. "What's not to like?"

"Well, yeah, he's got a great house. I'd expect no less," Marley retorted. "But how was *he?* Was it awful being stuck there with him for almost three days?"

Avery shook her head. "I wouldn't have believed it, but he was relaxed and friendly. Fun, even. The snow tapered off. The plow came by and, once the roads were sanded, Rhys drove us home. End of story."

"How was Anya?" Marley asked. "Was she terrified of Bella?"

"I thought I'd keep Anya shut in the bedroom, but, as a matter of fact, Bella was a gracious hostess. I let Anya settle in, and then I introduced them. Bella was very gentle. She's a gorgeous dog! By the time I left, she and Anya were curling up together on Bella's dog bed."

"So, what now?" Marley pressed. "Détente? Or—?"

"Or nothing," Avery responded. "I guess rescuing us was Rhys' good deed for the day, but I'm not sure he likes me any better."

"It's not that he doesn't like *you*," Marley said slowly. "He's having a hard time seeing another woman here, in Sloan's place. I'm just guessing, but it's pretty clear he's not over her. He probably feels it's disloyal to her somehow to move on, so he doesn't. I feel sorry for him."

"Maybe," Avery agreed. "Sloan is definitely the elephant in the room."

"That's why Rhys built a new house, one where he isn't picturing Sloan in all the rooms. Everyone knows that," Marley said. "A lot of single women consider him an eligible bachelor, but he's clearly not interested in dating."

"I'll be happy if he's *civil* from now on," Avery joked. "And speaking of eligible bachelors, I got a text from Johnny Zaika the other day, asking how I was faring during the storm and wanting to make plans to visit."

Marley raised her eyebrows. "Do tell!"

"Nothing to tell," Avery said. "I don't know if he'd drive up from Connecticut or fly into Burlington. What with getting to the airport, parking, getting through security, it's probably faster to drive."

"Will he stay here? You've got guest rooms upstairs."

"Not this time. He'll stay at the inn. I haven't seen him in about thirty-five years, so who knows if we'll even like each other? And there may not even be a next time."

Three weeks later, Avery stood in the pub's doorway at the inn, scanning the room. She had a mental picture of Johnny Zaika as the tall, handsome boy he'd been in prep school and wondered if she'd recognize him now.

It was a Friday evening, and almost every table was taken, but no one in the room looked even vaguely familiar. Avery wondered if he'd been delayed, but she hadn't heard from him. Just as she decided to go and ask the concierge if John Zaika had checked in, a man at the bar turned, and Avery's breath caught. Her mind reeled, and the intervening years vaporized.

"Johnny?" she whispered and then asked in a firmer voice, "John?"

He strode toward her and took both of her hands in his. "Avery! How nice to see you. I never expected to find you in Vermont."

"By way of Iowa," Avery told him as he guided her toward a two-top in a corner near the fireplace. She was acutely conscious of his hand on the small of her back. She hadn't been touched by a man in over a year, and it felt good to have someone taking care of her. "My late husband took a position there, and it turned out to be a career. We were there for twenty-six years."

"You must be used to crappy winters," John commented, and Avery felt a tinge of irritation.

"I love winter in Vermont," she protested. "It's like living inside the postcard."

"But don't you miss it? Living in a college town? There must have been a lot more going on there than in rural Vermont."

"I'm not exactly buried alive," Avery said, laughing. "Burlington isn't that far, and there's quite an active social scene at the ski resort. I'll take you sightseeing tomorrow, and I thought we'd stop in at The Slippery Slope tomorrow evening and have a drink with my friend, Marley. She's seeing the bartender, so she's a regular. Then we can have dinner on the mountain. There are so many good restaurants, and we can decide tomorrow what we feel like eating. I haven't been here long enough to have tried them all, so there isn't one in particular that I can recommend."

"Do you think you'll ever move back to Connecticut?" John asked. "Are you and your cousin still close?"

"Very much so," Avery replied. "I spent a month with Hailey and Jay after I left Iowa. She would have liked me to live nearby, but it felt too much like trying to reclaim the past. I wanted a fresh start somewhere new."

"I see," John said noncommittally, and Avery felt another flash of irritation, feeling judged.

"She certainly married well," he said. "Her husband is quite the local celebrity."

"She married well because Jay's a great guy, and they have a solid relationship." Avery was aware of a slight edge in her voice, and she attempted to change the subject.

"Tell me about yourself," she said. "Hailey told

me you got your degree at Yale and own a chain of pharmacies."

"That's right, undergrad and Pharm. D. at Yale. I own seven pharmacies. My wife passed away recently, and I have two adult daughters. That's it in a nutshell."

Johnny Zaika was as handsome a man as he'd been as a boy, Avery thought, but what he had in looks, he lacked in personality. She'd had such a crush on him as a schoolgirl but had never really known him. He was tall and still very lean, with the same thatch of thick hair that fell rakishly over one eye and a boyish grin. She acknowledged that he was very attractive, but she was less attracted to him than she'd expected to be.

"You look quite different," she heard him saying. "I remember you with fiery red hair."

"It's still red. Well, more or less—mostly less. It faded, and I wanted something a bit more dramatic, so I transitioned to silver."

"You color your hair gray? On purpose? My wife was obsessed with every gray hair that appeared and kept it blonde until the day she died. She spent a fortune at the salon."

Avery's initial irritation was turning to active dislike. *This might be a very long weekend!*

John arrived at Avery's precisely on the dot of nine the next morning, after he'd had breakfast at the inn.

"You have excellent taste," he complimented her. They were seated at Avery's kitchen table with mugs of coffee in front of them. "From the weathered outbuildings, I expected more of a run-down old farmhouse with faded Formica countertops and cracked linoleum floors. And a horror of an old electric stove."

"Not hardly! It was a pleasant surprise for me too," Avery agreed. "I looked at several rentals in the area, and each one was worse than the one before. This house was professionally restored and renovated by an internationally famous interior designer. Actually, she lived in Connecticut for a number of years. You may have heard of her, Sloan Williams."

John's eyes widened in recognition. "I didn't know of her, but I remember the media frenzy. She was killed by some teenage punk who was driving and texting. And then it was a big court case with a lot of news coverage. The kid got off with a slap on the wrist, as I recall."

"So I've heard," Avery agreed. "This was her house. Her husband rents it now."

"Well, you lucked out," John said.

The day passed pleasantly, although Avery's planned itinerary was abandoned when John asked about the Shelburne Museum.

"I looked it up on Mapquest," he told her. "It's just ten miles south of Burlington, so about an hour from here, up Route 116."

"Those times are given for ideal road conditions,

but we should be fine today," Avery said. "We'll be back before dark, but let me take a quick look at the hourly forecast. It's fine if the roads are dry, but I like to make sure there are no surprises. If there's any precipitation and then the temperature drops below freezing, it can get icy."

She stood and put both mugs into the dishwasher. "I'll just be a minute. My laptop's in the den. You can look around if you'd like."

A few minutes later, Avery and John shrugged into jackets. She eyed his thin-soled loafers but said nothing. "We'll take my car," she told him. "You'll see a lot of Subarus on the roads up here because they're so good in the snow."

"I've always wanted to see the decoy collection at the Shelburne Museum," John told Avery as she turned onto Route 100. "My dad was an amateur carver, but he had an impressive collection himself which I inherited."

"Are you a duck hunter?" Avery asked. The look of disgust on John's face told her he was anything but.

Avery took a deep breath and said cheerfully, "I haven't been there either, but I've read that the museum is known for its exhibits of American paintings and folk art."

She'd expected to spend a couple of hours there, but the museum comprised thirty-eight buildings, and both she and John found themselves so engrossed that the day slipped by. Avery was fascinated by the world-renowned quilt collection and by the print shop. It was two-thirty when they made their way into a cute bistro a mile and a half from the museum.

"We should probably get something light to hold us over until dinner," Avery suggested, perusing the menu. "We could just get an appetizer." When John nodded, she said, "I think I'll have the crab cakes with chipotle lime aioli." She smiled at him. "What looks good to you?"

"I'm not sure I've ever heard of 'Vermont Cuisine.' But here I am, so I guess I'll try Smoked Shelburne Farms Cheddar Fritters served with Vermont maple sriracha aioli.

"Whatever that is," he added, rolling his eyes.

"They have a creative chef," Avery commented. "If you don't care for it, we can switch."

As it turned out, the food was excellent, and they lingered over coffee, reminiscing about prep school classmates and mutual acquaintances. Avery was startled when John took her gloved hand as they walked across the parking lot to her car.

While they'd been in the restaurant, a lowering sky had spit snow, and it glinted on the asphalt as she turned on her headlights. Glancing at the lighted display on her dashboard, Avery swore. "Damn it! The temperature's thirty-four degrees. We could have black ice if it drops below freezing."

She drove carefully and was relieved to see that a sand truck had made a pass up Route 100.

"We should be okay to go up the mountain," she told John. "The ski area keeps the access road very well-tended, and it's probably the safest place around. Driving is actually better after dark, for me at least. I just hate that period of dusk when the shadows deepen, and it's hard to see."

There was a good crowd gathered at The Slippery Slope so early in the evening, and Avery spotted Marley at the bar. She shrugged out of her jacket and hung it over the back of the barstool next to her friend, motioning John to take the one next to hers.

"You got here just in time," Marley said. "Another fifteen minutes, and this place will be standing room only. Bluegrass starts at seven. You staying?"

"No, we just stopped in for a quick drink. I thought you'd be here, and I want you to meet John. Marley, this is Johnny Zaika. John, Marley Wainwright."

The bartender placed coasters in front of the newcomers. "Hey there, Avery. The usual?"

"Hey, Landon. Yes, please." She turned to John.

"Labatts."

Landon nodded and retrieved an ice-cold beer, expertly removing the cap and placing it on the bar in front of John. "Drinks are on Miss Marley," he said.

Forty-five minutes later, Avery looked at her watch and said, "We have a dinner reservation, so we're going to get going."

"Come on back for some live music." Marley addressed John, and he looked at Avery questioningly.

"Maybe," she conceded, but she knew they wouldn't return. She'd put music on the radio driving back from Shelburne, and John had expressed a preference for oldies, telling her he didn't like country or bluegrass.

Avery and John settled themselves at their table, and both ordered steak with peppercorns. Their server recommended a robust red and poured a small amount into John's glass. He swirled it and held it in his mouth before swallowing. He nodded approvingly, and the server filled Avery's glass halfway before returning to John's.

John held up his glass and touched the rim to Avery's. "To us," he toasted. "Better late than never."

Avery sipped her wine, struggling to keep her face expressionless. After a moment, John reached across the table and took her hand again, his thumb stroking her fingers.

"I'd like to see you again, Avery," he murmured. She was saved from responding when two servers approached. One opened a folding stand, and their waiter set a large round tray on it. He lifted the covers from their dinner plates and placed Avery's in front of her before serving her companion.

Avery closed her eyes as she savored the tender beef. The meal was exquisite, and they spoke little as they enjoyed the food.

The two servers reappeared, one swiftly removing their plates and cutlery and de-crumbing the table while the other maneuvered a dessert trolley into place. Avery was sated, about to decline dessert, but John was clearly considering the selection.

"Avery? What would you like? Why don't we get two, and we can share?" he proposed.

She smiled weakly and said, "They all look wonderful. You choose."

Avery reached out as John passed a dessert plate to her. She saw, over his shoulder, that the maître d' was leading Rhys Williams and a beautiful young woman to a table near theirs. Avery recognized the dark-haired woman from the chili cookoff and saw that Rhys was once again guiding her with his hand on the small of her back.

She sucked in a shallow breath, shocked at her visceral reaction to seeing her nemesis with another woman. Unable to drag her eyes from them, watching the way they leaned toward each other and appraising the adoring look in the other woman's eyes, Avery surmised that they were very much a couple.

So what's the big deal? she chided herself. *He was nice to you once, and he probably would have done the same for anyone in your situation. Another tenant would have been stuck in a freezing house without lights or heat or any way to cook, and Rhys would have felt responsible.*

Avery called Hailey on Sunday afternoon, minutes after John Zaika's car pulled out of the parking lot at the inn.

"It was awful," she said flatly. "He's a colossal

bore! I thought the weekend would never end."

"He's gone?" Hailey asked.

"Just now. We had brunch at the inn."

"So, what made it awful? I've been dying of curiosity all weekend. If you hadn't called me just now, I'd have been calling you."

"Ugh! Forget it! This is a classic case of 'Be careful what you wish for.' Was he always such an asshole, and I just didn't know it?"

"Well, when you're smart and good-looking, and your parents are rich, I guess you might grow up with a sense of entitlement," Hailey said. "So, yeah, he probably was."

"*We* were smart and good-looking, and *our* parents were rich," Avery protested. "I don't think we had such a sense of entitlement that we were assholes. But that's not it. Maybe 'asshole' is the wrong word. What's the word I want? He's just such a prig. He irritated the shit out of me. Plus, he has nice clothes and a good car, and he paid for meals, but I think he's cheap."

"Whoa," Hailey agreed. "Cheap's not good. What makes you say that if he picked up the tab and didn't ask you to split the bill?"

"I don't know. It was just things he said. I found myself feeling sorry for his wife. She probably thought she had it made, but he clearly considers himself the breadwinner, the head of the household, you know?"

"I do know," Hailey agreed. "Jay's the

breadwinner here, that's for sure, but I never for one instant feel like we aren't equal partners."

"Jay has such generosity of spirit," Avery complimented her brother-in-law. "He's secure, and he has a big heart. Andrew did, too. I could end up being alone for the rest of my life because I may never find someone like him."

"You won't," Hailey promised. "You have too much to offer. Someone will come along when you least expect it."

Just then, Anya jumped into Avery's lap and began to knead her thigh.

"*Someone* loves you," Hailey teased. "I can hear the purring from here. And *I* love you! I was thinking of coming up next week. The kids are looking forward to spending February break with you, but I don't want to combine a business trip with their school vacation. I've been making phone calls, and I have a lot to tell you. Do you think we could make an appointment to meet with your landlord and look at the space over the general store? Aw, crap, I have an incoming call, and I have to take it. It's Tish Chappell. She's the chair of the fundraising committee at Ivy's school, and she's trying to recruit me for the annual auction. I've been letting her calls go to voicemail, but she's persistent, and I can't avoid her forever. I'll call you tomorrow, and we can finish this conversation."

Avery decided to indulge in a long relaxing soak and opened the taps to fill the jetted tub in her bathroom. She'd just lit a few candles and poured herself a glass of wine when her cell rang again. Glancing at Caller ID, she saw it was Marley and pressed the button to accept the call.

"Hey," Marley greeted her. "I want to hear all about your weekend, but Landon's here, and I can't talk. I'm just calling to ask if you want to run down to Woodstock tomorrow with Sienna, Jerica, and me. Sienna wants to look at a horse, but we're going to have lunch at Baxter's and do a little shopping at Brigham's. I thought you might like to come along."

"I love Woodstock!" Avery exclaimed enthusiastically. "I'd love to!"

"Okay, great. We'll pick you up at eight-thirty. I'm guessing it'll be freezing in the barn, so dress warmly. Sienna and Jerica will probably ride out with the owner if Sienna likes the horse, but you and I can wait there. The farm used to belong to an Olympic rider, so it's a pretty upscale place, and I'm sure there's a heated lounge."

Chapter Twenty

Avery took in the scenery from her seat in the back of Sienna's Kia, noting the dark-green mailbox with its neat red lettering that indicated they'd arrived at Willow Farm. The car turned into a long drive, and Avery noted the pines bordering the road on the right and split-rail fencing outlining the fields to their left. There were several horses in the distance, their colorful blankets vivid against the snow-covered pasture.

Sienna pulled into a parking area, and the four women filed into the barn. Stalls lined a center aisle. Light shone through the glass pane on a door lettered OFFICE, and it swung open at once as a slender woman with glossy chestnut hair emerged. She approached the group, her hand outstretched, and said, "Welcome to Willow Farm. I'm Nancy Lawson, one of the owners. My partner, Kelly Ross, is teaching a lesson in the arena, but she'll be through in about fifteen minutes. You're here to look at Franklin?"

Sienna shook hands and introduced herself and then her friends.

"Yes. I've never owned a horse, but I've been taking lessons for several years. The barn recently changed hands, and I— well, let's just say I'm not on the same page as the new owner. My focus has been learning to ride well, and I enjoy trail riding. The new owner teaches hunters, jumpers, and equitation, and she seems to think she's preparing her students to compete, which isn't my thing at all."

Nancy looked sharply at Sienna. "You do know Franklin's gaited? He's not a jumper. Our focus here is on eventing. We teach jumping, and he's a round peg in a square hole. That's why he's for sale."

"How did he get here?" Jerica asked.

Before Nancy could reply, a set of huge doors at the far end of the barn slid open, and several horses were led into the aisle. The four riders put them in crossties and began removing their tack.

Avery watched with interest as each horse was covered with a lightweight blanket made of netting and led back through the double doors.

"Where did they go?" she asked Marley in a low voice. "And why are those blankets full of holes? Won't the horses be cold? How come half their bodies are shaved?"

"Those are called anti-sweat sheets," Marley explained. "Horses sweat while they're being worked, and they'll get chilled if they aren't cooled out afterward, so the riders took them back into the arena to walk them. The loose weave or 'holes' as you call them, allows the sweat to evaporate. It takes forever for horses with a full winter coat to dry, so the school horses are given a trace clip in the fall."

"A full body clip leaves hair on the legs and just under the saddle," Jerica interjected. "A trace clip leaves hair on top of the neck, the top of the horse's body, and on its legs. The demarcation along its sides is where the traces lay when a horse was harnessed. It's kind of a compromise because it removes hair only in the areas where horses perspire the most."

"Who knew, right?" Marley grinned.

A woman strode down the aisle, calling out, "Be right with you. Meet me in the lounge."

"That's Kelly, my partner," Nancy said. "She's the one who's selling Franklin, and she can tell you about him." Nancy led the group into the lounge and asked if anyone wanted coffee or hot chocolate.

"Avery and I are going to wait here while Sienna and Jerica go out for a short ride," Marley explained. "We'd probably love a cup of coffee."

"Do you all ride?" Nancy asked. Marley, Sienna, and Jerica nodded, and Avery shook her head.

"You don't ride?" Nancy addressed Avery.

"Nope. I don't know anything about horses, and I've never even been close to one. I'm just tagging along, looking forward to lunch at Baxter's," she admitted.

Nancy laughed aloud. "Well, maybe Franklin will change your mind. He's a sweetheart!"

"That he is. Hi there, I'm Kelly Ross. Which one of you is Sienna Calvert?"

After another round of introductions, Kelly said, "Tell me about your riding experience and why you'd be interested in this particular horse."

"My dad died a year ago, and his will has just been probated," Sienna explained. "I longed for a horse as a kid, but my dad was career army, and we moved a lot. Sometimes, there was a stable on post, and I could muck stalls in exchange for rides, or, sometimes, I could exercise horses when the owner got orders and hadn't yet sold or shipped the horse. Dad always felt bad, so he left me money to build a small barn, buy a tow vehicle and trailer, and get a horse."

Nancy and Kelly both nodded approvingly.

"How big is your barn?" Nancy asked.

"Not very big," Sienna told her. "It's not built yet, but it will have just two stalls."

"So, will you be getting a second horse?" Kelly inquired. "Horses are herd animals, and it's hard for them to be alone."

Jerica grinned. "I live about a half-mile up the road. The plan is for me to look for a horse, too, and keep it at Sienna's. I need to get out of the lesson barn before I'm kicked out. I've already had a few run-ins with the new owner myself."

Kelly eyed her quizzically.

"She's a bitch!" Jerica added. "It's just a matter of time."

"Who is it?" Nancy asked.

"Someone from Maryland. Her name is Taylor

Gantt. She thinks she's hot shit."

Nancy and Kelly exchanged a look. "You have *got* to be kidding! She's Roddy Llewellyn's daughter. Her mother used to be a working student here."

Now Sienna and Jerica exchanged a look.

"*Seriously?*" Jerica gasped.

"Yup. Roddy Llewellyn. He trained with Corey Bridges and got two individual Olympic golds, a silver, and two team bronzes."

"Was Taylor's mother an eventer, too?" Sienna asked. "She must have been if this is an event barn and she was a working student here. What was her name?"

"Asha Hamilton owned Willow Farm then. We were all working students. Taylor's mother was Kendra Van Baalen when we knew her." Nancy grimaced, and Kelly shuddered.

"Hoo, boy. Like mother, like daughter," Nancy declared. "So, on a more pleasant note, let's go meet Franklin."

"He's humongous!" Avery exclaimed as Kelly led a large black horse out of a stall a few minutes later and dropped his lead rope. She walked around him, unfastening the surcingles on his blanket and unsnapping the leg straps. In one smooth motion, she lifted the blanket over his hindquarters and folded it in half before sliding it over his head and handing it to Nancy. She clipped crossties to his halter and turned to Sienna.

"As you see, he ground ties," Kelly pointed out.

"And he has no problem with a closed-front blanket. He's a gentle giant."

"How big *is* he?" Jerica asked.

"He's 16.2, which is tall for a gaited horse. Most trail riders prefer a horse that's 15 hands or 15.1, 15.2 because they're so much easier to mount and dismount."

"How did he get here?" Jerica asked again.

Kelly puffed her cheek full of air and blew out in disgust. "We have a student. She's a great little rider, and her grandmother decided to buy her a horse. Well, granny lives in the south, which is gaited horse country, so she bought Franklin and had him shipped as a surprise for her granddaughter."

"Never mind the fact that the kid is eleven, and she weighs less than ninety pounds," Nancy snorted.

"She's not even five feet tall," Nancy added. "She's talented, but she looks ridiculous on Franklin, apart from the fact that he doesn't jump. And forget dressage! Can you imagine him trying to do a twenty-meter circle?" She groaned. "We need to find her a clever little horse about 14.3, and we will."

Nancy turned to Jerica. "So, if you're going to keep a horse in Sienna's barn, I'm assuming you'll be riding together. If she has a gaited horse and you don't, it's going to be hard on you when you have to do a lot of trotting and posting to keep up."

Sienna and Jerica exchanged glances again.

"Do you know much about gaited horses?" Kelly asked. "Have you ever ridden one?"

Both women shook their heads.

"We'll saddle up Franklin and take him into the arena so we can make sure you're comfortable with his tack, and then the four of us can go out for a short hack. The snow is too deep to ride on any trails, but we can go out a dirt road for a ways, and you can see what gaiting feels like and how Franklin covers ground differently than trotting horses. One of you can ride him out, and the other can ride him back. We'll help you get on and off."

Nancy had Franklin tacked up within minutes, and she led him into the arena and over to a wooden box.

"We stand on this box when we teach," Nancy said. "My husband's a carpenter, and he put a heat strip in it, which is a godsend during the winter. It also makes an ideal mounting block." She looked from Sienna to Jerica. "I'll bet you were taught to put your left foot into the stirrup, bounce on your right foot a couple of times, and spring up into the saddle." Both women nodded.

"Well, we recommend that you always use a mounting block or find a tree stump or a big rock— anything. If there's nothing handy, find a ditch or a low spot and stand the horse in it to give yourself as much height as you can. If you mount from the ground, you've got one hand on the pommel and one hand on the cantle, and you're yanking the saddle toward you as you try to get yourself up. That could pull the horse's spine out of alignment."

"I never thought of that," Sienna said.

"I wish we were closer and could take lessons with you," Jerica said.

Sienna stepped up onto the box and swung herself into the saddle with ease. "I think the stirrups need to come up a few holes," she said.

"I was the last one to ride him, and we're about the same height," Kelly said. "You ride a gaited horse with a long leg, so the stirrups look just right. This trail saddle has a western seat, and it's very comfortable." Pointing, she continued, "It has center-fire rigging, which puts the knot behind your leg after you do up the girth, and it also holds the saddle in place more securely because there are two points of contact, not just one. You're probably used to stirrup leathers, but you'll appreciate fenders during the summer because they keep your leg off the horse's sweaty sides and you won't need to wear half-chaps. And those are safety stirrups, so you can't get a foot caught in the event of an unscheduled dismount."

"This is so different from everything I'm used to," Sienna said. "Does he need those shanks on his bit? It looks like a medieval torture device."

"That's a walking horse bit. The mouthpiece is actually very mild, but the shanks give you the leverage to keep him collected so he can engage his hindquarters and gait. Go ahead, gather up your reins and lift them, sit down on your seat bones, and encourage him to move off."

Kelly directed Sienna through a series of

maneuvers, turning to the left and the right, stopping and backing up.

"Wow!" Sienna said, "He's so responsive."

"He's an experienced trail horse," Kelly told her. "He'll go through water, over bridges, through ditches, over rocks. This horse will take care of you."

"What kind of horse is he?" Jerica asked.

"He's a Tennessee Walker. But there are several breeds of gaited horses. There's Rocky Mountain, Kentucky Mountain, McCurdy Plantation Horse, Paso Fino, Spotted Saddle Horse, Missouri Foxtrotter, American Saddlebred, Racking Horse—. Most have a docile, amiable temperament, but some, Pasos and Saddlebreds, are more hot-headed.

"Are there any drawbacks to a Tennessee Walker?"

"Generally speaking, no. But they have a lot of Standardbred in their background, so they could tend to be pace-y. If they do pace, it's usually a stepping pace which is not uncomfortable. All you have to do is sit deep, wiggle your seat bones, and keep them collected; they'll usually pick up a running walk."

Sienna made a face. "It's like you're speaking Urdu. I thought I knew how to ride, but there's so much to learn."

Kelly smiled. "It's just like getting a new car. When you drive away from the dealership, you know how to drive, but you can't even turn on the wipers. After you've driven it a few times, you can turn on the wipers with your eyes closed."

Sienna leaned forward and patted Franklin's neck. "What a good boy you are."

"Put him on the wall here on the short side, Sienna, walk down the long side, and when you get to the long side on the other side of the arena, ask him to move out of a flat walk into a running walk. When he's gaiting, you'll see a head nod, and you'll feel the four beats."

Ten minutes later, Sienna brought the horse to a halt, slid off, and handed the reins to Jerica. "It's amazing! You won't believe it! You don't have to post! He's so smooth!"

While Kelly worked with both women, Nancy had three horses tacked up and waiting in crossties. Once the four of them set off down the drive for a short ride, Marley and Avery settled themselves in leather club chairs in front of the woodstove in the barn's well-appointed lounge.

"I'd say Franklin's going to be Winslowe's newest resident," Marley commented. "But tell me about your weekend while we have a few minutes to ourselves."

Avery grimaced. "It was awful. He's so staid and so un-fun. I always thought of him as 'Johnny,' but he sure is a 'John.' He has a lot to be proud of with a good education and a successful business, but he's so—I don't know—self-satisfied and smug, I guess. He has no sense of humor, and I mean *zero*. I spent less than forty-eight hours with him, and I was irritated and bored after the first three."

"Well, I'd say your teenage fantasy is shot in the ass." Marley laughed.

"I'd say!" Avery agreed. "He keeps texting and asking about getting together again. He wants me to come to Connecticut, and that is not going to happen. No way in *Hell*. I think he's the kind of man who needs a wife, and he's interviewing candidates for the job. He'll find someone who'll be grateful to snag him and delighted to move into his big house. I'll bet he never lets wife number two make any changes to his first wife's décor. He told me she had a cabinet in the garage with sets of holiday dishes for Halloween and Thanksgiving, Christmas, Easter, Fourth of July. Oh, God, spare me."

"I wonder what he's like in the bedroom?" Marley mused. "The missionary position once a week while he services the little woman, or he comes home from work and wants the missus to dress up in a naughty nurse outfit?" She giggled, and soon both she and Avery were laughing so hard, tears streamed from their eyes.

"He kissed me when we got back on Saturday night," Avery confided. "He drove to my house that morning, but we took my car. He walked me to the door, and I was planning to say goodnight and scoot inside, but he lunged, grabbed me, and shoved his tongue down my throat."

"Ugh," Marley commiserated.

"Worse. He has one of those huge rubbery tongues that makes you want to gag. Thank God, I

279

met him at the inn for brunch the next day, and then he left. We had a repeat of the lunge and grab in the parking lot, but it was broad daylight in a public place, so I could at least pull away with a peck on the lips."

Avery's phone rang. She glanced at the screen and groaned. "As we speak." She tapped the button to decline the call and let it go to voicemail. "He's probably on a lunch break. I'm just going to have to tell him it's not going to work out." Her expression grew solemn, and she said, "It's times like this that I really miss Andrew. Rhys Williams is the only one I've met in the last year who's available and remotely interesting. I saw a whole other side of him when I spent time alone with him during the blizzard. He's a fascinating man. But then I saw him with his girlfriend again when John and I were having dinner at Pepper Jacks. They were coming in as we were finishing up. I saw the way he looked at her, and they were obviously very involved. I saw them at the chili cookoff a few months ago, and it was the same thing. I could tell they were an item just by the way he touched her."

Marley stared at Avery, her face a mask of confusion.

"Rhys Williams has a girlfriend? That's news to me. I haven't seen him with anyone."

"You were at the chili cookoff," Avery protested. "You didn't see them together?"

"I saw him with Mira," Marley said slowly. "Is

that who you mean?"

"Who's Mira? Whoever it is, she's gorgeous. Petite, long dark hair. She looked young enough to be his daughter."

Marley laughed. "That *is* his daughter! Rhys and Sloan adopted Mira when she was four. It's quite a story. Her whole family was slaughtered right in front of her. An American journalist got her out of Syria, and she was staying with a French family outside of Paris, friends of Rhys', when he visited them and first saw her. She was very traumatized, and she's never spoken.

Avery's mouth fell open in shock.

"Rhys and Sloan had her DNA tested and determined that she's Yazidi. It's so sad that she lost everyone she knew and loved, and then she lost Sloan. She and Rhys are very close. She adores him."

Just then, approaching hoofbeats advised Avery and Marley that the group of riders had returned. Sienna and Jerica burst into the lounge a few minutes later and headed immediately for the woodstove, tugging off their gloves and holding their hands out for the welcome warmth.

"He's a great horse; I love him," Sienna proclaimed. "I'd take him home today if I could."

"Are you going to make an offer on him?" Marley asked.

Sienna shook her head. "I'm not going to dicker. He's worth every penny. He's going to stay here in livery until spring. Probably the soonest I can get a barn built is April. By then, I'll have a truck and a trailer, so I can come and get him."

"He'll stay here as a boarder?" Marley nodded in approval. "That's a good plan."

"He'll be in full livery," Sienna clarified. "Boarding is just stall rent, blanketing, turnout, feeding, shoeing, and de-worming. In other barns, owners either blanket their own horses, schedule their own farrier, and de-worm their own horse. Or there's an à la carte price list where barn help takes care of those items, but owners pay for each of the services, and it's added to the basic board. Here, all of that is included in the board bill so Nancy and Kelly can be sure each boarder gets what he needs and all the horses are on the same schedule. Livery's a little different because it includes exercising the horse. It's not training, but it keeps the horse in shape."

Nancy came in with Kelly right behind her. They, too, went straight over to the woodstove and stood with their backs to it, facing their visitors.

"Just give me a minute, Sienna," Kelly said, savoring the heat. "You can sign a purchase agreement and either give me a check for first and last month's board or mail it. It's of primary importance to Nancy and me that we match each sale horse with the right home, and we're delighted you're going to be Franklin's new owner."

"They're going to find me a gaited horse," Jerica told Marley. "Their former partner lives in Tennessee. She and her family all have gaited horses, and all her friends do, too."

"Asha Hamilton," Nancy said. "You may remember her from the Atlanta Olympics in 1996. Her husband was tragically killed, and she was forced to drop out a few days before the Games. There's no one I'd trust more or recommend more highly to find you a horse as nice as Franklin. You could fly down to try him, or she could send you a video and have him shipped.

Chapter Twenty-One

"I've been looking forward to this all morning," Avery said as she crumbled saltines into her bowl of chili. The four women were seated in a semicircular corner booth on the second floor of Baxter's. A huge window overlooked the busy street and afforded a view of the steady stream of customers going into and coming out of Brigham's General Store, just across the street.

They'd all ordered chili. Marley was busy spooning sour cream and shredded cheese into hers, but she paused, looking up with interest, as Sienna questioned Jerica.

"So, if this Asha Hamilton finds you a horse or a couple of prospects, will you go to Tennessee to look at them yourself? I wouldn't want to rely on a video, although a lot of horses are bought online now."

Jerica laughed. "Give me a minute here! Two hours ago, I'd never even seen a gaited horse and didn't know anyone who had one. I haven't gotten that far. I sure like Franklin, though. If you weren't buying him, I'd want him."

"Gaited horses are all over the place in the south," Marley said. "It shouldn't take long to find you one. You could look online yourself."

Jerica shook her head. "Nope. I don't know anything about gaited horses. I think I'll ask Kelly for Asha Hamilton's contact info to tell her what I'd like in a horse and go from there."

Marley's eyes glinted, and her mouth quirked up at the corners. "I wouldn't mind a trip to Tennessee. I've read about those rolling stoplight parties in Nashville; it's called 'transportainment.' There's a big green tractor that pulls a wagon full of people and a bus with massage chairs. The busses are roofless, and they have bartenders and light-up dance floors at night. There's even a truck with a hot tub in the bed."

"How's that any different from downtown Winslowe?" Avery joked.

"Seriously, wouldn't it be fun to fly into Nashville and stay a couple of days?" Marley persisted.

"Sounds good to me," Jerica said. "But I'll be working fourteen-hour days until April fifteenth. That's the downside of being an accountant—tax time. I shouldn't have taken today off!"

"You're lucky you have a profession where you can work from home," Marley pointed out.

"Well, so are you. And so's Sienna," Jerica pointed out.

"I'd go crazy if I had to commute into Burlington," Marley agreed. "Or live in a city. I love being able to pick my own hours. I do some of my best stuff in the middle of the night when I can't sleep."

"What about you, Sienna? Do you think you could get away for a weekend toward the end of April?"

"Probably. Sooner than that, I'd hate to go off and leave a work crew, but my barn should be done by then."

"Are you self-employed, too?" Avery asked.

"Yes and no," Sienna replied. "I work for a large bank as a loan originator, but I'm contract. I get paid by the number of transactions I close. My brother-in-law is a Vice President, and he got me hooked up with them. I do all my research online and fill out forms on the computer. I can work in the middle of the night if I want to, too, so I can make my schedule somewhat flexible."

"Well, that's three. What about you, Avery? Trip to Tennessee sound good?"

"I've never been to Tennessee. I'm not really sure where it is." She gave a vague wave. "In the midwest, somewhere, isn't it? Near Arkansas? Does that sound about right?"

Marley rolled her eyes. "No, honey. It's below Kentucky and between North Carolina and Missouri."

Jerica held out her phone. "Here's a map of the US. You see Tennessee? And there's Nashville, pretty much in the middle of the state. I've never been there either, but it's a pretty cool place, especially if you like country music."

"This is just an idea, so don't say anything to anyone, okay?" Avery looked around the table for assent. "My cousin, Hailey, was intrigued with the space over the general store when she came up for Thanksgiving, and she thinks we ought to lease it and open a clothing shop."

Sienna's eyes widened, and she reared back. "Sloan's shop? Re-open Sloan's shop? I wouldn't touch that with a ten-foot pole! No one's lasted six months."

"Wait," Marley said. "You said 'lease.' So, you *wouldn't* be reopening Sloan's shop; you'd be doing your own thing, right?"

"You'd still have to deal with Rhys Williams," Jerica pointed out. "He's a monstrous pain in the ass. He's such a control freak I doubt he'd even agree to a lease and it's not like he needs the money."

"Hailey wants to come up next week," Avery said. "She's been working on a business plan, so she'd be the one to approach Rhys."

"Why not you?" Sienna teased. "You mean you didn't soften him up when you spent three days tucked away in his cozy cabin?"

"And two *nights*," Marley winked.

"Not hardly," Avery scoffed. "I haven't seen or heard from him since. I bought him a bottle of Napoleon brandy and dropped it by, but he wasn't there. He must have been around somewhere because the door was unlocked, so I left it on the kitchen counter with a note."

"Whoa! That's an expensive bottle of brandy. He didn't even say 'thanks?' "

"I bought it to thank *him*," Avery said. "So, anyway, I have no idea whether he'll be receptive to Hailey's proposal. If he is, she'll want to be up and running by summer tourist season, so I'm not sure how committed I might be in April."

"It's just a weekend," Jerica pointed out.

"If the object is to go and look at horses, I won't be of any help. I got as close as I want to get to horses this morning which is to say I sat in the lounge and drank coffee."

"I remember reading about Asha Hamilton," Marley said. "It's coming back to me now. There was some big scandal. Asha's sister shot her husband or something."

"No, she didn't!" Sienna remonstrated. "There was an accident. I don't remember the details, but I remember that Asha's husband was killed, and she didn't get to ride in the Olympics, and the American team didn't get a medal."

"That's ancient history," Jerica said. "Regardless of what happened, I'm sure she knows her way around a horse, so let's see what she says. Right now, I have to go to Brigham's and have them send some maple syrup to my mom. She lives in Florida. Her boyfriend makes pancakes every Sunday morning, so I make sure they always have real syrup. It's no cheaper here than it would be there, but it impresses their friends that they have Vermont syrup sent to them from Vermont."

"Your mother has a boyfriend?" Marley laughed. "That's so cool."

"Yeah. My dad died years ago, and Mom started going to tea dances on Wednesday afternoons. She met Walt, and he moved in with her. All the ladies have boyfriends. They're all widowed or divorced, and they don't remarry so they can keep their late husband's pension and social security benefits or alimony from their ex-husbands. It's a substantial financial gain for both parties to cohabitate and combine their resources."

***

The following week, Avery and Hailey sat at a table in the general store in Winslowe.

"I'd love another cup of coffee." Avery glanced at her watch and sighed. "He should be here any minute, so we probably don't have time."

"You don't need any more caffeine," Hailey teased. "You're already wired. What are you so worried about? The worst he can say is 'no.' But, this prospectus is pretty convincing, and even if he isn't a businessman, surely he can see that prime real estate is just going to waste." She narrowed her eyes and studied her cousin.

"Or is there more to it? Something you're not telling me?"

Avery shook her head. "What's to tell?"

"Look, you don't have to like the guy to lease an empty space from him. I don't see you moving out of the farmhouse just because he irks you. Same difference! I'll be doing the books for a while, and I can send him a monthly check, or we can pay for a year upfront. You don't have to have any contact with him."

Emmie pulled out an empty chair and sat down. "Not here yet? It's not like Rhys to run late."

"I'm giving Avery a pep talk," Hailey said. "There are a lot of pros here and not a lot of cons."

"I, for one, would love to see a clothing store upstairs again," Emmie said. "It's a huge draw for our business." She reached over and squeezed Avery's hand. "And I'd love to see you every day."

Emmie laughed. "Jeez, Avery, you look like you sucked a lemon. You wouldn't have to go far for lunch; that's gotta be on the list of pros." She winked at Hailey.

She stood suddenly and whispered, "He just walked in. Don't turn around."

"Hey, Rhys," Emmie called. "Do you want coffee?"

"I could use a cup," he agreed. He eyed the mugs on the table, looking inquiringly first at Avery and then at Hailey. "Will you join me, or have you already had your limit?"

Hailey kicked Avery under the table.

"I'd love another cup," Avery said and mustered a smile. "Hailey, this is Rhys Williams. Rhys, my cousin, Hailey Betancourt."

Rhys' gaze sharpened, and he asked, "Any relation to Jayson Betancourt?"

"My husband," she told him. Hailey had never been afraid to use Jay's celebrity to further her own causes. She slid a folder across the table.

"This is our prospectus. I'm sure you'll need time to consider it, and you'll have questions. Today is a preliminary meeting and an opportunity for me to view the space."

"This is a partnership venture?" Rhys inquired. Hailey nodded.

"Equal partners, although Avery will be hands-on, and I'll work behind the scenes for the first few years. My two children are both in school. Once they're away in college, I'll take a more active role."

"How old are your children?" Rhys asked.

"Ivy is seventeen, and Wes is fifteen. They're both in prep school; Ivy is a senior at Loomis Chafee, and Wes is a sophomore at Deerfield."

"Good schools." Rhys nodded approvingly.

"Avery and I both went to Hotchkiss," Hailey replied. "We're only four months apart, and our parents lived next door to each other."

"You live in Manhattan now?" Rhys queried.

"No, Connecticut. Avery and I grew up in New Canaan; Jay and I are in Greenwich. A driver picks Jay up at an unspeakably early hour and drives him into the city."

After desultory small talk, Rhys turned to

business. "Do you have a background in retail, Hailey? Why a clothing store? And why here?"

Avery spoke up. "Because I need something to fill my days, and the location begs for it. A clothing store can't help but succeed."

Rhys spoke in a pleasant tone, but his eyes were sad. "That's exactly what Sloan, my late wife, said. She told me it would be a gold mine—her words—and indeed it was."

"Since then?" Hailey prompted. "You've had a succession of managers, and now the store is closed. Why is that?" She'd been apprised of the history, but she wanted to hear what Rhys had to say.

"People say I'm hard to work with," he admitted. "People find me, well, *difficult*, for lack of a better word."

Hailey met Rhy's eyes, and her gaze was unwavering. "Are you?"

A long moment passed before he spoke. "I'll study your proposal, and I'll get back to you in a couple of days. Shall I show you the upstairs now?"

Rhys opened the door and gestured for the women to precede him. Hailey stood in the middle of the floor and turned around slowly, absorbing the details. Floor-to-ceiling windows let in a lot of light but also reduced the amount of usable wall space. She made notes as she strolled around.

"There's a lot of inventory here," she stated. "We wouldn't be able to incorporate it into our line. I recommend putting some tables outside on a nice day in the spring and having a sale. Whatever remains could be donated."

"That was part of the problem," Rhys replied. "Managers needed to restock, and their choices got farther and farther from Sloan's taste. What you see here—Sloan would consider it a travesty."

"Maintaining a static inventory is almost impossible," Avery said. "Vendors change hands or go out of business, styles and colors are dropped or added. You were asking the impossible."

Hailey gestured to the folder in Rhy's hand. "That's why we propose leasing the space and opening a franchise. The company we intend to go with is headquartered in Texas. The flagship store is on The Riverwalk in San Antonio, but they have outlets in several upscale locations in the west. Jackson Hole, Park City, Aspen, Vail, Denver, to name a few. Those are company stores. The only franchise to date is on Nantucket, and that's because the founder's sister-in-law owns it, so there's a family connection."

"And why would the founder consider a franchise here, if I may ask?"

Hailey grinned. "Location, location, location. Vermont has a lot of cachet, and with proximity to two ski areas, business would be year-round and not seasonal."

Rhys nodded, and Hailey continued. "You may not have heard of it. The company is called Roundtop Ranchwear. Simple, practical clothes in sustainable fabrics.

"Where are the clothes manufactured?" Rhys asked. "China?"

"No, the factory is in Texas. It's all in there." Hailey gestured to the folder. "I'm sure you'll have questions, so you can call either Avery or me. My kids will both be on winter break in two weeks, and they're eager to experience the skiing at Mad River Glen, so I'll be back. We can meet again then if you'd like."

Three nights later, Avery was on the phone with Marley, discussing the timing of a proposed trip to Tennessee.

"What about the third weekend in April?" Marley asked. "That's the soonest Jerica can go. She absolutely can't get away during tax season, and we probably won't see much of her between now and the middle of April in any case. That would work for Sienna and me."

"I know zilch about horses," Avery protested. "Absolutely zero. *Nada*. You really don't need me to go along."

"You *have* to come," Marley insisted. "None of us has ever been to Nashville. It will be *so* fun! Sienna wants to do that tub-in-a-truck transportainment thing on Friday night, and I thought we could get tickets for the Opry on Saturday night. We'd see a few horses on Saturday. We'd stay over on Sunday night and fly back on Monday morning. That way, we'd have

Sunday if Jerica needed to take a second look or even look at more horses."

"It's hard for me to make plans," Avery said. "It depends on what Rhys says about the lease. If he rejects it out of hand, then, yeah, I'm free as a bird. If Hailey manages to persuade him, that's a whole other story. There'd be a lot of work to do if we were going to be open by Memorial Day. But he's a total wild card; it could go either way."

"I don't envy you having to deal with him," Marley said. "I'm not good with loosey-goosey. I like to know what's what."

"Me, too," Avery agreed. "I almost wish it were Hailey doing hands-on and me working behind the scenes. She had him eating out of her hand the other day. It's just *me* he dislikes!"

"That's what you did with your husband," Marley said slowly. "Didn't you? He wrote the books and went on book tours and gave book signings. You did all his research and got a mention in the acknowledgments. Why are you content to live your life in the shadows when you have so much to offer?"

Avery was startled by Marley's perspicaciousness.

"I—." She was relieved when her phone chirped to alert her to an incoming call, but that was short-lived when she saw the caller was Rhys Williams.

"Marley, I'm sorry, there's a call on the other line that I have to take."

"Okay, no problem. Talk tomorrow."

Avery pressed the green circle to accept the call

and took a deep breath, steeling herself.

"Mr. Williams."

"Rhys, please."

"Rhys."

"I've been looking over your prospectus. Your cousin has done an excellent job; it's quite comprehensive. But I do have a few questions. Is this a good time?"

Not really. Not now, not ever. "Sure. But you may want to talk with Hailey."

"I called her, but the line was busy and then still busy when I tried again."

"I'd be happy to help, "Avery lied, forcing an upbeat tone into her voice. "What concerns you?"

"I've looked at the Roundtop Ranchwear website, and I see that each of the stores has a similar look and feel. Each physical plant is different, of course, but it appears that identical materials and colors are used. That implies considerable renovation of my premises."

"Yes. One of the company's co-founders is married to an industrial engineer, and he's responsible for the specs. Materials can be sourced locally and local workers hired, but we'd have to adhere to their standard if a franchise is granted."

"I see."

"There are some proprietary elements as well with a black awning and a window box containing acrylic cactus."

"I see. And where would this awning and the

windowbox be located?" Rhys asked.

"Every store, including the Nantucket franchise, has display windows at street level. We would be constrained in that regard with a second-floor location, so we envision a sort of bay window, if you will, grafted onto the front of the building. Signage would direct customers upstairs. Emmie Clayton assures us that the clothing store upstairs was very popular."

"I don't dispute that," Rhys said. "I'm well aware. That's one aspect you don't have to convince me of."

Avery waited for him to continue.

"So, let me make sure I understand this. You want a five-year lease, renewable in increments of five years. You modify the site to conform to the look the franchisor demands and obtain a line of goods from Roundtop Ranchwear. Is that correct?"

"Yes, exactly."

"How familiar are you with this company?" Rhys asked. "Have you visited any of their stores? Do you order clothes from their website?"

Avery sidestepped the question. "Hailey and her family ski at a different resort out west every year at Christmas. She's been to almost all of the stores except the ones in San Antonio and Vail. She orders frequently, and she introduced me to the online catalog."

"I see. And you've approached this company about granting a second franchise in the east?"

"No. We haven't. It's not that we want to open a

clothing store as much as we want to open one co-located with the general store in Winslowe, Vermont. The first step seems to be securing the venue."

"I see. And what would the second step be?"

"Approaching the company with a prospectus. If the CEO and COO find it a viable prospect, their marketing and merchandising managers would conduct a site visit and make a recommendation."

"I see," Rhys said again. Avery gritted her teeth, struggling not to let her irritation show.

"And then?" he asked.

"And then their facilities team would make a site visit. The industrial engineer is responsible for traffic flow and placement of displays, and he'd be accompanied by the stylist and the webmaster who would work on promotion. And then we'd work with the merchandising manager to order goods and schedule deliveries."

Avery cradled the phone between her cheek and her shoulder while she got a half-full bottle of wine and pulled the cork out with her teeth. Reaching into the cupboard for a wine glass, she poured a generous amount and took a surreptitious swallow.

"I think you've answered my questions, Avery. I didn't mean to grill you, although it probably felt that way," Rhys said and then startled her by adding, "You should probably sit down and have a glass of wine. You deserve it!"

Chapter Twenty-Two

The next month sped by. Hailey, Ivy, and Wes drove to Vermont with four pairs of skis in Hailey's roof rack for a week of skiing during spring break.

"My dad's going to fly to Burlington on Wednesday night," Ivy told her aunt. "That's why we brought his skis. He'll drive back with us on Sunday."

Every detail of the planned visit had been thoroughly discussed, so Avery was well aware that Jay had scheduled two rare weekdays off to join his family.

"I wish we could show him the space we have in mind," Hailey said. "He's been to the general store, of course, but he hasn't been upstairs. No word from Rhys?"

Avery shook her head. "Not a whisper."

"And nothing from the grapevine?" Hailey persisted. "Todd and Emmie don't know anything?"

"Not about that. They said Rhys was away, but neither one knew where or why."

"He seems to be pretty much a recluse," Hailey observed.

"Nice of him to go off and leave us hanging," Avery grumbled.

"We didn't specify a timeframe for him to respond," Hailey countered. "We didn't make him an offer that would expire within a specified period. We gave him a prospectus to read, but we don't know what else is going on in his life. We'll hear from him when we hear from him."

"There's a lot to do, and every day we don't hear is one day less we have to do it," Avery lamented.

"That's true, Cuz', but the ball's in his court. There's nothing we can do but wait to hear from him."

With the proposed partnership in limbo, Avery and her guests spent every day on the slopes. Jay and the kids took the lift to the peak first thing Thursday morning and skied the most challenging and demanding trails, while Avery and Hailey adhered to their routine of warming up on easy beginner cruises. They re-grouped at lunchtime in the lodge's cafeteria.

Hailey watched fondly as her son and daughter leaned their skis and poles against a rack, ran a cable through the bindings and wrist straps, and closed the padlocks.

"They'll order the same thing they had for lunch yesterday, chili in a boule. They never get tired of it." She laughed.

"That's easy enough to make at home," Avery said.

"Ah, but it's not the same." Hailey rolled her eyes at Avery.

The two women chose intermediate trails for their afternoon runs as the group split up again. When Avery stopped on a crest and perused the slope below, Hailey asked, "You tired? Let's rest a minute."

"No. I've been taking lessons all winter, and my legs are in pretty good shape. I just always have to stop here and figure out how to get down the rest of the way. It's a little too steep for my abilities. I usually traverse from side to side and eventually get there. But you go ahead. Just wait at the bottom."

Hailey shook her head and keyed her helmet mike to reply. "You shouldn't have to stop and look. You want to ski straight down the fall line. Don't look at your skis; focus on where you want to go. Carve a turn if you have to slow your speed."

Hailey skied to the bottom ahead of Avery and watched as her cousin made her way painstakingly down.

"Avery, I'm going to tell you something that will make it so easy for you to turn. You have shaped skis, so you're halfway there. An instructor told me this years ago, and it was the best lesson I've ever had. When you want to turn, press down with your big toe."

"That's *it*? Press down with my big *toe*?"

"Yup. Let's say you want to make a turn to the left. Press down with the big toe on your right foot. That'll put your weight on the inside edge of your right ski. With your feet parallel, your weight will automatically shift to the outside edge of your left ski.

Try it! Don't think about your edges, just press and let it happen."

Two hours later, Avery set two steaming cups of hot chocolate on one of the long tables in the cafeteria and sank onto the bench where Hailey waited with their helmets, jackets, and gloves. She was exhilarated, grinning from ear to ear.

"That was so fun! I can't believe it. I loved skiing from top to bottom without stopping. But, man, am I tired."

"Let's look at Pepper Jack's menu online and call in a to-go order," Hailey suggested, setting her cell phone on the table. "I'm buying; we'll get something wonderful for dinner that won't require any effort."

"Twist my arm," Avery agreed. "Unless you're eager to ski Mad River tomorrow, why don't we take the day off and go to Burlington? We can meander through the Church Street marketplace and have a long lunch somewhere. There are so many good little restaurants, it'll be hard to choose."

"That sounds absolutely great. I don't know how those three do it, but they'll be up and out early. They've been talking about the Glen for weeks. I'm sure they'll each buy a bumper sticker, two for dorm rooms and one for Jay's office. I had no idea it was such a cult thing," Hailey said.

"We can all ski Mad River Glen on Saturday," Avery said. "They want to go two days in a row. You can get your own bumper sticker."

Hailey laughed. "And where would I put it? On

my refrigerator? Actually, that's exactly where I *will* put it. It'll be a reminder of what a fun week we've had." She put her arm around Avery's shoulders and pulled her cousin in for a one-armed hug. "I'm so glad Jay rearranged his schedule and could come, too. Thank you so much for having us."

"I just hope you have another reason for coming to Winslowe soon, "Avery said tartly. "I'd forgotten all about Rhys Williams today. I'm starting to feel really pissed that he's left us hanging."

But Rhys hadn't deliberately left Avery and Hailey hanging. He'd read their prospectus thoroughly and found no fault, but he wasn't sure he wanted to see someone else's clothing shop replacing Sloan's. Reminders of his dead wife were everywhere, and he wondered if agreeing to the proposal would rip the scab off, would not allow him to heal, not allow him to move on.

His indecision was a clear sign he needed professional help, and he promised himself he'd make an appointment with a therapist in Burlington as soon as one was available. But the call from Connecticut wiped all thoughts of prospectuses and appointments from his mind.

"Rhys Williams?" an unfamiliar male voice had asked, late-morning on Tuesday. "My name is Delonte Kimble. I'm a colleague of Mira's, and I'm calling on her behalf. She slipped on a patch of ice in the parking lot at work and was taken to the hospital by ambulance. It's not life-threatening, but she's hurt, and she's asking for you."

"Hurt, how?" Rhys demanded. "Did she hit her head on the pavement?"

"I don't think so," Delonte replied. "I saw her slip and rushed over to help her. She was conscious and cognizant but in a lot of pain. She'll have a CT scan to rule out a concussion or any kind of head injury. She went down on all fours and cut her knees and the heels of her hands pretty badly. There's a lot of embedded gravel that will have to be debrided. And she may have a broken arm. That's all I know right now."

"What hospital?" Rhys demanded. "I'll be there as soon as I can get there. In about four hours. Tell her I'm on my way."

"I will, sir. I rode in the ambulance with her, and I'll stay at the hospital with her," Delonte told him.

"Thank you. I appreciate that," Rhys said and disconnected the call.

He drove straight through and had just signaled an exit from the interstate when his cell rang, the incoming call overriding the GPS. He tapped the green circle to accept.

"Rhys Williams," he said tersely.

"Mr. Williams, it's Delonte Kimble again, calling to let you know that Mira's been treated and released. She had a dislocated elbow and a lot of cuts, scrapes, and bruises. She tore one knee open badly enough to require fourteen stitches. She's on heavy-duty pain meds, and she's at home now, in bed.

"I see. I just got off the interstate at the State Street exit. I'm only a few miles from the hospital. I'll double back and come straight there."

"Mira's pretty drugged, and she's sleeping," Delonte reported. "So there's no rush. I'll be here."

"Is there anything I can pick up on the way, in that case?" Rhys inquired.

"She might be hungry when she wakes up. Some soup would be good. And some comfort food like mac and cheese for later, I guess. Maybe some ginger ale if the meds make her nauseous."

"What about you, son? Is there anything you need?"

"Me? Nah, I'm good. But thanks for asking."

"This happened in late morning, you said, and you were at the hospital for several hours?" Rhys probed. "Did you get any lunch?"

"No. I guess I didn't. I didn't even think about lunch," Delonte admitted.

"I left as soon as you called and drove straight through," Rhys told him. "I didn't stop for lunch, and I'm starving. How about I pick up something for the two of us at the deli, and I'll get a few things for Mira."

Over roast beef sandwiches, Rhys asked Delonte about his job.

"You're Mira's colleague? That's what you said on the phone," Rhys inquired. "You both work as translators for the governor?" He frowned, looking quizzically at Delonte.

"You mean because I'm not hearing or speech impaired? My sister has acquired deafness. She had meningitis when she was four and nearly died. She's been profoundly and permanently deaf ever since. Fortunately, she'd developed language skills by that age, so she has no difficulty articulating. But my entire family had to learn ASL so we could communicate with her."

"Mira lived with a French family for a time and learned some French Sign Language," Rhys explained. "Then, my late wife and I adopted her, and she came to live with us in London, where I was posted with the diplomatic corps. Mira learned British Sign Language as a young child and then American Sign Language when we returned to the States. She has selective mutism and doesn't speak due to her childhood trauma. She may have shared some or all of that with you. Sloan and I always hoped that with time and therapy, she would start speaking, but Mira has never uttered a word."

Delonte stared at Rhys for a long moment. "You might not believe this, but I think she spoke this morning. Or at least made a sound. One of the women in our office turned thirty today, and we were planning a birthday party in the break room at lunchtime. We all chipped in for a gift, and Mira had it in her car. She went out to get it, which is when she slipped and fell. I had a dentist appointment and was coming in late to work. I'd just arrived and, as I pulled in, I saw her fall, so I rushed over to help. I knew enough not to move her, and I called 911. I thought she might have broken her arm, and I told the dispatcher to send an ambulance." Rhys listened raptly as Delonte continued.

"I was afraid she'd go into shock, so I took off my coat and covered her with it. Her lips moved, and I thought she said something. Or tried to say something. It sounded like a foreign language but not anything I could identify. I don't know. I'm not even sure now that I heard something."

"If she did speak, what do you think she might have been trying to say?"

Delonte shook his head. "I don't know. I put my coat over her, and I thought she said something," he repeated.

"Do you think she could have been trying to say 'thank you?' That'd be the most likely, I'd guess," Rhys said.

"I have no idea what she might have said, but I think she said something," Delonte repeated again. "I wish I could be more help."

Rhys opened Google Translate on his iPhone. After a moment, he asked, "Could it have been *sipas ji were?*"

Delonte's eyes widened, and he shook his head again. "I don't know. I don't think so. But, maybe."

"You know Mira is Yazidi?" Rhys asked. "Sloan and I had her DNA tested. Mira may have been born in northern Iraq or Syria, but it's impossible to know what country she's from. Most likely, she's Kurdish, and her language could be Kurmanji. Or Arabic."

Rhys tapped again. "Did it sound like this? *Ashkuruk.*"

Delonte shook his head again. "I don't know. It was just a whisper. Maybe I imagined it."

When Rhys went in to check on Mira two hours later, she had just awakened, looking around the dim room. She turned, her eyes searching for the time on her alarm clock, and a bolt of pain shot up her arm. She gasped, and Rhys hurried to her side.

"Mira? Honey?"

She attempted to draw her arms from under the covers, to sign and ask why she was at home on a weekday afternoon and why her father was at her bedside. Anticipating her questions, Rhys gently explained.

"You had a bad fall, sweetheart. Your co-workers planned a birthday lunch, and you went out to your car to get the present. You slipped on a patch of ice and were taken to the hospital by ambulance. Do you remember that?" Mira shook her head weakly.

"You had a dislocated elbow and a badly cut knee that required fourteen stitches. There are deep abrasions on your knees and the palms of your hands. They were embedded with gravel and had to be debrided. Your colleague, Delonte, was in the parking lot when it happened, and he saw you fall. He called 911 and rode in the ambulance with you, and stayed at the hospital with you. He brought you home, and I got here a little while later. You've been asleep for a couple of hours."

Mira drew her right hand from under the covers and, palm facing her father, inserted her thumb between her index and middle fingers, rocking her fist from side to side. Rhys clearly understood the sign for needing to use the bathroom.

"Okay, honey. Let me help you up." Rhys drew back the covers and put his arm around Mira's shoulders, careful not to jostle her injury. He saw that her elbow was encased in an L-shaped splint and supported with a sling.

"Here, let's get your legs over the side of the bed. Scoot forward until your feet are on the floor. I've got you." Rhys helped Mira stand and waited as she gained her equilibrium.

"Lean on me," he instructed. "I'll help you into the bathroom."

"Delonte?" he called after getting his daughter settled. Delonte appeared in the doorway, and Rhys told him, "She's awake. She's in the bathroom now, but she may be hungry. I'll get her settled back in bed and give her some more pain meds. Can you heat some of the chicken soup I brought? I stopped at a pharmacy and got a plastic mug with a bent straw; it's in a bag on the couch. Let's get her some water, too; she'll need to stay hydrated."

Delonte improvised a bed tray with a short stack of books on either side of Mira and a cookie sheet he found in a kitchen cabinet.

Mira took several mouthfuls of the savory broth, then set her spoon down. With a flat palm, she placed the fingers of her right hand against her lips and moved them forward and slightly downward, first toward Delonte and then again toward her father.

"You're welcome," the two men said in unison.

"I'm going to stay until Mira's ready to go back to work," Rhys told Delonte. "She'll be in pain for a few days, so she'll be out for the rest of this week. After the weekend, she may be feeling well enough to go into the office, but I'll probably stay a few more days and drive her to and from work."

Delonte nodded. "Let me know if there's anything I can do. I'll call tomorrow to see how she is."

"Thank you, son," Rhys said, putting a hand on the younger man's shoulder. "I'm glad you were there when the accident happened, and I appreciate all you've done. It's a relief to me that Mira has such a good friend."

"I like your friend," Rhys told Mira that evening after she'd slept for a few more hours.

"D-E-L," she fingerspelled into Rhys' palm.

"Del? Short for Delonte? He seems like a nice young man."

Mira gestured to her nightgown and held her hand palm up in a questioning gesture. Rhys laughed aloud.

"Yes, I'm afraid he was the one who undressed

you. He did leave your underwear on so your modesty is preserved," he teased. Mira blushed furiously and rolled her eyes.

"Ordinarily, I'd take exception to someone removing your clothes without your consent," Rhys said, winking at Mira. "But, in this case, we're lucky he was in the right place at the right time.

Mira was still in considerable pain but much improved the next day. She was desperate for a shower, so Rhys found some bubble wrap and some duct tape, fashioning a protective sleeve around her arm, both knees, and both hands, leaving her fingers free to handle a cake of soap. "Close your eyes," she signed when it became apparent he'd have to undress her and help her under the stream of warm water.

Rhys wrapped a towel around Mira's head in a turban. "Tomorrow, we'll figure out how best to shampoo it," he told her. "Right now, I'll wait outside, and when you're ready, I'll close my eyes again and help you get dressed, okay?"

The phone rang just as Rhys settled his daughter on the couch a short while later.

"Rhys Williams," he said into the receiver.

"Mr. Williams, good morning. This is Governor Robert Reynolds. I'm calling to see how Mira is this morning."

The two men spoke for several minutes with Mira's employer assuring Rhys that she should take as much time as she needed to rest and heal. An hour later, a huge floral bouquet was delivered with a card indicating it was from the office of the governor. That afternoon, Del and his sister Tyesha came by with flowers and a box of chocolates.

"Usually, you get the flowers and the candy before men take your clothes off," Del signed, teasing Mira. When Mira pulled a corner of the blanket over her face in mock horror, Tyesha giggled, and Rhys guffawed.

Chapter Twenty-Three

It was late on Monday afternoon when Rhys arrived back in Winslowe. Although the days were rapidly lengthening, it had been spitting rain all day, and the low sky was gray and gloomy. Rhys found himself unable to face his empty house and pulled into the general store, attracted by the lights in the windows and the people moving around inside.

"Hey, Rhys," Todd greeted him cheerily. "How's Mira feeling? Emmie and I were glad to hear she wasn't seriously hurt."

"She went back to work today," Rhys replied. "She dislocated her elbow when she fell, and it was very painful for several days. There's nothing you can do except ice it, take painkillers, and support it with a sling. She skinned both palms and both knees pretty badly, and one knee had a cut deep enough for fourteen stitches, so she was stiff and sore."

"I can relate." Todd grimaced. "I fell out of a tree when I was eleven and dislocated my shoulder."

Overhearing the conversation, Emmie called from the walk-in cooler, "I'll be back in two minutes. Todd, why don't you take a break and have a cup of coffee with Rhys?"

Once the two men were seated at a table, Rhys continued, "I drove Mira to work this morning, and then I did some grocery shopping and stocked her fridge. I left a week's worth of deli meals so she won't have to think about cooking for a while. Then I changed the sheets on her bed and did a load of laundry."

"Can she drive?" Todd inquired.

"She probably could, but I'd rather she didn't. I arranged for an Uber to take her to work and back for the rest of this week."

"She's lucky to have you," Todd said.

Rhys' expression was suddenly so bleak that Todd stifled a gasp.

"Mira was so damaged, and she's come so far," Rhys said. "It's just heartwrenching that she lost Sloan. I've been her mainstay for the last six years, but this job has been good for her. I met her co-worker, and I think he's instrumental in drawing her out of her shell. He saw her fall and called for an ambulance. He stayed with her in the ER, and when she was discharged, he took her home and got her settled in bed. Apparently, he undressed her, and when he and his sister came to visit the next day, he teased her about taking her clothes off. I was so shocked, I almost fell off my chair! Mira's never had a boyfriend, although she's had her share of admirers. She's never had a close friend of either sex, for that matter. But she seems comfortable with this young man. I think he and his sister will provide a good support system for Mira."

"Where's Bella?" Todd asked. "Did you take her with you?"

Rhys shook his head. "No. I hated to do it, but I boarded her. I wasn't sure what the situation was or whether Mira would be admitted to the hospital. I didn't want to find that I was needed inside, leaving Bella in the vehicle for a lengthy period. There's security in the parking lot, but the hospital isn't in the best section of town, and I didn't want to have to worry about her."

"Where's she now?" Todd asked.

"Outside in the truck. I just picked her up, and I haven't been home yet. I thought I'd stop in and pick up something for supper."

"We have stew today," Emmie called. "And some great bread to go with it."

"That sounds ideal for a day like today," Rhys agreed. "May I have a take-out order?"

Then he added, "Emmie, can you join us when you have a minute? I'd like to talk to you both."

When Emmie was seated, Rhys looked from her to Todd, meeting their eyes and holding their gazes for a moment.

"I think I've had somewhat of an epiphany this past week," he told them solemnly. "When I saw Mira interacting with her visitors, I realized that she's finally starting to blossom, to emerge from her shell.

She's happier than I've seen her in a very long time, and I realized that what I want for her, I also need for myself."

Emmie reached across the table and placed her hand on Rhys', encouraging him to continue.

"I need to make some major changes," he acknowledged. "I'd like to start by apologizing to you both." Emmie started to shake her head, but Rhys held up a hand, silencing her. "Hear me out. I've been distant and unapproachable at best, churlish and ill-tempered at worst. You are fine people and ideal tenants. I'm very impressed with the way you've built this business and very proud of your success."

Emmie's eyes widened, and her lips parted in surprise. "Th-thank you," Todd stammered.

"I'm aware that the clothing boutique upstairs was a huge draw and contributed a lot to the store," Rhys said. "Sloan had an exceptional flair for design, and it was unrealistic and unfair to expect a manager—a succession of managers—to maintain an inventory as she would have. I feel like a dog in the manger for refusing to rent it since, but that's about to change."

"Does that mean—?" Emmie blurted, but Rhys held up his hand again.

"Yes. I've had a very comprehensive proposal for some time from someone who wants to lease the space and install a franchise. I've been unfair in not getting back to her with a timely response because I'm sure she'd like to be open for the start of the tourist season on Memorial Day weekend, and there will be lead times in renovating the space and ordering goods."

Todd looked Rhys in the eye and asked, point-blank, "You said 'someone.' Is that someone other than Avery Markham and Hailey Betancourt?"

"What? No. That was a figure of speech. Avery and Hailey would operate as a limited liability company, and I was thinking of an LLC as an entity."

Todd nodded in approval, and a broad smile transformed Emmie's face.

"They'll do a wonderful job, you'll see," she gushed. " It will be such a success! Everyone who stays at the inn will come in. It will be such a draw for our business. And it will be great to see Avery every day."

It was almost ten o'clock when Hailey called Avery, unable to repress her excitement.

"I hope you have a bottle of champagne handy because we have something to celebrate! Rhys told you he's accepting our proposal?"

"I haven't heard from Rhys," Avery said flatly.

"You—*what?* He called me at about seven," Hailey said. "Why would he have called me and not you? There must be some mistake."

"I've been out," Avery said. "I just got home. I was at Sienna's. She's going to be building a barn, and she just got plans today from the contractor. I went to Woodstock with her and Jerica and Marley to look at a horse a couple of weeks ago—."

"A *horse?*" Hailey interrupted. "I didn't think you knew anything about horses."

"I don't," Avery protested. "But I love Woodstock, and who could pass up lunch at Baxter's? I was just along for the outing."

"So, Sienna's getting a horse? Is that a sudden interest?"

"No. She said she's always wanted one, but her dad was military, and they never stayed in one place for long. When he died, he left her money to buy a horse, a tow vehicle and horse trailer, and put up a small barn."

"That must have been a nice surprise," Hailey said. "What a wonderful way to remember her father. So, did she buy one? A horse?"

"Yup. He's black, and he's huge. Better her than me." Avery laughed. "Sienna's barn will have two stalls, so Jerica's going to get a horse too and keep it there.

"Good thing there aren't more stalls," Hailey said. "Or you'd have to get a horse, too."

"Oh, no. Nope. Never happen."

"Rhys might have called while you were out," Hailey pointed out. "No message on your machine?"

"I didn't even look," Avery admitted. "I've given up waiting to hear from him. Asshole."

She crossed the room and saw that the red light on her answering machine was flashing. Rhys' voice filled the room when Avery depressed the button.

"Avery, it's Rhys' Williams. I'm calling to discuss

your proposal. Sorry I missed you; I'll try again tomorrow."

"You heard that, right?" Avery asked Hailey. "I take it back, calling him an asshole. Apparently, I did hear from him. What did he say to you?"

"He apologized for waiting so long to respond and said he's decided to accept our proposal. He said he'd sign the lease agreement and get a copy to you tomorrow, and his attorney would drop a copy in the mail to me. Once he provides you with a signed copy of the lease, advise him that we'll contact Roundtop Ranchwear about buying a franchise. Our attorney stated in his cover letter that the lease would not take effect unless or until the franchisor is on board. If it isn't Roundtop Ranchwear, we'll have to come up with Plan B."

"I hate Plan B," Avery said. "To my way of thinking, Plan B just means you're settling for second best."

"I don't think it will come to that," Hailey said reassuringly. "Let's make sure it doesn't. I suggest we call the owners of the Nantucket franchise and ask to pick their brains. It would strengthen our case if we included projections. Their shop is seasonal, and they both live in Boston during the off-season. You'd come down I-89 to 93; it's about a three-hour-and-fifteen minute drive for you. It's two hours and forty-five minutes for me, up I-91 to the Mass Pike. It would be a long day, but we could each get an early start and do it in a round trip. Or,"—Hailey waited for several beats and drew out the suspense—"we could each get an early start, plan a meeting for mid-morning, and have part of the day to do some shopping, have a nice dinner somewhere, and spend the night. There are a lot of new boutique hotels. It'd be fun!"

"I love it! That would be fun."

"So, you're going to talk with Rhys tomorrow, and I'm going to get contact info for the owners of the Nantucket franchise and try to set up a meeting," Hailey summarized. "Is there any time that doesn't work for you?"

"I love Boston!" Emmie Clayton said the next day when Avery stopped in and ordered a sandwich. "I'm so envious. Everyone here gets 'cabin fever' after the winter's dragged on and on, and a change of scenery sure appeals to me right about now." Avery nodded.

"I hear ya'. Hailey and I are planning to combine business with pleasure and make it a little overnight getaway. There are two partners in the Nantucket franchise, and we'll be meeting with them." Her face darkened and she shook her head, clearly aggravated. "It's going to be tough to open by Memorial Day. It would have been nice if we'd gotten a response from You-Know-Who soon after we gave him our proposal. There's not a minute to waste now so Hailey and I are both going to leave early tomorrow morning and get to Boston around ten. It's about the same amount of time for each of us, and the timing should work out really well. I came in to pick up a selection of pastries to take with me. I texted the hostess to tell her I'll be bringing them because I'm sure she'll offer coffee when we arrive."

"Nantucket is the high-rent district." Emmie frowned. "Do they have houses there? Surely they can't commute from the city if they both live in Boston."

"I spoke with Meg Hallowell. No, that's not right. Hemsworth? Hollingsworth, that's it. Meg Hollingsworth. Her husband is the managing partner in his family's law firm in Boston, and they've had a cottage on Nantucket for several generations. She's partners with her daughter-in-law. They both spend the summer on the island, managing the store, and both husbands take the high-speed ferry over on Friday evening for the weekend."

"So, there's some kind of family connection to the clothing company?" Emmie asked. "If that's the only franchise, what makes you and Hailey think they might let you have one?"

"The daughter-in-law is from Round Top, Texas. Her father manages Round Top Ranch. They raise and train Quarter Horses, and when her sister-in-law saw the wealthy women who came to the ranch to buy horses, she recognized a market for a certain kind of clothing. She has a degree in fashion design, so there you have it."

"Western clothes? Why would they sell on an island off the east coast, and why do you think they'll sell in Vermont?" Emmie shook her head.

"Where's your laptop? Is it handy? I'll pull up the website and show you what I'm talking about," Avery told her.

"The clothes are classic and timeless," Avery stated as Emmie scrolled through the pages. "They're simple and functional and elegant all at the same time. They use a lot of Tencel which drapes beautifully, doesn't wrinkle, and can be machine washed, for the most part."

Emmie's eyes widened. "I see what you mean. I want one of everything! Oh, my God, those one-of-a-kind belts! If Todd asks you for a suggestion for my birthday or Christmas this year, show him this website."

Avery laughed. "Hopefully, this stuff will be right upstairs. And you'd probably get a deep discount."

"Noooooo." Emmie giggled. "This could be bad!"

Avery stood, picked up her keys and the bakery box, and said, "Wish us luck."

The next morning Hailey arrived first at the hotel and surrendered her car to the valet. She'd already confirmed the reservation online, so now she waited in the lobby for Avery.

"You made good time," Hailey said as she slid into the back seat of the Uber she'd called as soon as Avery pulled in and handed her own car keys to the valet.

"There wasn't much traffic until I got into the city.

I missed the worst of the morning rush hour, but I doubt there's ever really a lull," Avery said. "I'm an early riser, so I headed out before dawn. More accurately, I should say that Anya is an early riser. If I'm not up by five, she tries to dig me out from under the covers."

Hailey laughed.

"I like to get coffee, then sit in bed to look at the weather and peruse the *New York Times* and the *Washington Post* online," Avery continued.

"How does Anya feel about that?" Hailey asked.

"She loves it, especially at this time of year, with flannel sheets and a heated mattress pad. She burrows under the comforter and curls up under my knees. I can feel her purring."

"She's okay left alone overnight?" Hailey inquired.

"Anya's been to Marley's, and she feels comfortable, so I dropped her off on my way out of town this morning. Luckily, Marley's an early riser too. She says she gets a lot of work done before most people have had breakfast. Marley bought a little bed for Anya, and she curls up next to Marley's keyboard."

"We're here," Hailey said, blinking. "That was a short ride. And we're right on time."

"It's very generous of you to pick up the tab for the hotel," Avery said. "I'm sure it's not cheap."

Hailey grinned. "Harborside is a splurge, but we don't get here every day. Let's buy something fancy to wear to dinner, and splurge on a nice restaurant, too. We deserve a treat."

"On the condition that you let me pay for dinner," Avery insisted.

"I wish this were a celebratory occasion," Hailey said. "But I feel like we still have a long way to go. I would hate it if we were able to secure the location and fail to get the franchise."

"Fingers crossed," Avery whispered as the door opened and they were ushered into the foyer of an exquisite Beacon Hill home.

Hailey's fears were allayed within minutes of meeting Meg Hollingsworth. She was warm and welcoming, and her house was comfortable and looked lived in.

"This property has been in my husband's family for three generations, going back to the day of gas lamps in Louisburg Square," Meg explained. "As a bride, I found it daunting, but we grew into it and it's been perfect for a family of five. Three boys took their toll in terms of wear and tear, and I've been refurbishing it little by little, so it's a work in progress. I had the walls repainted and the floors refinished as soon as our youngest went off to college."

"How old are your sons?" Avery asked conversationally as Meg removed the pastries Avery had brought from the box and arranged them on a plate.

"Whitney is the oldest; he'll be thirty this summer.

He and Elena live in Weston. It's about fifteen miles outside the city. My middle son, Prescott, is twenty-one. He'll be graduating from Brown in a few months. And the youngest, Chadwick, is nineteen. He's at Tufts, so none is far from home, and we see them often. Elena is the daughter I've always wanted. She came to us as nanny for Scotty and Chad when she was sixteen, and she's been a family member ever since. Now, *literally*." Meg laughed. "She and Whit were married right after he graduated from law school and passed the bar."

"Is Elena the family connection to Roundtop Ranchwear?" Hailey asked.

"Yes. Her sister-in-law, Stephanie, founded the company. She's married to Elena's brother, Antonio, and they live on the ranch. Elena missed Texas terribly in the early days of her marriage to Whit, to the point that my husband and I wondered if he might agree to move to Texas. But his roots here are deep. He and Elena lived in an apartment downtown for the first several years, but they bought a home in the suburbs when Whit made junior partner, and they were trying to conceive. Elena's pregnant with their second child now, which is why she's running a little late this morning. She's in her second trimester, and the morning sickness is just starting to abate."

"I read recently that Weston is the ninth most-affluent ZIP code in the entire country," Hailey said.

"Whit and Elena have a lovely home, and it's a wonderful place to raise a family. My husband is the managing partner at Hollingsworth, Bowen, Benson & Lowe, and Whit is being groomed to succeed him. We've talked about downsizing when Holt retires, and Whit may want this house when the time comes. Fifteen miles doesn't sound like much of a commute, but winter driving can be pretty ugly. There is a train which passes through Weston but it no longer stops so, even if he took the train into the city, Whit would have to drive a few miles to board at Kendal Green. Even then, he'd arrive at North Station and still have to get to the office. So, we'll see what the future holds."

"Tell us about Nantucket," Avery said. "How did you and Elena come to open a clothing store there?"

Chapter Twenty-four

Meg's face lit up. "I've always loved Nantucket. It's one of the most special places on earth. My family's had a house on the island for as long as I can remember. It's a big, old, rambling thing with eight bedrooms and five baths. I've spent every summer there for decades. When I was a kid, the rooms were tiny, and there was only one bathroom, but when I inherited it, Holt and I had some walls knocked out and bigger, energy-efficient windows put in. The house was originally a dark brown, but we had it repainted a creamy white and the plumbing *completely* overhauled. As you can imagine!" She laughed.

"Elena spent two summers with us as nanny for Scotty and Chad, as I said, and then she was off to college," Meg explained. "She graduated from Wellesley at the same time Whit graduated from Harvard Law, so they were married at the end of that summer. He became a first-year associate at the law firm and put in inhumanely demanding hours. Elena had a good job, but it was very unfulfilling, and they rarely saw each other. Since she couldn't spend time with him at home, I persuaded her to consider summering on the island with me, and Whit could come on whatever weekends he could manage, as Holt does. A clothing boutique in a very desirable location had just closed, and the premises were available for lease. I knew it wouldn't last long, and I suggested to Elena that we snap it up and go into business together. It seemed like it was just meant to be."

"So, why a franchise?" Hailey asked.

"Well, I knew Roundtop Ranchwear would be a huge success with such a wealthy clientele, but Stephanie's dad is her business advisor, and I was sure he wouldn't have wanted her to get overextended, expanding too quickly. All her stores are company stores, and they're all out west. With a franchise, she'd have no capital investment and no risk. It seemed like a perfect way for Elena to connect to Texas and her family. Whit wanted her to be happy, so he was fully in favor. It was win/win any way you looked at it."

"When is Elena's baby due?" Hailey asked. Before Meg could reply, the front door opened, and, a moment later, Elena rounded the corner.

"Hey, there," she greeted the group. "Sorry I'm late. There was a construction delay, and traffic was backed up. Whit always uses Google Maps because it alerts drivers to issues and suggests an alternate route. He keeps telling me I should use it." She sighed. "I guess he's right.

"You're here now; that's all that matters." Meg smiled fondly at her daughter-in-law and introduced her to Avery and Hailey.

"I thought we'd show you pictures of the ranch, the offices, the factory, and the flagship store on The Riverwalk so you can get an idea of who's who and what's what," Elena told the visitors. "I've got a million pictures on my Ipad, and I'll mirror them on a much bigger screen in the TV room," she explained.

"We have a lot of pictures from the Nantucket store, too, of course," Meg added.

The women spent several hours in deep discussion.

"What do you think?" Avery asked, looking from Elena to Meg. She hadn't realized how much she wanted this until now, and now she wanted it badly.

"I think Stephanie will be amenable to opening another east-coast franchise in the right location," Elena said. "She'll want Luc, her dad, to look over your prospectus, and her business partner, Alison, will have to sign off, but my recommendation and Meg's will go a long way."

"I have an idea," Meg said slowly, a gleam in her eye. "I love Vermont. It's only a three-hour drive." She turned to Elena. "Why don't we take a little road trip and check out the Winslowe General Store? We can take Vivi with us, and we'll be back the next day."

"We'd love for you to see what we have in mind,"

Avery told them. "There's a lovely inn just across the street where you'd be very comfortable. They have an elegant restaurant—." Avery broke off in mid-sentence at the horrified expression on Elena's face.

"—and also a casual tavern downstairs with pub food," she added.

"As long as they have mac 'n cheese, Vivi will be happy." Elena rolled her eyes.

"Is that your daughter's name? Vivi?" Hailey asked.

"V.V. are her initials. Her first name is Victoria after Whit's paternal grandmother and her middle name is Valeria after mine," Elena explained. "Victoria Valeria Hollingsworth."

"V.V. Hollingsworth sounds like *she's* going to be the managing partner of something someday." Hailey laughed.

"That's what Whit says," Elena agreed, nodding. "He sees a pinstripe skirt suit in her future."

Meg made sandwiches and, after a working lunch, Elena glanced at her watch.

"I hate to leave, but I've got to pick up Vivi soon. My neighbor's daughter is only a month and a half older so we take turns helping each other with daycare. She has a vet appointment at three-thirty and I told her I'd only be gone for a few hours."

"We can't thank you enough for meeting with us today, Elena," Hailey said. "Your pictures are incredibly helpful and I took a lot of notes, so Avery and I have a lot to work with now."

"If we can get Steph and Alison on the phone before I take off, Meg and I will have a quick conference call and recommend a Vermont franchise," Elena promised as the four women hugged in the front hall. "It will mean a lot to them that you took the time to come here to learn as much as you could."

"I wish you could come to Nantucket to see our store," Meg said, her expression pensive. She turned to Elena. "We still have to decide if we're going to open for Daffodil Weekend." Turning back to Avery and Hailey, she explained, "Holt and I don't usually open up the house until the middle of May, but Daffodil Weekend is the official start of spring, and it's a big deal on the island. It's always the last weekend in April. I hate to miss the opportunity to start the season with strong sales."

"I have an invitation to go to Nashville with some friends that weekend, but we're going to be up to our eyeballs in renovations if Stephanie accepts our proposal," Avery said. "I might not be able to spare the time because we'd want to be open by Memorial Day, and the timing will be tight as it is."

"Roundtop Ranchwear's assistant designer is from Tennessee," Meg exclaimed. "Mia Hadley. We met her when she was a senior at Rhode Island School of Design, RISD. She helped us put together a beachy collection for our store." Meg lightly smacked her forehead with the palm of her hand. "She's Mia Miller

331

now; I keep forgetting to use her married name."

"She brought her horse to college and boarded him nearby, and her fiancé leased a horse in the boarding barn," Elena added. "Mason was taking weekend courses for his CPA and didn't have time to ride, so Mia invited me to ride with her on Saturdays. Growing up on a ranch, I learned to ride as soon as I could walk, and I had a horse all my life. I missed it, and when Mia and Mason moved to Texas, I took over the lease. It's a half-lease now because Gus' owner has a little time to ride him herself now that her kids are older. Works out for both of us."

"Small world," Meg commented with a smile.

"One of my friends in Vermont just bought a Tennessee Walker," Avery said. "Her riding buddy wants one too, so they're going to Tennessee to look at some. I don't know anything about horses, but I've never been to Nashville, and it sounded like fun. We all love country music, so we were planning to get tickets for the Grand Old Opry on Saturday night. I hate to miss it but this is so much more important."

Less than two weeks later, Avery and Hailey sat on the folding chairs Todd had mustered in the empty space above the general store, in what would soon become Roundtop Ranchwear's second east-coast franchise. Meg and Elena had expressed their enthusiasm in a call to Texas the afternoon of Avery and Hailey's Boston visit and wasted no time in arranging an overnight getaway to see the town and the venue firsthand a few days later.

They arrived in mid-afternoon, checking into one of the rustic family rooms at the inn. Eliza Clayton was at the general store when they walked across the street for a cup of tea and a pick-me-up pastry and she immediately fell in love with Vivi, offering to babysit for a couple of hours that evening so the women could enjoy a leisurely dinner with Avery.

"Liza is a lovely young woman," Meg commented as they waited for their appetizers.

"The whole family's lovely," Avery said. "Todd and Emmie were the first people I met when I arrived in Winslowe. They're quite a bit younger than I am but they've been very kind to me and we've become very good friends."

"Emmie seems pretty excited about the boutique re-opening upstairs," Elena said.

Avery nodded. "She knows better than anyone how well a clothing shop did under the previous owner. She's said many times that every woman who comes into the general store is disappointed that it closed."

***

Now, Hailey had come up for the site visit by the contingent from corporate headquarters. Tinh, Simon and Damien, Calla and Canna had arrived at the Burlington airport and rented a car, checking into the inn just in time for dinner. Hailey spent the night at Avery's and the cousins watched and waited the next morning as Tinh measured, sketched, and made notes. Simon and Damien were rapturous about identifying scenic spots in the local area for photoshoots and planning a marketing campaign. They left with Calla to drive around and promised to return in an hour. Canna sat with her laptop open on a small folding table and went through inventory items one by one as she, Avery, and Hailey strategized about what to order and when to stock it.

"These Tencel shirts are our best-seller, hands down," Canna said. "You can dress them up or dress them down. They sell well year-round; you can't go wrong. And resupply won't be an issue as the factory rarely runs low on stock. The handmade one-of-a-kind jewelry and belt buckles are another matter."

"I've been poring over the layouts on your web pages and the products you offer," Hailey said. "I see a lot of skirts worn with cowboy boots."

"Well, yeah." Canna grinned. "That is definitely a 'thing' in Texas. It kind of epitomizes the whole ranch wear look. Throw on a shirt with the tails out and cinch the waist with a belt, add a pair of boots. Any boots will do. A skirt sale will upsell itself in no time." She laughed. "Stephanie bought the leather shop next to her flagship store on the Riverwalk in San Antonio, so now we have a whole line of boots, sandals, bags, and belts."

"My head is spinning," Avery said.

"I thought we'd have dinner tonight on the

mountain," Avery said as she and Hailey stood at the register downstairs. They'd all made their selections and placed a to-go order for lunch from the deli counter at the general store.

"Good idea," Todd said, placing a stack of styrofoam containers on the counter. "Let them see how busy it is around here during ski season. If you guys can carry these, I'll bring drinks." As he started up the stairs, Todd called over his shoulder, "Better make a reservation."

"I called Pepper Jacks," Avery told Hailey an hour later. "They're slammed! They won't have a table until 8:45, but we can go to The Wayward Peacock at 6:30 for pub grub. That'll put us at The Slippery Slope just as the band warms up."

"I don't know where they get their energy," Canna said later that evening, watching Simon and Damien clogging up a storm. "Those two sure can dance."

"You're not so bad yourself," Hailey complimented her. "I enjoyed watching you and your sister doing the two-step with them."

"Everybody in Texas does the two-step." Calla laughed. "Honky tonkin' is a way of life. We usually go out on Saturday night. You should see the looks we get when we dance with our husbands." She pulled her phone out of her pocket, scrolled, and handed it to Hailey.

Hailey's mouth fell open in astonishment. "You married twin brothers?" She handed the phone to Avery.

"Wow! Did you find them on some dating website that matches twins?"

"Not hardly." Calla and Canna exchanged glances and burst out laughing.

"We've known them all our lives," Canna said.

"Family friends. They were right under our noses," Calla explained. "They're a few years older, so they never paid much attention to us. Canna and I both skipped two grades, so we were undergrads when they were in vet school at A&M."

"So, how *did* you get them to notice you?" Hailey asked, intrigued.

Calla and Canna exchanged another meaningful glance and burst out laughing again.

"We seduced them," Canna said. "Simple as that."

"Wait," Hailey said, a thoughtful expression on her face. "Calla Sauseda and Canna Sauseda. Stephanie Sauseda. You're her—?"

"Yup," Canna said smugly. "Sisters-in-law by marriage. Marco and Mateo are Steph's husband's little brothers. We had crushes on them for years and we finally did something about it."

"Stephanie likes to do business with family members," Calla said. "It's something she learned from her dad. He's always believed it engenders an uncommon degree of loyalty."

"She liked the idea that you two are cousins, as well as business partners," Canna confided.

"I'd say the site visit went very well," Hailey said

the following morning over breakfast at Avery's. "It's going to be so much fun working with Roundtop Ranchwear if that crew is any indication. They're so interesting, each in their own way."

"They're all so attractive. And so talented. And so personable. They all seem to have a dream job," Avery said.

"Simon and Damien are clearly the 'creatives,' with what seems to be total latitude in planning layouts and photoshoots. And the twins! Can you imagine landing jobs like that right out of college? It sounds like they get quite a bit of travel to some pretty upscale locations throughout the west. Canna said neither had ever been out of Texas before they were hired. This was their first trip to the east coast."

Hailey didn't miss the note of wistfulness in Avery's voice. "Are you thinking that you might have had a dream job if you'd gotten a law degree? You'll never know what might have been; there's always a road not taken. You might have absolutely hated it. But look what you did have, those years of collaborating with your husband and traveling somewhere every summer to get background for plots."

"That was never really mine," Avery said. "Andrew was an established writer before he ever met me. We were good together, but I always felt a little like I was riding on his coattails."

Hailey hugged her cousin. "*This* could turn out to be a dream job for you. You've found a great place to live, and you'll be in a pleasant space handling gorgeous clothes all day and meeting a lot of people." She rose from the table and took her dishes to the sink. She picked up her overnight bag where it waited by the door and Avery walked her cousin out to her car.

"We've got a good handle on merchandising," Hailey said "We can place an order for delivery—what do you think? —third week in May?"

"Sooner if renovations are complete. You may not know this, but Emmie's first job after she graduated from college was as a travel writer for the Boston *Globe,*" Avery told Hailey. "She still has a contact there who said she could get us a feature the Sunday before Memorial Day weekend if Emmie would submit it on a freelance basis with a few photographs. Emmie would be paid by the column inch and, for us, the publicity would be priceless.

Hailey nodded approvingly. "That's fantastic! But we'd need renovations to be done around the beginning of May. That sure doesn't give us much time."

"And that's assuming all goes well," Avery said, her tone glum.

"Why wouldn't it?" Hailey frowned. "Oh. You mean—"

"That's exactly what I mean," Avery said flatly. "Him. Rhys. Our landlord."

"Who has to sign off on Tinh's plans. I get it," Hailey said. "But we're not making structural changes to the building. We need wall space, not windows, but Tinh's recommending boxing the windows on the inside to give us three sides instead of a flat wall and leaving the windows intact. And each box will serve as a dressing room, so he's addressed two issues with one solution. We would never have thought of that. We'll be adding interior walls but they'll be moveable, like stage flats, so we can keep reconfiguring the layout. It's brilliant. I don't see anything objectionable."

"I'm not worried he'll object," Avery said. "I can't even put my finger on it. We got off to such a bad start, and he makes me really uncomfortable. I dread having to see him, never mind getting his consent."

Hailey shrugged. "It goes with the territory; it *is* his building. Why don't we have our attorney send it to him? Nobody says you have to do it yourself."

"I'm not sure that wouldn't be worse." Avery chewed her lip. "That might feel like a slap in the face. No, I'll have to call him. I'll ask him to meet me here to go over Tinh's recommendations and have him sign off."

"You know, this should be straightforward. We're leasing the premises and this is what we need. You see signs on every commercial property saying 'Will build to suit.' It seems like common practice."

"But developers don't have all the emotional baggage." Avery sighed. "I wish we were opening a hardware store, or an electronics store, or a toy store. Anything but a clothing store like Rhys' dead wife's clothing store only different." She sighed again.

"Do you want me to do it?" Hailey asked. "I can stay an extra day. If we're going to be camera-ready by the middle of May and open at the end of May, we need to get going. I can call him now and meet with him tomorrow morning if he's free."

"No. Not that I don't appreciate the offer. We told him I'd be running the store day-to-day, and you'll be a silent partner for a few years, working behind the scenes. It will seem funny if I don't handle this myself and probably make things even more awkward. I'll do it." She scrunched up her face.

"I just don't want to."

Chapter Twenty-Five

The grand opening was everything Avery and Hailey hoped for and more. They'd set up a long table on the porch of the general store and hired Liza Clayton to sell off as much of the old inventory as possible on a busy holiday.

By mid-morning, it was clear she was slammed with no sign of letting up as Route 100 was thronged with sightseers and tourists enjoying a glorious spring weekend. Cars were parked every which way in the parking lot and along Main Street. Every woman who was headed into the general store stopped to peruse the goods on sale, often waving husbands and sons ahead to save them a seat or place a takeout order while they browsed.

The Betancourt family had arrived at Avery's on Friday night and drove to the general store shortly after eight the next morning. They all sat on the deck eating an early breakfast and enjoying each other's company before going their separate ways.

"Oh, my God, Dad! You should see the line at the register," Wes moaned. "I gave them our order but who knows when they'll get to it."

"We should have made sandwiches at home and packed your lunch," Avery replied. "I had no idea they'd be this busy this early."

"Enjoy your breakfast," Jay advised his son. "We have all day." He turned to Ivy.

"Are you sure you don't want to come, Princess? The view from Mt. Abraham is supposed to be spectacular. Three-hundred-and-sixty-degrees. You can see Lake Champlain." He cocked an eyebrow quizzically at his daughter.

"No, thank you. No, no, no. I read the reviews. The trail is steep and you have to do some 'scrambling.' It's rated difficult. You boys are welcome to it!" She snorted derisively. "Sounds too much like work."

When Jay and Wes had stowed lunch, snacks, and drinks in their insulated day packs, they took off, eager to begin hiking.

"Judging by the number of people out and about, we might as well open now," Hailey said. She turned her wrist and glanced at her watch. "It's only nine-fifteen, but why wait until ten?"

Roundtop Ranchwear's newest store was thronged with eager shoppers and sales were steady throughout the morning. By eleven, Ivy had been dispatched to pitch in on the porch and help Liza who was overwhelmed.

"This stuff's just flying out of here," Liza told Ivy, rolling her eyes.

"That's the whole point," Ivy said knowingly. "My mom said they wanted to start with brand-new inventory and not have any leftovers from the previous boutique. The owner was killed in a car wreck and the upstairs was closed up for a long time. They'll donate whatever doesn't sell this weekend."

"I don't think they'll have to worry about that," Liza said. "It's like a plague of locusts. There won't be anything left!"

"So, you're going to work upstairs this summer?" Ivy asked during a brief lull just after lunch.

"Yup. My brother and I've always helped out in the store but I'll be sixteen in two weeks so this is my first real summer job. I love clothes. I'm so excited. My dad says I'll probably spend more than I make, smack in the midst of all that temptation. I've already seen ten things I want."

"My aunt will be a good boss," Ivy promised. "She's cool."

***

"I've hardly seen you all summer," Jerica said to Avery a few months later, laying a shirt on the counter.

"I know. I had no idea a little boutique could be so busy. Thank God Hailey does inventory control and ordering. Liza accepts delivery when we get a shipment and steams the garments before stocking them. She's been a godsend; I don't know what I'd do without her!"

"You're going to have to figure that out soon," Jerica replied. "It will be really busy all through foliage season and pretty busy through ski season. You're going to have to hire someone when Liza goes back to school."

As Avery folded the shirt into a sheet of tissue and slid it into a bag, Jerica said, "I couldn't decide which color to get. I was really torn between this one and that deep forest green." She bit her lip. "Maybe I should get them both."

"Special occasion?" Avery asked.

"Yup." Jerica grinned. "Sienna and I are going horse camping. We joined a trail riders' group and they're sponsoring a ride in New Hampshire."

Avery looked puzzled. "Camping as in *sleeping in a tent*? Where do the horses stay?"

"Sienna's borrowing her cousin's pop-up camper. We'll sleep in that. I'll tow it and she'll trailer the horses. There are corrals but they're open so we're paying for a site with two covered stalls in case it rains."

What about a bathroom?" Avery asked. "Tow-behind campers don't usually have bathrooms, do they?"

"Only the big ones do. But the campground has a bathhouse with toilets and showers. And there's a little porta-potti in Jeremy's camper if we need it in the middle of the night."

"So, why the shirt if you're just going to be riding and camping?"

"Meals are included at this ride. We'll eat breakfast and dinner at the pavilion and they'll give us a saddlebag lunch. There'll be a band both nights with line dancing." Jerica looked thoughtful, then she said, "You know what? Ca-ching! I'm going to get both shirts. Maybe I'll meet a handsome cowboy."

Avery smiled. "For you, there's a 'friends' discount."

"No rest for the weary," Marley commented as she and Avery sprawled on her couch one rainy Sunday evening after a simple supper of lasagna, garlic bread, and salad. "Kids go back to school at the end of August but Labor Day weekend is like the last gasp for families and Route 100 will be almost bumper-to-bumper. September is considered a 'shoulder season' but it's surprisingly busy with all the sightseers and vacationers who want to avoid families with kids, and then foliage season gets more and more frenetic as the colors get better. Columbus Day weekend will be wild! And then comes ski season."

"I've been warned." Avery laughed. "That's what Jerica told me."

"If you're in business, though, what could be better? Look at the inn; it's always packed. And the general store; Todd and Emmie work hard but, man, they just rake it in."

"I'm still running on adrenaline," Avery admitted. "But I must admit I need to hire someone full-time and start carving out two days a week to be off. Any suggestions?"

Marley shook her head. "Not offhand. It should be someone local, though. No one will want to drive very far in the winter if they don't have to. Why don't we make up a flier? You can put it by the register at the general store and one by your register. See if you get any takers."

"Thanks, Marley. I'll take you up on that."

"I can't believe I've been here almost a year," Avery said. "I haven't come up for air since we opened the boutique and the time has gone so fast."

"Are you happy?" Marley asked. "Do you feel at home here, like you've settled in and started sinking some roots?"

Avery looked thoughtful. "Yes and no. I love the area, I've made some wonderful friends, and my partnership in the boutique with Hailey is very rewarding. I expected my education to provide a career and I sure didn't see myself ever working in a *ladies' clothing store*. But Roundtop Ranchwear is a delight to work with and it's very rewarding to have the clothes so well received that they just fly out the door. And I love them. I seem to want one of everything and now ninety percent of what's in my closet came from the shop."

"You're a walking advertisement," Marley teased. "When your customers see how good the clothes look on you, it makes them want to buy."

"I'd have to agree that wearing the clothes in the shop is a plus. I get asked ten times a day whether my shirt or my pants or my skirt is something we carry. And the various pieces go together so well that a sale usually includes several items, with an expensive belt or piece of jewelry thrown in at the last minute."

"But?" Marley probed.

Avery looked puzzled. "But what?"

"There's more to life than that. What about romance? Don't you ever get lonely?"

Sadness filled Avery's eyes and Marley leaned over, taking her hand and squeezing it. "I shouldn't have asked. I didn't mean to make you sad. I know you're still grieving for your husband."

Avery shook her head. "It's not that. I know Andrew is gone and I miss him. I miss having someone to lean on, someone to share my life with. If the right person came along, I'd be receptive, but I'm not looking. I'm not about to get on an internet dating site." She gave a mock shudder. "And I'm not about to look up any more high-school crushes."

"And you're probably not going to have a seasonal fling with a bartender half your age," Marley teased.

Avery gasped. "Are you kidding? Landon was half your age?"

Marley chuckled. "He still is. My little boy toy. Some of the best sex I've ever had, I'll say that. But he's long gone and I'm going to be coming off a dry spell when I see what possibilities the mountain might offer up this winter."

"I guess there's a lot of turnover in ski areas,"

Avery said. "Didn't Landon go out west somewhere?"

"Yup. One of his fraternity brothers got him a job at a big resort. They've been guiding whitewater rafting trips this summer and Landon will start tending bar there once the snow flies." Marley shrugged. "It was fun while it lasted. I'm still feeling burned after my last serious relationship and I'm not looking for a commitment."

"So, life is good for the most part," Marley summarized. "Will you stay in the farmhouse or look for a place of your own?"

"I'm going to get a kitten," Avery said in a seeming non sequitur. "I'm sorry; that was a train of thought. Rhys was adamant that no pets were allowed when I rented the farmhouse from him. I told him it was a deal-breaker and insisted he write a clause into the lease agreement saying I could have two cats. I wasn't about to give Anya up, and I didn't want her to be lonely all day if I ended up working somewhere."

"Which you have," Marley pointed out. "So, is she lonely?"

"I'm guessing she is. I think she'd be a lot happier if she had someone to play with and snuggle with."

"There are always free kittens," Marley said. "Check the bulletin board at the vet's."

"I want another Siamese. I've been emailing with a breeder in Massachusetts. She just had two litters two weeks apart. Hers are so young she can't tell what colors she has yet but I'm hoping for a chocolate. Siamese are born pure white and the colors develop after a few weeks."

"Chocolate? Is that a sealpoint?" Marley asked. "With the black face and legs and tail?"

"Chocolatepoint is a dilute. Sealpoints' coats darken with age and chocolate stays light. They still have a dark mask, legs, and tail and, sometimes, you can't tell them from a seal. There's a difference in their paw leather and nose leather, too. Seals have dark brown noses and paw pads and chocolatepoints have cinnamon-colored noses and paw pads."

"What color are Anya's nose and paws?" Marley asked. "It never occurred to me to look."

"She's a bluepoint so her nose leather and paw leather is dark gray."

"So, if there's a chocolatepoint in the litter, when do you think you'll get him? Or her."

"In about two months. The breeder doesn't let kittens go until they're about ten weeks old. I know cats sleep most of the time but I feel so guilty all day, knowing Anya's home alone."

Just then Marley's big marmalade cat leaped up, landing in her lap. Marley grinned. "As we speak."

"Since Rhys has agreed to two kittens, it sounds like you plan on staying right where you are," Marley observed.

"I don't see why not," Avery said. "The farmhouse is lovely and I feel at home there. I pay the rent upfront so I won't have to deal with Rhys and sometimes I forget that I'm a renter. I renewed for an additional six months but I made arrangements through Apex Realty and gave Daisha a check."

"You renew in six-month increments?" Marley shook her head. "That would make me nervous. I'd want a long-term lease, at least a year."

"The original agreement was for six months, renewable for an additional six. I haven't seen or heard from Rhys but I can't imagine that extending would be objectionable."

"I thought he'd be curious to see the boutique in operation," Marley said. "He didn't show up for your grand opening, though, did he? And he hasn't been in at all?"

Avery shook her head. "Nope. He was decent about accepting our proposal to lease the premises but Hailey handled that, for the most part. I haven't had any contact with him, and I'd guess he doesn't want to see someone else running a clothing shop in his late wife's space. Her death is obviously still very painful. Some people never get over a loss like that."

"He must have been a swan in a previous life," Marley joked. "You know, mates for life."

"Swans aren't known for their temperament." Avery snorted. "That fits."

"Have you seen Rhys Williams?" Avery asked Emmie a few days later when she ran downstairs to pick up her lunch order for a salad. Emmie shook her head.

"Why? Do you have a problem at the house? I have a list of the plumbers, electricians, carpenters, and handymen Rhys uses whenever we have an issue here."

"No, it's not maintenance or a repair. I just need to talk to him about something and I realized I haven't seen him for quite a while."

Emmie bit her lower lip, wrinkled her nose, and shook her head. "Come to think of it, I haven't either. But that's not unusual. He's kind of a recluse. I can go months without a glimpse of him. Our paths don't usually cross unless I run into him at the grocery store or the gas station or something. The bookkeeper pays our rent and utilities so I don't even have to mail him a monthly check. Let me ask Todd."

"No," Avery said quickly. "That's all right. Thanks anyway. I have Rhys' cell number. I'll probably try to reach him when I get home this evening."

Concern clouded Emmie's face. "Is something wrong?"

"Not at all," Avery told her, reaching for her to-go box. "I don't mean to cut you off but I've got to dash back upstairs."

"Have you seen Rhys lately?" Emmie asked her husband as he backed the truck out of its parking spot behind the general store that evening.

"Nope. Why? Should I have?"

"Avery asked me earlier if I'd seen him and I realized I haven't actually seen him all summer," Emmie replied.

"Why's she looking for Rhys? Is something wrong?"

"I don't think so. I didn't get that impression. She just said she needed to ask him something."

"Maybe she wants to ask him if he'll sell her the farmhouse," Todd said. "She's been here almost a year and she might be tired of renting. If this summer's any indication, it looks like the boutique is a huge success. She seems really happy every time I see her. I'll bet she's decided to stay and wants a place of her own. I would."

"Me, too," Emmie agreed. "The boutique sure has been good for our business. It's a big draw." She put a hand on her husband's knee. "Do you think he'd sell it to her?"

"Who? Oh, Rhys. That's anybody's guess. I've fantasized about him selling the store to us for years. The building, I mean.

"You've reached Rhys Williams. Sorry I missed you. Please leave a message, and I'll return your call."

"What the Hell?" Avery sputtered, holding her phone away from her ear in disbelief. "That's the *fourth* time I've gotten voicemail!" She and Marley were standing in the hallway but Avery slid the phone into her pocket and they rejoined the group of women seated on the long sectional couches in Merritt St. Johns' living room.

She was hosting a wedding shower for Brandi

Tyler who was marrying Larry Hughes at the end of the month. Two years of dating proved them compatible and her sons were in favor, readily agreeing to move out of their small house and into Larry's large home.

Brandi glowed with happiness as she gazed at her closest friends, Marley, Sienna, Krista, Emmie, Jerica, Gina, and Avery who would serve as her attendants.

"There'll be more people in the wedding than attending it," Krista teased.

"Oh, Avery, I'm so glad you chose Winslowe," Brandi said, looking directly at her and holding her gaze.

"You mean you're so glad we all chose gifts from Avery's boutique," Sienna quipped.

"Between Larry and me, there's not one household item we need," Brandi said. "But all I have to do is put those clothes in a suitcase, and I'm ready to leave for my honeymoon."

"Has anyone seen Rhys Williams?" Marley asked. "Avery's been trying to reach him. She just left a fourth voicemail. His message says he'll call back, but he hasn't."

"Rhys? Hmmm. I haven't seen him all summer, come to think of it," Merritt said. "I kind of had a thing for him for a while but it was mostly wishful thinking. I haven't really thought about him since I started seeing Greg. I can't honestly remember the last time I saw Rhys."

"I saw him in July," Krista said "I was in line for an oil change and his truck was ahead of me. I wanted the deluxe service where they check all your fluids so he was gone by the time I finished." She shrugged. "I haven't clapped eyes on him since."

Jerica threw up her hands. "Not I. No clue. Sorry."

"He comes into the general store occasionally," Emmie said. "But more in the winter. We're so slammed all summer I hardly look up. I wouldn't know if I'd seen him or not. Just kidding. He hasn't been in for quite a while."

"We sent Rhys a wedding invitation," Brandi said. "Larry's known him for years. I don't think he sent the RSVP card back yet. I haven't seen it but I still have a bunch I haven't opened yet." She turned to Avery. "You might see him then."

When the party began to break up several hours later, Avery stood.

"I want to thank you all for including me in your group, and for your friendship," she said. "You have no idea how much you've helped me through one of the worst years of my life. I feel so welcome here in Winslowe."

Emmie reached for Avery's hand with her left, and for Jerica's hand with her right. In moments, each of the women clasped hands, standing in a circle, tears shimmering in several pairs of eyes.

"We're so lucky to have found each other," Brandi said. "When a special relationship comes along, you grab it with both hands."

ABOUT THE AUTHOR

Linnhe McCarron is the pen name for Leslie Helm who lives in an equestrian community near Big South Fork, Tennessee. Originally from Connecticut, she lived in Maine for 15 years and Vermont for 10, but she has had horses most of her life, wherever home might be.

She rides gaited horses now, a black Tennessee Walker named Luc, and a buckskin McCurdy Plantation Horse called Jax.

If you enjoyed this book, please support the author by leaving a review.

Made in the USA
Columbia, SC
20 July 2022

63741284R00198